Roger McKnight
HOPEFUL MONSTERS

Roger McKnight is from downstate Illinois.
He has lived and worked in Chicago, Sweden and Puerto Rico.
He now lives in Minnesota.

"Roger McKnight is a very slick writer with an incredibly quirky sensibility. Miss him at your own peril."

– Mark SaFranko –

Author of Hating Olivia, Lounge Lizard, God Bless America, Dirty Work, and The Suicide

"Roger McKnight is an extremely talented writer, and among his many gifts is an ability to maintain, even though his characters struggle in an America fraught with lousy jobs, racism, busted relationships, damaged war vets, and homelessness, a subtle but believable hint of optimism that things will turn out alright in the end. 'Hopeful Monsters' is one of the best collections of linked stories I've ever read."

– Donald Ray Pollock –

Author of Knockemstiff, Devil All The Time, and The Heavenly Table

"These are stories full of compassion and humanity that beautifully evoke the plains of Minnesota from an exciting and authentic new voice in American letters."

– James Miller –

Author of Lost Boys, Sunshine State, and Unamerican Activities

"Hopeful Monsters is my kind of collection: stories that feature an array of intriguing characters brought to life through elegant, often gritty specificity that illuminates what it is to be human."

– Adam Lock –

Author of Dinosaur

"Roger McKnight writes with compassion, precision and humour about Minnesota and its people. In the carefully rendered world of this collection, chance and circumstance bring disappointment and struggle, but also moments of precious hope."

– Wendy Erskine –

Author of Sweet Home

"Authentic slices of Midwest 'thick-time', a place where time hasn't stood still but marches to a different beat. Open-ended stories of how change comes to those that wait. Loved these stories. Off-kilter and hopeful."

– Wayne Holloway –

Author of Bindlestiff

"My favourite thing about reading Roger McKnight's stories is that you forget you are reading fiction. In Hopeful Monsters you encounter real people who vibrate with life, with mystery, and also with pain and humour. This collection shows me why I read stories - to see beneath the surface of real lives and remember that I am not alone."

– Jason Brown –

Author of Driving the Heart & Why The Devil Chose New England For His Work

"Like a stranger in a bar regaling you with stories of his past, there is a whiff of fact and fiction, along with an overwhelming sense of unease."
– Josh Denslow –
Author of Not Everyone is Special

"Roger McKnight encapsulates the chill and uniqueness of Minnesotan culture. His prose tip toes across a vast landscape of sentiment, leaving the reader curious to learn more and hopeful like his monsters."
– Michelle Blair Wilker –
Author of Chain Linked

"Roger McKnight takes us on a riveting societal tour of Minnesota in this beautifully realised collection. We're granted a peek of life through the eyes of the downtrodden – war vets, immigrants, and homeless among them – but one of McKnight's greatest achievements is the ability to find hope even in the darkest places. These are stories to savour."
– Tomas Marcantonio –
Author of This Ragged, Wastrel Thing

"McKnight knows that every story is many stories, that every life touches many lives. These powerful stories artfully braid the stark narratives of strangers into something wondrous and transcendent. Indeed, *this is what we talk about when we talk about hope.* The prose is incandescent, the characters riveting, the themes complex. Roger McKnight is one savvy, lyrical, and fearless writer."
– John Dufresne –
Author of Louisiana Power and Light, Johnny Too Bad, No Regrets, and Coyote

"Roger McKnight is not afraid to discuss sensitive topics such as suicide, homelessness, addiction, and mental health, creating an array of intriguing characters and scenarios that give a voice to the forgotten in our society."
– Dan Stubbings –
The Dimensions Between Worlds

"Like the great writers of dialogue – Greene, Carver, Moore, and others – McKnight's thoughtful expressions and turns of phrase equip his characters with a sense of agency that never tells the reader how to feel, but instead guides them to that perfect crux of empathy where we are surprised not to be reading characters that seem realistic; but to be reading characters that feel like ourselves; who have the same thoughts, feelings, and reactions that we do. In this way, reading this book feels like being in a series of intimate conversations with your closest friends."
– Proffesor Wu –
Nothing In The Rulebook

STORGY®
BOOKS

First Published in Great Britain in 2019 by STORGY® Books

Copyright © STORGY® Books 2019

London

Grateful acknowledgement is made to the following publications in which some of
these stories were first published: Passager, 'Genuine Souls'; REAL: Regarding Arts
& Letters, 'September Mist'; Toasted Cheese, 'Basic Skills'; Conceit Magazine,
'Loving Søren'; Down in the Dirt, 'Down the River'; STORGY Magazine, 'Iago';
Garbanzo Literary Journal, 'A Place in Space'; Lost Lake Folk Opera Literary
Journal, 'Burnt Potatoes'; The Fictional Café, 'Forgetting She Forgot'; Avalon
Literary Review, 'Paying Her Way'; Fixional, 'Rain Shadow'; Sweet Tree Review,
'Sixteen'; Adelaide Literary Magazine, 'Victoria'.

Published by STORGY® BOOKS Ltd.
London, United Kingdom, 2019

10 9 8 7 6 5 4 3 2 1

Cover Art by Savannah Bieg
Cover Design by Rob Pearce

Edited & Typeset by Tomek Dzido

A CIP catalogue record for this title is available from the British Library

Trade Paperback ISBN 978-1-9998907-4-2
eBook ISBN 978-1-9998907-5-9

www.storgy.com

HOPEFUL MONSTERS

STORIES BY
Roger McKnight

S T O R G Y
LONDON

£9.99 (new)

For Helena,
who encouraged me
to write these stories.
and Barb, who read
them all.

CONTENTS

A world neither
shrinking nor growing,
only begging to be
embraced.

GENUINE SOULS

STAN SCRIBBLING TOSSED under a woolen blanket one frigid August night. The shivers catapulted his thoughts ahead to November, but he went with the flow thinking, *so this is Minnesota summer*. By the time he stumbled on Minneapolis' Lake Nokomis the next afternoon, he was luxuriating under a reawakened summer sun. Crystallized before him in the bright light was a cheerful woman with a furry dog. She sat in the grass under a leafy maple, with both legs tucked under her skirt and a portable radio propped against the pooch's rump. Over the airwaves a baseball announcer raved about "Killer's monstrous homer" and described a hometown slugger rounding the bases.

Stan remembered that same voice on the U. S. Armed Forces Network from the last day of the 1967 Big League season. At an Army base near Stuttgart, he'd listened to the man's dejected description of a decisive Minnesota Twins defeat, the second in a row. The only thing left, the commentator lamented, was another long, gruelling Northern winter.

That was then. Now, in 1968, Stan found himself exploring the Twins' home city as hordes of flaxen-haired school kids crowded the beach and a pentathlon team swam sprints across the lake. South of the beach a few ducks paddled past a quay with gaily bobbing sailboats.

"Yankees. We beat them!" the woman said. She spoke over the shouts of the youngsters and their frantic splashing.

After eight years in Germany, Stan was now enrolled in grad school at Minnesota's only big-time university. Following a week of orientation meetings, he was embarking on an unguided tour around town. For starters, he'd followed the Mississippi till Nokomis caught his eye. With no city map, he struggled to concentrate and get his bearings.

"How do you like that?" the woman asked to recapture his wandering attention.

"What? The weather?" Stan asked while glancing at the sky.

"No, our weather never changes, we get four seasons every day," she said with a chuckle. "I meant the game."

"Crazy place," Stan replied. Realizing he hadn't answered, he added, "Love baseball."

Gently stroking the dog's back, the woman studied Stan carefully, inviting him to say more but in no hurry.

He stepped off the path and introduced himself, half expecting the mutt to bark at him, but it only yawned and wagged a friendly tail. Without saying her name, the woman took off her sunglasses and nodded presciently, as though she'd seen Stan coming. When she leaned farther into the sunlight, her blue eyes sparkled and her hair turned a deep blond. At the same time, he noticed a dark birthmark on her forehead which fell along her left eye and down her cheek. Not wanting to stare, he concentrated on her bonding with the dog. He bent down to pet the pooch. "What's your name?"

"This is Thor, the god of thunder," she said. Thor opened a drowsy eye and blinked. "He's totally misnamed, as you can see."

She glanced down at Thor, who dreamily stretched his legs, while she switched off the radio. Then she looked up at Stan and smiled.

Here I am, he thought. A different city. An erratic climate. A new school year. An aging baseball season. Otherwise, all he knew of this place came from the mellow vibes of a glittering lake and this striking woman with her lazy dog. He thought of moving on but stayed put, suspecting he'd reached his destination without knowing he had one.

***

4

Unhurried, the woman gathered up her things and put a locate on Thor, who had woken up and gone for a dip. He shook so strongly the water splattered on her. Seeing her bare legs glisten, she motioned to her open backpack. Stan handed her a towel from within the pack and watched while she shed her sandals. She whapped them against each other so the sand flew. Stan noticed her toes were even in length, except for the second toe on each foot, which was longer than her big toes.

"Sorry," she said. "Thor's part Newfie. He smells water a mile away."

Having nowhere to go, Stan hesitated. "Where you heading?" he asked.

She didn't answer, but put a leash on Thor, then tossed the towel back at Stan, who stuffed it in the backpack. When she made no move to retrieve the pack, he slung it over his shoulder.

"I'm Kristine," she said. "This lake's always buzzing. Spelled with a K, by the way."

"What? Your name or the lake?"

"Both," she replied. "A bit abrupt, but you wanna join us and walk around it?"

"I was about to ask you the same."

Stan handed her the backpack. While she strapped it on and slipped into her sandals, he took Thor's leash. The dog continued along the same path Stan arrived on, stopping to sniff at rocks and tree trunks, like he was greeting old friends.

"We come here all the time. It's two-and-a-half miles around, but only two from here to where you came from," Kristine explained.

"So I'm not even halfway? Story of my life," he said in a mock-facetious tone.

She shrugged, meaning to say she wouldn't know.

"At least I remember where I started out from," he added.

"Early pioneers called this Lake Emily," Kristine explained, turning to glance at him so her hair fell over the birthmark. She acted relaxed but maintained a distance, out of politeness, Stan assumed. He quickened his pace when she upped hers, so he understood she'd been this way before.

"They named it after an early settler's wife." Her statement sounded halfway like a question that requested affirmation. Stan saw her watching him, like she awaited a signal that would cement their friendliness. He nodded. "Or his daughter. Then they changed it to Nokomis, after an Indian in a Longfellow poem. Used to be all marsh here, no more than five feet to the bottom. So they deepened it, my granddad remembered that. It's 30 feet now, in places."

Settler's wife. Or daughter. Thirty feet deep. Stan caught that, but struggled to filter her other words. This place felt dreamlike, a city with 10,000 lakes and greenery that would surely fall prey to asphalt anywhere else in urban America. Growing up outside Paducah left him with memories of pot-holed roads through Kentucky forests or past humble tobacco farms. By contrast, his thoughts drifted to prosperous communities in Germany, with their manicured parks and genteel burghers wearing tweed coats or ladies bedecked in Sunday dresses. Such sights had taught him what bourgeois meant.

Comparing three cultures at once was hard, and Germany wasn't any utopia either. Somewhere from those well-ordered folks' bosom Nazism had sprouted in the '30s. Stan remembered Kentucky folks his parents' age saying such horror could never happen on America's side of the pond, thank god, even if his own soft-spoken people seldom hid their own skewed ideas about race and religion. There must be anomalies in Minnesota, too, he guessed.

"You wonder why I'm so friendly?" Kristine asked. "Too forward, even?"

Her switch of topics from the lake to herself once again interrupted Stan's wandering thoughts. She glanced up at him, and he guessed her height at five eight against his six feet. She was thin at the waist and strode on long, straight legs, which caused her skirt to rustle as if on puffs of a wispy breeze.

"You mean, did I stop for you on the path, or did you stop me?" he wondered. He didn't know the answer himself, but had learned in Europe that the first strangers to greet him in new places were nearly always hucksters or genuine souls. The key was telling the difference.

"It was spur of the moment, I figured why beat around the bush," she mused. "You know, I'm 26. I sit here like a lonely spinster, which I'm not, listening to ball games that mean something to some, but not much to me. I love the solitude, despite the radio and hullabaloo on the swimming beach. You think I'm out of line?"

"More like a fresh breeze. Traveling alone, I learned to look before taking a leap. Sometimes you need to go out on a limb. See what happens."

"Gotcha. But it wasn't me caught your eye," she observed. "You're a true dog lover."

"Thor-lover. It was how you leaned your radio against him," Stan replied, though her sensuous pose in the summer grass was really his strongest impression. He was wondering whether to tell her that, when Thor lurched after a squirrel.

"Shall we?" Stan asked, relieved the dog made his decision for him.

Kristine pointed at the taught leash and they hurried on. Stan realized he had only two short miles to cement his first friendship in Minnesota.

***

South of the beach, a combined car and walking bridge crossed the lake. To his left, Stan saw the waters spread out in summer glory. Sunlight hit the rippling waves and reflected onto the bridge. Stan shielded his eyes.

"It was built by WPA in the '30s," Kristine said pointing to the sturdy bricks on the bridge's underside. "They're Kasota stone, from south of here."

Only a roar from the airport disturbed their peace. Planes rose above the lake and disappeared over the city. South of the bridge reeds grew in profusion in a protected wetland. Birds with red patches perched on the stalks.

"Red-winged blackbirds. Aren't they lovely?" Kristine asked. "They lay eggs in the marshes and the males guard the approach. Rare to see them so late in the summer."

"I saw *Tosca* in Potsdam once. The stage costumes were red and black like theirs. Never see birds like these where I come from."

"Which is where?"

"They call it the Bluegrass State. Kaintuck."

"What brings you so far north?"

"Study. Teaching, too. I get to lead a class on Modern Lit, but I want to study Goethe. Nobody in Paducah gives a damn about the wild hairs I've got. I told myself, if I'm back in the States, I'll get as far from home as possible. Besides, this is the only place that wanted me."

Stan waited to see if Kristine understood his self-spoof, but Thor eyed a gaggle of geese who dared him to charge, and in his eagerness to take the challenge the dog slid on their droppings. Kristine grabbed the leash. Using Stan's vein of light raillery, she chastised Thor while wiping his paws. Near them a few old-timers passed on a bike path.

"Heading where?" Stan wondered, nodding their way.

Kristine shot him a Eureka look, which told Stan she'd figured his mind was drifting hither and yon in prolonged jet lag. He wondered how to tell his story.

"My college was Bible Belt," Stan explained. "A righteous mix of Southern Baptists and Black Panthers. Sounds weird."

"And I act older than I am. Till I take off my glasses. Does that sound weird, too?"

"Acting older keeps young punks from hitting on you, that's my guess. But why back there?" Stan asked pointing at the grassy spot she and Thor abandoned to show him around the lake.

"Not so fast. What got you to Germany? Nobody just appears there out of the blue," she protested.

"I wanted to play baseball, but became the disaffected athlete. That's what sociology gurus call guys like me. There was this prof."

"Who took you from Paducah to Potsdam? Likely story," she jested.

Stan stopped walking so their glances gently collided. She caught on intuitively, he felt, though precisely which things she understood best he couldn't figure. As before, her knowing smile showed there was no rush to find out.

"I got a taste of your world once, down South. Long before I got him," she said, pointing to Thor. "I read Catherine Marshall and dreamed of Appalachia, then got into Med School. I applied for a summer internship in eastern Kentucky. Thought I'd help folks. When I got there, they said they never knew they were poor till outsiders like me started telling them. I dropped out. Been looking for my next step ever since."

"Kinda my story. This prof."

She nodded yes, meaning, finally, this prof.

"I beat jock logic and took Lit. This guy said to understand the great writers we had to see Europe. Like your folks in Kentucky, I didn't know what I was missing till he told us. So I tried joining the Army *if* they'd station me in Germany. Took their rinky-dink physical, then told the recruiting sergeant, sorry, no dice."

"You'd do more good in the classroom?"

Stan waited while Thor snooped among the reeds. Two geese flapped out of the slew and swooped down on the open lake. Stan observed them bobbing on the ripples.

"Tumult in my soul," he explained. "I compromised and did student teaching. Lucked out and hooked up with Army schools. Travelled. Read *The Sorrows of Young Werther*. Followed Goethe from Frankfurt to Weimar. Got as far as Sicily."

"Quite a trek. His sorrows didn't do you in?"

"No, *Werther* caused a stir, honorable suicide and that stuff. But I'm still here." Stan didn't know why he was telling her this, but Kristine's ability to walk straight ahead and look his way put him at ease.

Around the bend from the reeds they stopped at a marker showing they'd gone 1.5 miles. A flock of white birds rose from the water and glided along the opposite bank. Against the dark green oaks and maples, the flock made graceful passes.

"Land gulls," she said. "They came here and saved farmers from ravenous grasshoppers."

"Biblical locusts. In the middle of a continent?"

"Yes, way back when."

The gulls turned and flew opposite the ascending jets, their slow flapping a contrast to the planes' deafening roar. Near the bank, the fowl settled in the marsh where they pecked for food.

"Kristine Fahn, that's me," she said.

Stan wondered why she chose that moment to give her full name. He decided she'd grown impatient with him for not asking.

"Sounds German," he said, turning his gaze from the gulls.

"It is, but my name means 'devil' in Swedish."

She let her comment hang, so Stan fell silent. Unlike the gulls, he searched in vain for a place to settle. Kristine found them a bench at the one-mile mark. She tied Thor to the back support and relaxed against it while gazing at a spot across the water.

"I sit here and wonder what a person could build over there and still preserve the natural setting," she said.

"Only that?" Stan asked.

"To assuage my melancholy. I saw you coming and thought, he's got a good face," she added. "Your fair looks could pass for German."

Stan looked into her blue eyes, which absorbed the light but still reflected some brightness. Her forehead bore only the slightest worry crease.

"You view the distant shore like an architect," he said.

"You're smart!" she exclaimed and rose to her feet to continue the walk. "Urban planning, that's my next dream. I see spatial lines. I'm a quarter Swede. My great-grandmother immigrated from Bohuslän, on the coast of Sweden."

Stan wondered at Kristine's mixing of topics, as if her wires momentarily got crossed, from baseball to Bohuslän or buildings to birthplaces.

"Great-Granma came over on a rickety steamer. Uneventful, till they hit a storm off Newfoundland. The boat sank. They never found her folks or little sister, but she floated to a craggy rock. Rescuers found her hanging on so tight her hands cramped."

Stan wondered if Kristine imagined that, or some similar, ocean tragedy occurring on this placid lake. As if anyone could drown on Nokomis, he thought.

"First she stayed with relatives in New York," Kristine continued. "Then she came west. Lots of Swedes were here."

"As far from the sea as she could get?" Stan guessed.

"My mom says her grandma had nightmares ever after. Waters were her woe."

"So that's why you got a Newfie? 'Cause they save drowning sailors?"

Kristine flashed a taut smile that said her thoughts had left the Newfoundland rock her great-grandmother clung to. The mental turf she now tread was hard-and-fast hinterland, but her footing tenuous.

"Thor saving me? Fat chance," she said, joking. "Ocean rescuing's being bred out of Newfs. He's a wüss. In a pinch, I'd have to save him."

With under a mile left, they neared a smaller beach on the northeast side. The pentathlon swimmers arrived and rested before turning back. Halfway they paused at a buoy, then continued to a grassy spot on the far side. Once on land, the swimmers shook so water flew Thor-like from their bodies as Stan imagined rainbows in the spray.

"Thor's my buffer," Kristine said, turning serious again.

"Between you and what?"

"Me and my thoughts. The beauty of here and the other side."

"This is the other side," Stan added. He pointed to the pentathlon buoys. "It's opposite where we started from."

"Not that other side. The murky one. I cringe as storms rise up. Thor's my rock," she repeated.

Around the next bend the trees were a darker shade of green as they strolled beneath them. Thor meandered out on a fishing pier where mid-afternoon somnolence ruled and Stan thought back to his first glimpse of Kristine and Thor in the grassy glade. It reminded him of the Frenchman Seurat's pointillist painting *La Grande Jatte*, which he'd seen a reproduction of in Paris. It pictured a summer afternoon on the Seine with Parisians at river's edge. Two women flashed fishing poles, while a staid couple walked under a parasol as their monkey and pet dog approached a larger black dog. A small girl in a white dress stared straight back at the viewer. Stan had read that the women were prostitutes, but nobody knew why the genteel couple kept a monkey.

Like the figures in that Parisian scene, no one spoke at this end of Lake Nokomis. The calmness reminded Stan of the enticing differences he'd experienced in German cities, yet his recent decade shift—he'd just turned thirty—caused a rumbling of self-doubt. Prospective employers were beginning to cast a doubtful eye on his hopping from job to job in city after city. At the same time, he knew years of routine would never suit him. Recently he'd struggled through Dickens' *Bleak House* and likened school teaching to the novel's dire description of banking one's future on stifled hopes. He himself imagined bleak years ahead if he didn't seek structured intellectual renewal, and soon.

"Do you want to know what really brings me here?" Kristine asked. The humidity curled her hair and beads of sweat formed on her forehead. She swept her skirt around and returned to the path. "This," she said. She pulled back her frizzled hair to show the birthmark close-up. "It's this and Great-grandma at sea. They run deep in my soul, they're why Thor and I come here. I mean, baseball's only my elevator music."

So, it's true, Stan thought. There's a story hidden by the lakeside, like in Seurat's painting. The Parisians had a reason for being at the Seine that summer day, but all we get from the painted scene are silent hints. It's like Kristine tuning in ball games without truly listening or caring much who wins; hers is a separate tale.

"My sister and me, we were twins," she announced suddenly.

"Were?"

"Caroline, she drowned here."

Kristine blinked as though she expected Stan to be shocked. He wondered instead what a drowning had to do with her birthmark.

"C and K, that was us. Identical, but no sense trying to fool people who was who, I bore a mark, she didn't. We were fourteen, took the same classes, but split up in rec. I tried soccer. She went for cross-country. Their practice runs led this way, so one day her team came here to cool off. Some of the girls headed for the deep part. Out there."

Tears welled up as she pointed toward the smaller bathing spot.

"Eight girls launched off, seven came back. C was missing. No panic at first, then they yelled. Divers found her snagged to a submerged tree limb. Nobody saw her, nobody heard her. No nothing."

Since crossing the walking bridge, Stan felt the talk drift away from his comings and goings. He'd seen Europe far and wide, but Kristine's world, with its silent sojourns, was grounded in this single park.

"I felt guilty," she said. "C and me, we came from the same egg, the same womb. She was lithe and nimble, but couldn't loosen herself from a dumb tree limb? And I wasn't there? It's a waking nightmare. Like I'm drowning with her. I know I'm dead, but holding Thor tells me I'm still alive. Who can be both?" She pulled the dog next to her and ran a hand the length of his spine.

Stan reflected on her tense words, feeling strongly, as he had before, that she sensed things deeply. Only this morning we were unknown to each other, he marveled.

"But it's more complicated than that?" he guessed. He took the leash and let Thor wander its full length to give Kristine more space to think.

Realizing his ploy, she looked him straight on. "C had it

all. Popular, smart, but I was lovelier, even if just a smidgen, or would've been, except for…"

She pointed to her birthmark and paused, as if seeking the truth.

"Well, we were equally lovely, inside, where it matters."

From his youth Stan remembered hearing folk tales of pregnant women in the Kentucky hills, who'd been deprived of proper nutrition and then bore babies bearing emblems of what their mothers craved. Like poor mothers that yearned for strawberries had red-haired children. He could think of nothing Kristine's mother might have lacked that matched her daughter's birthmark, except dark chocolate. He realized the birthmark set off the magic of her fairness, chiaroscuro maybe?

"Our docs guessed the capillaries formed wrong on my skin at birth and never dissolved, yet I lived to adulthood. C didn't," Kristine said.

"Meaning what? You wish it the other way around?"

"Nothing's that simple. This lake has taught me as much. Watching the clouds, soft or angry, and the quiet of this place, even with the jets, gives me peace, but the uncertainty sets me awry."

"Like the weather? Four moods in one day?"

"Everything's a jumble. It occurred to me that maybe C wanted it this way."

"She killed herself? C'mon."

"No, but I think she realized, deep down, that I was blessed. Some all-seeing force laid a hand on me. She was fated to be perfectly formed, but people admired my courage. I know you can't follow this, but she carried that realization with her. I know she did. And I failed her when it mattered most."

Kristine slowed down. "Life plays strange tricks."

Stan couldn't deny it. This morning he'd had no idea where he was heading and now he was here listening to an intriguing woman's unexpected tale and wondering where it was leading. He called Thor, who started them on the last stretch around Nokomis. Me, he thought, calling her dog.

***

Soon they crossed a pedestrian bridge over a creek. A few steps ahead lay the beach with the towheaded kids, who hit the water en masse to escape the sun.

"Sometimes I imagine a crowd like this 80, 90 years ago," Kristine said. "They'd be jabbering away in European tongues. The State brought in New England schoolmarms to teach them English. Now everybody talks alike."

Stan thought of the summer day eight years past when he sailed the opposite direction, Boston to Bremen. Lots of gray Novembers, like he'd imagined going to bed with last night, had followed, but in Europe folks looked and acted different from country to country and he adjusted.

"It made immigrants feel at home, learning the language." Kristine paused before continuing. "For those who made it. Lives were lost along the way."

"Here, too," he said, nodding toward the lake. "You carry that with you, your sister."

"I felt like one of those old-world immigrants after C drowned," she replied. "I had to learn how to live all over again. On my own."

As she spoke, a blustery wind blew up. Stan sat down in a lakeside picnic shelter. Kristine took a seat opposite him. Fiercer gusts rattled the corrugated tin roof, so Thor crept under the table.

Kristine nodded toward the approaching downpour. "You've almost completed the weather cycle," she said whimsically. "Chill, heat, wind, and rain. The only season you've missed today is winter. You'll get home before then."

"Yes, home," he agreed. With nowhere to go save an empty apartment, he paused. Meeting Kristine, he'd forgotten his self-absorption. Her own history could have led down the same suicidal path as Goethe's generation, but she strove to gain from her losses.

"We've had Decembers without snow. It usually comes, though," she said.

"If I wait long enough?"

"No guarantees. I thought if I waited, I'd figure out why Great-grandma was the only one who reached that rock, or why it was C that drowned, and why I got this birth mark and she didn't."

"Answers," Stan countered. "I wonder a lot, what if I wake up one day and—just like that—I'm alone and forty?"

"Is that what Goethe wrote about, ideal love, disappointed dreams? What about stumbling onto something simpler?" she asked, pointing to Thor and herself and their simple shelter. Thor moseyed around to Kristine's side, where the two looked at Stan, like here you have us, our story.

Stan imagined those words spoken for real, so he asked, "Where does the energy to tell your story come from?"

Thor whined impatiently, before Kristine responded. "Water, an Atlantic rock, a submerged tree trunk. They have no meaning unless we invent one. You know the line about conflicts? Once we reach a resolution, the story's over." She wrinkled her brow, wondering whether she'd understood his question and answered right.

Stan wondered if his wanderings in Europe had been a search for serious answers, as he always told himself, or if those travels, like the fickle Minnesota weather, were merely whirlwind distractions.

"I flee," he declared. "Or am put in perpetual motion. In Germany, they sent me out as a traveling school inspector. I spent a year-and-a-half without being in any town more than three weeks."

The troublesome gusts slackened, but approaching clouds gave Nokomis an eerie glow.

Seurat-like, Stan and Kristine gazed at a last gaggle of geese skimming to rest on the surface.

"You know," she began in a reflective tone, "in life there aren't any resolutions. That's only in books or movies."

The calmness of her words matched the tenor of the scene until the clouds grew angry. Thor yelped when his namesake sent jagged bolts of thunder and lightning through the darkening sky. Wind swept madly across the lake so bells on moored sailboats clanged and rain swept horizontally through the shelter, forcing them to dash for a nearby clubhouse.

The cloudburst buffeted the clubhouse wall, which Kristine leaned against. When she stepped out into the open, a torrent drenched her. The water cascaded down her face till Stan draped the beach towel over her head and dried her off, as she had done to Thor. With the towel hanging down to her waist, Kristine backed off and stood like a headless apparition. Stan stared awkwardly, seeing nothing but the drenched sheerness of her wet skirt and the long straight legs it clung to.

As if sensing his uncertainty, she laughed and let the towel fall to the asphalt. With a self-concerned smile, she next rummaged in her backpack till she produced a brush and ran it through her hair with long careful strokes, so the strands fell over her shoulders but without the former lustre. With each brush stroke she tilted her head so she revealed the birthmark, which made that side of her face appear doubly dark in the fading light.

On an impulse, Stan gently touched her face. He let his fingers glide down her left temple, slowly brushing her cheek and grazing her lips. Her birthmark was soft like the rest of her skin, so he felt the difference in hue was only capillary deep. He ran a hand through some ringlets by her ear. She glanced up at him, and her expression changed from concern to guarded surrender. He leaned forward to kiss her, but she backed away, a tempting smile still on her lips.

Kristine turned again to her backpack. She clicked the radio to see if it worked, folded the wet towel, and searched in vain for her sandals, which Stan said the wind had whooshed away. He found them nearby and stuffed them in her backpack, after which he assessed his dripping clothes and hair.

"We survived," he said with a chuckle once the storm had blown away.

"Not everybody does," she replied. "I saw a guy's sailboat tip over in a storm once."

She stared pensively toward the lake but abandoned

the sailboat story, deciding she'd talk of death no more. She looked down at her bare feet. "My toes," she said. "C's were the same. Perfectly even, save for a too-long toe on each foot. Embarrassing."

"We make do," he replied.

A sliver of daylight remained. "Winter coming," Stan said.

"I always wonder, where do geese go in a storm like this?" Kristine interrupted.

Stan shrugged. "Hunker down, like us?"

They returned to the picnic shelter in semi-disarray. Stan sat on the tabletop. By a dim ceiling light, he watched Kristine sort through her backpack yet again, take out the sandals, and straighten Thor's fur with a bristly brush. After each stroke, she removed his thick fur with her thumb and forefinger. As she let one gob fall to the floor, she looked up at Stan.

"Yes, they make do," she said.

He smiled. After that they returned to the path where Kristine whispered a few words to Thor. Then she lingered, Stan beside her. They spoke to each other softly. It was summer and her radio still worked, she told him.

"Good. We'll tune it in together," he answered. "Tomorrow. Same time?"

"Yes, same place. New ball game."

After a pause, she whispered, "So long," and led Thor away.

Stan watched until she was out of sight. Left alone, he hardly remembered where he parked his car or what to make of the unexpected thunderstorm, but he shrugged merrily at the bother of sudden change. From now on, he guessed, it'd be four seasons every day.

OUT
THE
WINDOW

IT WAS LATE afternoon in Sweden, 1973. Ewen Knighton had just got Beckman, the cross-eyed giant, to lie down in a separate room when Ben jumped him from behind. He clamped his good hand on Ewen's neck and squeezed so the American cringed in pain. "Not throw him out the window, not?" Ben said in staccato Swedish, his dark brown eyes squinting with pleading intensity.

"No, Ben, not throw you out the window, not," Ewen replied in the Swedish he'd picked up during a long winter at Ward B of Vapentake Mental Hospital. As he spoke, he tried to wiggle free, but Ben tightened his grip. "No," Ewen repeated, "not throw you out the window, I promise."

"Not lock him in the bathroom, not?"

"No, no way. Never."

Ewen finally pried himself loose and hurriedly checked what was happening around him in the dayroom, where he was alone with 32 developmentally challenged adults. Some were rowdies from the violent ward, others mute and docile. His glance fell on little Dick, who was born with syphilis. Though now in his twenties, Dick still had the hairless features of a toddler. Dick shed his pyjamas and lurched toward the toilet. With an innocent smile, he left a trail of drool and yellow pee on the dayroom floor, which Ewen had just finished mopping. Motala, the ward B gymnast, was doing somersaults on the therapy workbench. He sent a stack of picture books and a checkerboard flying. Some checker pieces slid to rest by Hasse, a balding but ageless soul, who was rocking back and forth on a bench against the far wall. Ewen dashed over to look for the scattered pieces, praying his boss Kalle wouldn't show up and discover the mess he'd sent him to prevent.

"How's it going?" Ewen asked Hasse while he searched around his feet.

Hasse stared ahead. Out through the windows he saw— or Ewen imagined he saw—a bright point of light. Hasse leaned forward, then pulled himself upright, and slammed the back of his head against the wall, an act he repeated hour after hour. Over the last thirty years he'd created a bloody halo on the plaster behind him.

As Ewen stood up from Hasse's bench, somebody gave him a bump. It was Osby, another broad-shouldered behemoth, whose thick lips spread in a friendly smile, revealing three of his front teeth were missing. "Hak...la, hak...la," he stuttered.

"You want a bib? A *haklapp*?"

Osby nodded, so Ewen led him to a cupboard, removed a cloth, and fastened it around his neck. "Hot chocolate coming up," he fibbed.

Osby fingered the bib and smiled even broader. He sat down and waited expectantly for his cocoa and rolls, still two hours from delivery.

With that, Ewen made everyone happy. Even Beckman was quiet. Ewen approached the doorway and peered in at the sleeping Swede, whose eyelids were barely closed and twitching so he appeared awake.

"Beckman'll fool you," Börje, the night manager, had said. Any time Ewen doubled up on the evening shift, Börje corralled him for coffee and talked in his soft south Swedish dialect. "You'll figure Beckman's awake when he's dead to the world. If you think he's dozed off, he'll snap your neck like a pretzel. Won't know what hit you."

"Funny. What made him that way and not you or me?" Ewen asked.

"Yeah," Börje agreed and stirred his coffee. "Could be us, but it's not."

"So what's he like on a rough day?"

So far Ewen had only grappled with Beckman when he grabbed the others' food or lunged for dessert. Beckman had never fought back.

While thinking these matters over in his relative solitude, Ewen took a vacant window seat opposite Hasse, who mumbled but never blinked. Meanwhile, Motala continued gyrating on his rubbery joints until he leapt over a table and skidded to a halt by Kalle's office. Despite the commotion, Ewen went on considering Beckman, blond, muscular, and pug-nosed.

"When he swallows his pills, he's tame as a kitten," Börje continued over coffee one night. "Stares around like a tranquilized cave bear."

Other times, Beckman had fits. The docs said it was epilepsy or St. Vitus Dance. "Old-timers I used to work with had no idea what those ailments were," Börje said, "so they made up strange names for them, like black blood or pooey-balls. That's when Beckman bugs his eyes out like billiard balls and strikes his head with his knuckles. It cracks like a rifle shot. Skull's thick as a...."

"C'mon, get off it," Ewen kidded him.

"Once he jerked a toilet stool from its moorings and slammed it through the wall. I saw him rip out the workbench, which was screwed to the floor. He smashed it to smithereens. Motala was on the stool and flew off like a spider monkey."

Ewen listened but had trouble knowing what to believe. Swedes were full of urban legends about Slavs and Greeks finding asylum on their shores then keeping goats and sheep in their apartments and turning to crime or murdering their daughters for dating Swedish men. Crimes of honor, the locals called it. Börje loved legends too, but Ewen had never known him to invent wild tales about the patients under his care. Besides, when Ewen arrived earlier today, Beckman was wearing his cave bear look and calmly gulped his pills down.

Nonetheless, scuttlebutt floated around. Co-workers remembered Kalle ordering staff to toss Beckman in the Storm

Room when he was at his worst. Throwing 300 pounds of maddened flesh around by main force? Ewen decided to lay low. "Stay out of the way, that's me," he remembered saying.

"Well, maybe you'll end up like the rest of us anyway," Börje replied. "Despite everything."

In his day room reverie, Ewen rested against the wall and peered absently at Hasse. Despite myself? Meaning what? As he got up and gathered stray picture books off the floor, Erik, a soft-spoken orderly, led a patient in.

"Go sit over there," Erik said mildly to Skarpheden, a thin, dark-haired patient about thirty, who loped toward a bench and slipped on a checker piece. Like Osby and Motala, he didn't go by a proper name. The staff called him Skarpheden because that's where he came from. The name linked him to a Swedish community recognized for its Nazi sympathies in the 1930s. Ewen watched as the fallen figure pounded angrily at the checkerboard, whose pieces caused him to tumble. He got up, kicked the books out of Ewen's arms, and flashed a threatening Loki-like grin.

"Go sit down!" Ewen shouted.

Skarpheden stood still. The only sound he made was a cackling laugh that gave off a smell of rotten teeth and bad breath. Erik was on his way out, so Ewen wondered desperately about his next move, when Dick pranced out of the toilet, naked. Several checker pieces stuck to his feet and he slipped and hit the floor by Skarpheden. Ewen reached out to help Dick when Ben seized him by the neck, once again from behind, and pleaded, "Not pour scalding water on him, not?"

At that instant Kalle's door opened and a tall, solemn man with curly hair shouted angrily, "What the hell's going on here!"

"No clue," Ewen muttered. He kept a wary eye on Skarpheden as he lifted Dick to his feet.

***

Lucky me, Ewen thought. He had a couple hours off in mid-afternoon but by six he was back to help Börje. After getting the residents to bed, Börje sat talking by the faint light of his John Silver cigarettes and the glow of the office coffeemaker. He showed Ewen the ropes but surely wondered what quirk of fate had landed the young Yank in this corner of the world. The shadows left Ewen squinting across the table and wondering how he'd answer if asked.

"Coffee?"

Ewen shook his head.

"A Long John?"

No again.

"What then?"

"I came here to Sweden to clear my mind from political troubles at home. You know, Vietnam. Watergate. Richard Nixon. Couldn't stand to see his face on TV again. Anti-war protests were going nowhere. Now I've been here forever and still wonder what I'm up to at Vapentake," Ewen told him.

"Because of Kalle?"

"Strange guy. Whadda I do, tough it out?"

"Like you say, no clue. This hospital's been open for forty years and nobody like you's ever worked here before."

"War, you know. You think you can escape it."

"Kalles are everywhere." His curious look urged Ewen on. "Where's your home?"

"Ever hear of Minnesota?"

"Yeah, lotsa Swedes."

"I mean the university there."

Börje lifted his cup slowly and swallowed so his Adam's apple bobbed in the coffee maker's crimson light. "Universities are like Kalle."

Ewen's first thought was a wise-ass reply, but he stuck to the facts. "I showed up for grad school there a couple years ago. Drunk on modern lit. You know?"

"Yeah. *The Old Man and the Sea*? *Den gamle och havet*, we call it."

Ewen fixed his gaze on Börje, who anticipated the next question.

"Yeah, I've read them all, the classics," Börje continued and smiled gently. "What next?"

"The war protests brought armed cops out, beating us with nightsticks. The profs. Like you say, they're Kalles, the whole bunch. They bogged me down. Endless glosses of *Paradise Lost*. Memorizing Old English grammar."

"Which is what?"

"*Beowulf*. Like Old Norse. You know?"

"I do," he said. "How'd *Beowulf* get you from there to here? C'mon."

"Met this Swedish girl."

"In Beowulf class?"

"No, in Studies of *Paradise Lost*."

"The old story."

"Well, not quite. Johan, her boyfriend, liked to tag along."

"And so they invited you here, to Swedish Utopia?"

"Johan said to me, 'Come home with us. Sweden's no paradise, but…'"

"But meaning he wouldn't share Birgitta with you?"

"Meaning there's no college tuition in Sweden. So I went to my Minnesota advisor and talked about taking a year off abroad."

"'Well, why not, confusing times these,' my prof figures. 'But who knows,' he says, 'you might even learn something.'"

"And here you be," Börje sighed. "So what do you think?"

"About?"

"This boring country, and all."

"Where do I start? Stockholm? I packed up my bags and followed Johan and Birgitta to the promised land. We hit all the parties. Great time."

"So when did doubt rear its ugly head?"

"In September. I showed up for classes at the university but was greeted with a teachers' strike. I needed something to do. So Birgitta told me to apply at Vapentake. 'They'll hire anybody,' she said. 'Jobless, college students, foreigners even.'"

"'And you're all three,' Johan chuckled. So one gray Monday morning I showed up here, at Ward B, from a country in a hated war, bearing a foreign name, which nobody could spell. 'You'll find your rhythm,' Kalle said and shoved me into the dayroom. Ward B."

Ewen thought back to the scene that first day. "Who woulda thunk it," he mused. "The sights. The smells."

"Yeah, gets some guys down," Börje agreed. "Like Bengt. He's the oldest and kindest of us all, goes out of his way to help, but the years take their toll."

"'Us old orderlies, we never live to see retirement,'" Ewen told Börje he had heard Bengt shouting one day. "'We end up kicking the bucket in this damn place just like the patients.' Bengt wrung his hands and screamed to high heaven."

Börje looked down at his coffee and jiggled the cup. Having trouble figuring what the evening manager was thinking, Ewen concentrated on Bengt's frustrations, which matched his own. The orderlies' only task, he'd decided, was keeping the residents clean and safe within a ward bombarded by the chaos they themselves created. The hospital planned their schedule immaculately. Staff woke them up at seven, dressed them, and served breakfast. At ten came cocoa and rolls, followed by lunch, and another whopping round of hot chocolate and pastries in the afternoon. Börje's evening shift put them to bed at seven.

"Vapentake's on permanent lock-down," Börje agreed, reading Ewen's thoughts. "No one gets a new lease on life here."

***

Twice a day, Ewen helped scrub the linoleum. The residents were given showers once a week, and beyond that, their only chance of getting clean was to wet their pants and be returned to the shower.

Even the joy of extra bathing can turn bad, Ewen thought, but decided not to say. Instead, he reflected on what was alluded to in Ben's maddening fear of being dangled upside down from a second-story window or dumped naked into a tub of ice water. When Dick refused to lie still, Ewen had watched co-workers force him to the frigid linoleum and jump on him or crook his arm. He'd watched a sadistic orderly dip Hasse's hand in scalding water. He'd seen others dowsing patients with freezing water, while the shower muffled their screams.

As a foreigner, Ewen was denied access to the residents' files, but Börje turned a blind eye when he peeked on the sly. Vapentake was built in the 1930s as a military base. The huge brick building that housed the featureless rooms of Ward B was once a barracks for Army recruits, but the authorities turned it into an institution for "crippled unfortunates." An old record book showed former bosses pointedly described patients as "uneducable retards" and "hopeless imbeciles."

"Lots of 'em are buried here. It costs too much to send their bodies home. In the '30s and '40s, most patients were sent here from the far north to distance them from home and make parental visits rare," Börje explained.

"Incest?"

"Yes. Lots."

While patient numbers continued to grow, employees became hard to come by, especially when word leaked out that Vapentake was a developmental dead-end. That perception gained ground when a nasty medical doctor told a Stockholm newspaper he turned down a job at Vapentake because he wasn't an animal keeper and had no desire to work in a cattle stall, clean though it was.

"So where do these patients come from nowadays?" Ewen asked.

"Near and far. Ben's one of your own."

"An American?"

"Italian Yank. Part Swede, too."

"With only one good arm. From where?"

"Somewhere, your state maybe. A car crash killed his parents, the mother a Swede, father from Milan. Ben suffered brain damage and partial paralysis on one side of his body."

"No relatives?"

"Only an uncle in Stockholm. The uncle turned the kid over to us, so he's grown up here, within these walls."

"Learning to talk Swedish in the third person? Like royalty?"

Börje changed the subject. "Your friend Hasse, then. Wanna hear about him?"

"Okay, Hasse," Ewen replied, "another guy that can talk, but nobody knows what he's saying."

"Right. He came down with fever as a kid. Zapped him. His parents delivered him to Vapentake, then disappeared. Some medical guy from way back described him as a living vegetable."

"Not much more can be said for Osby."

"A congenital idiot, calm and perpetually hungry."

At six feet six, Osby towered over everybody in the institution. Strangely, no one knew where he came from. His file described how a delivery truck from the town OSBY arrived at the hospital and sped off, leaving an unidentified youth standing in its wake. "Officials suspected he was a Pole that somebody ferried across the Baltic and dumped in Sweden. We've housed and fed him ever since."

"He's bigger than Beckman," Ewen said.

"True, but no match. Beckman's a northerner," Börje continued, "born to a backwoods Finnish girl. Some Swedish forester assaulted her and look what she got. A boy from the primeval forests, his mind infested by Lappland sorcerers and pagan spirits."

"St. Vitus Dance?"

"Worse. Beckman made it to pre-school before his seizures started. They brought him south and delivered him to us."

"I get it, but it's Skarpheden gives me the heebie jeebies," Ewen admitted. "The Evil Eye."

"Nonsense. He's harmless. A bunch of farmers found him as a naked baby under an oak tree. A band of Roma put him out to die. The farmers that found him were holding a neo-Nazi rally so they didn't want anybody to identify them. They left the baby at a police station and bombed off."

"Skarpheden's glare probably scared them out of their wits."

"Not Erik, he takes good care of him."

"Skarpheden's got it in for me. Like an inborn rage."

"It's you, not him, but if anybody's got a beef about life, it's Dick."

"The mellowest of all?"

"The saddest. Fetal alcohol syndrome, not just syphilis. His mother was a street hooker."

"Swedish?"

"In Stockholm."

"The playful puppy," Ewen said thinking of how Dick lunged for everything that caught his eye, a habit that caused staff to seek increasingly sadistic ways of forcing him to bed. "Few days go unpunctuated by Dick's screams."

"Anywhere people go, once they get absolute power over somebody, they'll abuse it," Börje replied.

He studied Ewen, long and hard.

***

Ewen hardly noticed Laila, the only woman orderly in Ward B, until she looked him up and asked about an English word in a magazine article on the British Royals. She was a twenty-five-year-old single mom. Her daughter's father was a young Brit she'd met while backpacking after her first year of study at the university, so she called her newborn Lis, short for Queen Elizabeth. Undecided about her studies, Laila had been an orderly at Vapentake for the last three years.

The evening after Ewen first put Beckman to bed all by himself, he and Laila went to see *Bonnie and Clyde*. The movie was old and they'd both seen it, but afterwards they ordered a bottle of Danish Elephant beer in a local pub and discussed the film. Sharing drinks was a Swedish habit that bugged Ewen no end. He wanted his own beer and offered to buy Laila one so they'd both have their own bottle.

"A great idea for a movie," she said, "just way too violent for my taste."

"America, all right. Violence and apple pie," he replied.

They sat fingering the rims of their glasses. Round

and round. His tongue never loosened up in Swedish before a couple of beers.

"Well, how long's it been?" she finally asked.

"What? Sex?"

"No, you. Being here. Long enough to be homesick?"

"A little. Now and then."

"So what do you think?"

"About?"

"You know. Vapentake. This boring country. The whole schmeer."

"Hard to know."

"What is?"

"What's going on, below the surface."

"Behind the scenes, you mean?"

"That, too."

"For example?"

"Börje, for beginners."

"The language? His south Swedish bothers me, too."

"No, I get what he says—not always what he means."

"Like?"

They finished the beer and he went for another. He returned and filled their glasses, recalling his favorite 3.2 joints back in Minneapolis, like a hole-in-the-wall called Stella's. "They should have free pitchers here, too," he mumbled.

She looked up perplexed. "Nothing's gratis. Free, as you say."

"So I've discovered."

"And Börje? What is it you don't get?"

"Like he's egging me on. Needling me."

"He thinks you're smart. You learn fast, but act impatient. You don't see what's going on," she explained, nodding at their beer bottle.

"What? What's going on?"

"He explains, but you don't read him."

"What's to read?"

"What he says."

She looked at Ewen expectantly, hoping he'd catch on.

"I understand," she continued. "It's hard for you to read between the lines in our language. Börje thinks we're all alike. Once you get…"

"Yeah, yeah, I know, total power. I've heard it all." He killed the rest of his beer with one gulp.

"Hospitals like this might not exist much longer," she said, pretending not to see his irritation.

"Why not?"

"They want to spread the patients out in community homes. We take it in stride, for better or worse."

"So?"

"So what do you think about it?"

"Can't say I do. What's to think?"

Silence followed while Laila sipped her beer. "Well, maybe Vapentake's more for the worse than the better," she said. "But know what?"

"What?"

"Lis has a new puppy. Wanna see it?"

"Sure."

They bicycled to her place in the winter darkness. Before leaving, the babysitter woke Lis up and Laila brought the girl her puppy. They watched as Lis gently stroked the tiny creature and held it close.

"His name's Buster," Lis whispered.

"Is this absolute control?" Ewen asked Laila.

"Lis and Buster? We call it love," she answered with a smile.

***

The university strike eventually ended, but Ewen stayed on at the hospital. Laila was there and, well, 'Why not?' as Johan put it. On the other hand, Bengt beat the odds and escaped Vapentake. Acting on an impulse, he took early retirement and left to live on Spain's Costa del Sol. Hasse was also gone. One afternoon in late winter, a rare glimmer of sunlight lit up the day room and Hasse's gaze brightened. He leaned forward and fell face down, dead. A lone relative showed up to claim the modest bank account the hospital kept in Hasse's name.

Another day Ewen was standing against the wall opposite Hasse's vacant seat pondering his Swedish work permit, which was soon to expire, when he thought he heard a rifle shot. Then two more echoing through the ward. Next thing he knew Beckman was in the room rolling his eyes so only the whites were visible. St. Vitus, Ewen thought and pressed the alarm.

Beckman was shedding his clothes when Kalle, three orderlies, and two Securitas guards barged in. The guards clipped Beckman at the knees and knocked him down. Beckman kicked and sent the orderlies sprawling across the room till Kalle stepped in and pressed him down. Beckman spewed out garbled words, mucous, and puke that splattered on the face of a guard pinned under him. Furious, the guy rolled Beckman over onto his stomach while the orderlies pounced on his back and beat him with fists and clubs. A silent, desperate struggle followed. Beckman lurched to his feet. He flailed at the guards and they hung on for dear life, eventually pulling him back to the floor. Blood, spittle, and primordial cries all melded together. Ewen looked on as Beckman fought like a preternatural savage exacting brutal revenge on humanity.

At last the Securitas guys subdued the exhausted and panting giant and slung him into the Storm Room. They left Ewen standing outside and listening as Beckman roared, banged, and kicked. When he finally stopped, the orderlies returned, strapped a straight jacket on him, and rolled him away on a gurney.

"That's it?" Ewen asked.

"Go get a bucket!" Kalle commanded.

"What for?"

"Just do it," another worker said.

When Ewen returned, Kalle opened the Storm Room again. "Clean it up!"

Beckman had defecated and eaten his feces or rubbed some on his face. The rest he smeared over the walls, floor, and ceiling.

Ewen mopped the room slowly, pausing each time he wrung the mop to gag and spit and vomit in the bucket, creating an ever fouler concoction as he went along. Soon he reeked of excrement. He stopped to clean the slime from his glasses, the effluvia dripping into his eyes.

When he left the room, Skarpheden stood in the hall grinning. Ewen tried to walk around him but Skarpheden blocked his way. Ewen grabbed him, tore off his clothes, and slung him in the shower room, cursing at the top of his lungs.

Ewen turned the cold water on and set the nozzle to an explosive stream that knocked Skarpheden to his knees. As Ewen sprayed him, Skarpheden crouched in the corner. The water battered him against the wall, on and on till his strength drained away. Finally, the wretch Ewen had turned him into scrunched down to nothingness, dowsed and discarded like a dying dog, but still glaring out in wordless hatred.

Ewen continued spraying him till he saw himself reflected in Skarpheden's mania. Me, he thought, like all the others?

He let the nozzle droop, but didn't drop it. Erik entered the shower room and turned the water off. Ewen watched his co-worker towel Skarpheden down and rub some life back into him. Still reeking of Beckman, Ewen wandered back to the dayroom to Hasse's old place, and took the seat.

"Not throw him out the window, not?" Ben said and clutched his arm.

Ewen was still there when the day shift left.

"You need a shower," Börje said when he came in. He waited in vain for an answer.

***

Ewen's work permit expired a few days later. The boss called and said Immigration wouldn't renew it, but he could finish his shift. Laila met him after work, and they biked over to see Johan and Birgitta. Ewen hadn't been there much lately, so they wanted to hear his news. He described Skarpheden.

"I explained it to our Yank," Laila said. "He got to see…"

"No, you're wrong," Ewen interrupted. "Vice versa. The situation gained total control over me."

Johan frowned, then nodded. "Who controls who," he said. "You need a beer."

"You bet, one of his very own," Laila joked.

The next day Ewen went to Vapentake and turned in his keys. Back outside, he looked up at the building. Behind a window in Ward B, a face appeared. Ewen squinted at the pane till the figure backed away. "No, Ben," he whispered, "not throw him out the window, not."

Leaving the hospital grounds on this first spring day of 1974 made Ewen's memories of Vapentake winter fade and his steps feel light. A breeze wafted between the stodgy old army barracks, lending them a joyous mien for once. In America prosecutors had exposed the White House Plumbers and Richard Nixon was under mounting pressure. For a moment, Ewen considered returning, maybe he was ready now, yet similar, or worse, troubles could pop up in D. C. any time, he suspected. What's more Laila and Lis were here and Buster no longer a puppy. Continuing on, he felt the gravel crunch cheerfully beneath his feet and saw the lilacs in full bloom. He stopped and touched them and other flowers, breathing in their irresistible essence. Small stuff like this is what Laila calls love, he thought, and stuck to his path toward home. He didn't look back.

A
PLACE
IN
SPACE

IT'S TRUE, John Dustman used to be a movie actor, but now he spends his time zapping squirrels. They scamper up his chimney on Oak Avenue and rummage in the attic. "Darned flibbertigibbets, there's no stopping them," he complains around the neighborhood, to all who will listen.

Hearing John now are his guests Noel and Belle, who called the other day and said they'd be passing through the Midwest from California on the way to a branch meeting of the Screen Actors Guild in Chicago. "We found you on People Search, and thought how nice to catch up with our old Hollywood pal," Belle had told John in her cheerful voice.

"Ah, yes, the Golden West," John replied, clicking uncertainly on his new cell phone. "Come up for a weekend in the Twin Cities, won't you?"

"Delighted. It's been years."

After a good night's sleep and a hearty lunch on John's screened-in porch, Noel and Belle are now exchanging puzzled glances as he describes the ongoing plague of furry-tailed rodents. "But why squirrels?" Noel interrupts and sneaks a peek at the towering trees in John's spacious yard.

"I get no rest."

"But, John..." Belle repeats in support of Noel's question.

"The place is lousy with 'em, I tell you, but there's this one...snowy white."

"In South St. Paul?" Belle wonders, as she studies the neatly arranged lawn furniture John has surrounded his house with.

"Legion!" he answers and blinks his watery eyes. "Like the locusts plaguing Charlton Heston and Max von Sydow in *The Greatest Story Ever Told.*"

"Oh, I remember the picture so well," Belle tells him and places a reassuring hand on his arm. "You were the Roman soldier carrying the banner in that big decisive battle. So brave."

Belle sees John getting even more misty-eyed and worries where his thoughts are heading next. She heaves a quiet sigh when Noel steps in to guide the conversation gently on. "Gee, John," her husband says, "with those bristles in your helmet you looked a noble Roman, for sure."

"We were all wet behind the ears in those days," John continues, "but we learned, didn't we? Like when Mike Nichols gave us roles in *The Graduate.*"

Noel and Belle turn toward John and laugh together at the memory. So nice to move on from chatting about squirrels, Belle thinks, as Noel says, "You bet. I just missed out on the role I wanted most, playing the hotel clerk in *The Graduate,* the guy that asks Dustin Hoffman, 'Are you here for an affair?'"

"And that line wasn't even in the original script," John is quick to add. "I mean, didn't you make it up for the other actor, Noel? And here the guy's still famous for it?"

They chuckle at the ironic twist, and Noel turns the reminiscing John's way. "And you were the morose guy at the table, smoking, when Dustin and Katharine Ross come into a strip club."

"Yeah, me, who never even smoked? And Belle played the bouncy stripper in that club," John adds with a tease.

"I did *not!*" Belle says with a huff of pretended indignation.

"And I was on the bus at the end," Noel adds.

"Wow, what a team," Belle laughs. "Noel's character

looking so confused when a young girl boards a city bus in her wedding gown, and then…" Belle pauses and considers her words, "Katharine acting so happy and then seeing John play such a grouchy guy."

John looks away, his expression frozen between a smile and a frown.

"But morose wasn't the real you, John," she says, picking up the slack. She looks at her husband and sees him shrug and take another peek at their host's tree-lined yard so nicely encircling the white frame house. John gives a cursory wave out across the lawn.

"The real me? What's here to remind me of the real me?"

"John, you were such great fun!" Belle insists.

"Fun? Here they think I'm just a loony old squirrel squelcher. Last summer, I invented a squirrel-proof birdfeeder, but the varmints broke into it. So I got a book on magic. Know what it says?" John looks at Noel and Belle, who shake their heads. "It says squirrels, especially albinos, are a witch's evil genius. This guy up and tells me the problem's the bats in my belfry, not the squirrels on my roof."

"Evil?" Noel asks.

"Yes, dear," Belle jumps in to explain. "Witches have those little mischief makers in fairy tales to cause grief. That's how you mean, isn't it, John?" She realizes John's only half listening.

"I greased the pole to the birdfeeder, but they climbed it anyway. I chased them into the neighbors' flower garden."

"What'd they say to that?" Noel wonders.

"I said the same to everybody. Squirrels don't have any right." John shakes his flowing white mane and motions out back, where they glimpse an empty doghouse. "Only my boy Spike kept them at bay."

"Kept?" Noel asks in surprise.

"So this is where you were born?" Belle interrupts, trying softly to deflect her host from his fixations. "All you talked about in California was the sea this, the sun that. You never mentioned St. Paul."

"I was so young when we left here. Besides, I grew up in the City of Lakes."

"Across the Mississippi?"

"The Father of Waters."

"So the Golden West?" she asks, her patience giving way to annoyance at John's circumspection.

"Sand and surf was my dad's dream. So he piled us kids into the ol' Dodge and..."

"Off you went?"

"You got it, ratty old Route 66. Straight to the City of Angels. That's where I met you."

"In Tinseltown," Noel says with a touch of sarcasm.

"Well, John, you certainly dreamed big," Belle continues.

"Didn't we all," Noel adds. "In the beginning."

"I was born for it," John explains. Belle hears his voice grow melancholy as though sepia tones of past events blend with the bright sunshine of this late summer day in a new century. "I grew up a go-getter, but unsettled. Hung around the studios running messages for John Ford and Howard Hawks, other directors, too."

***

Belle sees Noel stifling a yawn and remembers first hearing this tale ages ago. Hollywood was staging a banquet for Sam Goldwyn, but John couldn't afford a plate, so he asked the M. C. how he could get in. The guy told him to rent a tux and he'd sneak him in by the kitchen. Once inside, John found a table with Burt Lancaster and Tony Curtis when they were busy filming *Trapeze.*

"I talked to them all evening about filming the movie and later got to be an extra in some episodes with El Zorro."

"Ah, yes, Don Diego and all those whips," Noel agrees distractedly.

"We used to see you in old Zorro reruns," Belle says, "swinging on bullwhips between big, high city buildings." After El Zorro they made John a cowpoke, she remembers. He got to ride with Randolph Scott and shoot it out with a pack of Mormon sheep farmers. It was a range war and they drove the bigamists right off their cattle range. John always told that tale with gusto, but he loved winding it up on a serious note.

"Imagine, pretending they could love more than one woman at a time," he says in summary, like he's been retelling the story to Noel and Belle inside his head, in silence. "That was just before you and Belle came West for film school."

"Astrid, though?" Belle blurts out. "Before her, too?"

As she speaks, Belle senses Noel's alarm. They vowed not to utter a word to John about Petronella Tysk, the blonde starlet known to Hollywood as Astrid. Though claiming to be a Swedish farm girl from Iowa, she had no memory of the Midwest countryside and thought corn was the same as barley. Those mysterious quirks and her stunning beauty gave Astrid a celestial quality, which made her impossible to forget. She was John's only love.

"Burt was stupendous," John replies, ignoring Noel's momentary frustration with Belle. "He got his start as a trapeze catcher for the stars of the big top and performed his own stunts for *Trapeze*. He'd have made a great flyer for any circus, swinging from trapeze to trapeze."

"My, you never saw such a gentleman as Burt," Belle says.

"He starred with Gina Lollobrigida, remember? She stole the show in *Trapeze*."

"Hard to think, they're all gone now," Noel responds with a shake of his head.

Noel's tone leads Belle's thoughts even further away from Astrid. As she lets his sad words sink in, three squirrels, including John's white one, scurry under his enormous oak tree while a tomcat stalks them. The tom slowly lifts one paw at a time, his unblinking look fixed on the prey. When the cat finally makes his lunge, two of the squirrels scamper up the oak. The albino leaps toward another tree, like a bird gliding effortlessly on a summer breeze.

"Yippee, we're rooting for you," Belle yells.

"How about that white one?" Noel says happily to John. "A real flyer, huh?"

"Astrid, my one and only," John replies. The corners of his mouth droop down.

***

Astrid. Realizing John connects the white squirrel with his past love, Belle thinks back to the early 1960s and the Avenue of Stars. John was energetic but impetuous. He got a break helping Burt in *Trapeze*, but meeting Petronella was his real shot in the arm. She'd come to Hollywood from the Hawkeye Gymnastics Academy, or so she said. Her chimerical bearing and mesmerizing flair on a trapeze wowed crowds in the make-believe capital of film. "Just look!" Belle heard one boss exclaim in wonder. "That girl's out of this world."

Sure enough, Astrid swung like an angel on the bar and was fearless in the air, but what hopes and wishes she brought with her to Hollywood, or even who her parents and former instructors were, Belle never learned. She seemed as shrouded in mystery as she was covered in radiance. Only one thing was certain. In those first days, she was John's rock and undying flame. She made him feel at home on the streets of Hollywood. He bought a Corvette and rented a beach house. Belle recalled him telling in excited tones how he and Astrid swam far out in the Pacific on moonlit nights. It wasn't long before he drove them to Reno and they tied the knot. Astrid's devotion fed his lust for success.

"Now we're reaching for the stars," Belle remembers John saying, while Astrid smiled at his side. John wanted them to make a trapeze film on their own, this time with no Gina—and her Italian accent—or Tony—and his Brooklyn brogue—but a real Midwestern blockbuster. Noel and Belle went with them to ask Burt for backing. He was considerate but wouldn't help, so John decided to go it alone. Against the odds, he scraped together financial backing— it didn't hurt that Astrid had scads of new admirers— and rented a small filming studio.

Then came Hugo, the trapeze catcher, a dashing younger model of muscular Burt. He had gigantic, unfailing hands, and he was Swedish, too. As a teenager, he'd run off to the circus and was soon working under the big top in California, where John discovered him. *"Hej,"* Belle remembered him saying to Astrid in Swedish when John introduced the two. Astrid had replied with schoolgirl delight to his simple greeting.

High Flyer John would call their picture, with Astrid, Star of the Firmament, in the lead. He wrote a script with an even more daring love intrigue than Burt, Tony, and Gina's. What's more, aging film stars were sure to gape when Astrid pulled off a triple somersault, the first woman ever to do so on a Hollywood set. John wrote the picture's culminating scene in a Chicago big top, though they completed the actual filming in a cramped rented warehouse space in Hollywood. Caught up in John's enthusiasm, Belle helped him broadcast Astrid's planned triple far and wide.

The squirrels' bark-like grunting jerks Belle from her reveries. The two grays are chiding the cat, who's licking his paws in feigned disinterest after his failure at pursuing them up the tree. The three squirrels return to the ground and dash around madly. Finally, they climb up again and leap to a telephone pole, using its sagging line as their high wire.

***

"I've used everything on them," John says.
"But why would you?" Belle asks in astonishment.

"So what can you do?" Noel asks cautiously. "To stop them?"

"Guys call 'em tree rats, so I started out with rodent poison. Great on rats. But squirrels? Just makes 'em sick."

"And if you leave the poison out, pets'll find it, too?" Noel suggests, as John furtively looks away. "Spike?"

John bows his head.

"Oh, John," Belle sighs.

"Some guy online makes poison out of baking soda."

"Yeah, sure," Noel says skeptically, "and it works great as toothpaste, too."

"Then I soaked peanuts in strychnine. The squirrels died. Slow but sure."

"And you watched that?" Belle murmurs, nearly speechless.

"Only a couple."

"So I bet you had a last trick up your sleeve," Noel guesses. Belle hears the impatience in his voice. "What was it?"

"Car exhaust. I caught a couple in my garage, but they slunk out the tiniest holes." John gets up to clear the dishes and Noel and Belle watch as the gray squirrels abandon their merriment and bite the white one's head and nip at his tail.

When John returns, Belle coaxes him into a walk. She and Noel talk about their long drive from the West Coast and their life in real estate after Hollywood. "Have you ever regretted leaving us?" Belle asks.

John shows a melancholy smile. "My career bottomed out. Before its peak."

"Like ours," Noel agrees.

"There wasn't going to be any peak," Belle adds. "We lived with it."

They round the block and stop in John's front yard.

"You two had each other," he says. "I stayed on. You remember...all those years...till after *The Graduate*...but it wasn't the same. I came back here to Parks and Rec. I'm..."

"Yes, dear, we know, you're a one-woman man," Belle consoles him. And what a woman, too, she thinks. Or girl. Astrid made a tragic mistake with Hugo, but easy to understand. It wasn't just Astrid's otherworldly looks. On the trapeze, she took everybody's breath away. "Don't think on the bar," Belle recalls the experts telling her, "just do it," but she defied them, combining her athleticism with sure-fire decision-making. She brushed up on single somersaults and followed with doubles.

Only yesterday, Belle thinks, and pictures Astrid posing confidently on the pedestal board. Once or twice she swung with only the bare ground beneath her. Onlookers *ooooohed*! as Astrid cast out at the far end of the first swing, did her beat-back, swung high and into her breathtaking trick at the end of the second swing. She met Hugo in midair and clasped his hands. Time and again they were welded together till he released her and she swung back to the pedestal. Hugo's timing went with his perfect catches.

"The triple's next!" John told all of Hollywood, and Belle believed him. "Astrid has the world at her feet."

But Belle learned a triple was trickier than John imagined. She eavesdropped as he argued heatedly with Nomar, the wily cuss they brought in to consult. "She has to break extremely hard and let go in a straight position," the old-timer explained.

"Then we'll have to make the roof look higher," John argued.

"Don't you hear me? Look at her, this girl ain't earthbound. She needs space, tons of it."

"I got it figured," John countered.

"I'm tellin' ya, so much rotation, she'd never pull it off on a normal circus rig, let alone this," Nomar continued, waving dismissively at the make-believe Hollywood circus tent.

John explained he'd make it look like a true big top by zooming out with the cameras.

"But I'm telling ya, schmooze, no joke. We need distance, in real space," the consultant insisted.

The studio John rented was so cramped Astrid and Hugo had only mats under them, till Nomar improvised a safety net, more taut than normal. One day Noel and Belle took Nomar aside and asked him what he was so afraid of. "In plain English," Belle remembers Noel saying.

"You do a triple at such high speed," Nomar said, "your brain can lose track of where it's at in time and space. Some guys rotate so violently they never reach out for the catcher. I saw one crack his neck. Rigs like this'll kill even tough guys. Never know what hit 'em."

"Your brain can't keep up?" Noel had asked in dawning realization.

***

Oh, the danger of it, Belle thinks, as a lump forms in her throat all these years later. She's had a long fascination with triples, so much so she's watched them on YouTube, marveling at how flyers defy gravity. Belle imagines them abandoning all care as the worries of life on the ground and the dangers of open space dissolve into weightless freedom.

"I'll show you what I chase them with now," John says. He leads Noel and Belle out back, opens his garage door, and switches on the light, erasing Belle's lump of fear and excitement. The garage is empty, save a narrow carrying case on the workbench. John reaches for it and removes a rifle, its barrel strangely shortened.

"My .22. Sawed off. See what I added?"

"Good Lord, man!" Noel exclaims.

"A laser sight. I read up on it. Clean the weapon and install batteries, attach a slide. See? It focuses lightning fast. A red circle appears on their head. Squeeze and…"

"How many have you hit?" Noel asks.

John peers at the .22 and runs his hand along the smooth shaft. He looks up intently. "I'm supposed to see 'em hundreds of yards away."

"So you haven't hit any at all?" Belle guesses. Maybe the laser sees squirrels from several football fields away, but she realizes John can't hit the broad side of a barn with his fading eyes and a sawed-off .22. "It's a miracle you haven't killed yourself."

"Let me see it," Noel says and picks up the .22.

"I'll show you," John intercedes. He leads them to his backyard, where last summer's failed birdfeeder stands alongside Spike's forlorn doghouse. "Squirrels come out mornings and look around. I use the lawn furniture. Get a good aim."

John rests the rifle on his picnic table and gazes out at the garden. Noel and Belle plop down and swat at late-afternoon mosquitoes. "Oh, these darn things," she complains.

"Quiet!"

A squirrel emerges. It glances every which way, then jumps up on a tree stump and stares at the birdfeeder. John aims the rifle, but before he fires another squirrel scampers up a nearby tree in pursuit of the albino, who's hiding between branches. The white squirrel sails to the oak, climbs up to its highest limbs, and leaps for an impossibly far-off tree in a neighbor's yard, spreading its legs like wings and extending a long bushy tail. Outstretched, it hangs suspended between the opposing trees, gazing at the distant heavens.

Like the gods themselves, Belle thinks, before just as quickly fathoming that John is drawing a bead on the animal. It's his moment! He can let the squirrel fly to safety in the beckoning branches or—with good timing or a lucky shot—send him crashing down to earth. Belle wills him to pull the trigger and end the infernal gnawing in his head forever, but the albino sails on toward the tree. The squirrel grabs a branch, wiggles its snowy tail, and disappears in among the leaves.

John lowers the rifle. He rests his face on one arm and weeps, silently. Belle understands. He's seen Astrid. The albino has transformed his species, in John's mind, from a daily annoyance to a life emblem. He's remembered Astrid, like the albino, in mid-air. She's completed her triple and is hurtling toward Hugo. Belle intuits John's insidious vision of the event, how his life stopped when Astrid's neck snapped and the crowd hushed in horror. Today he could have exorcised the dreadful sight. He didn't have a prayer of hitting the squirrel, but he needed to pull the trigger on it despite everything.

"I couldn't," he says at last.

"We know," Belle replies.

***

Slowly the three stand up and walk back to the house, their expressions somber like the encroaching darkness. Belle roots in John's kitchen cabinet and starts brewing some fresh coffee. John adds cream to his cup and stirs it round and round.

"She fell, you know," he finally says.

"Yes, dear, we know."

"I couldn't face it."

"For forty years?"

"That's the way I am."

"What were you holding onto?" Belle asks.

"Our place. Always the same. Unchanging."

"We all saw her fall," Noel says.

"I imagined she didn't."

"Hugo didn't drop her on purpose."

"He didn't drop her at all. It hit me today, as I was ready to fire. She never reached out for him."

"You mean?" Belle says. "But Hugo always blamed himself."

"Or her brain didn't keep up," Noel suggests.

"She made her own decisions," John concludes.

"Yes, maybe," Belle says. "A perfect triple? What do you do after that?"

They sit in silence while twilight envelopes the room. A red light on the coffee maker casts a faint glow and reflects off their faces. To Belle, it makes John look younger, so she remembers his youthful dream of hastening to the top. That's probably what kept Burt from funding him, she reflects.

"She had her charisma, my beloved," John sighs, "but once in the air she was like the white one, far distant from us mere groundlings. She knew I needed something."

"A different place?" Belle asks.

"An inner life. She was here to set me free, from myself. She looked up…"

"At you," Belle interrupts.

"No, at the lights, before she launched off the pedestal."

"At the stars," Belle muses.

"If only I'd understood."

After John falls silent, Belle's thoughts drift back to South St. Paul, a town so languid not even John can invent nicknames for it. The humid night air lies like a blanket over them, and their thoughts become heavier. In through the open window comes the chirping of crickets. John reaches for his .22. Slowly he dismounts the laser sight and stashes the rifle in a closet behind him. At last he goes to the coffeemaker. He switches off the red light and turns to his guests. "A breath of air?"

"Sure thing," Noel agrees and follows John. Belle joins them outside later, just as a shooting star flashes across the sky.

"Hmm," John comments wistfully, "do stars fall all the way to earth?"

"I wonder," Noel answers.

"No, they burn out in the sky or find a permanent place up above," Belle explains.

In the general stillness, all they hear is the squirrels thumping along John's roof as they head for nests in the highest reaches of the mighty oak. Noel places his arm on

John's shoulder and Belle holds him around the waist. The three old earth-bound friends gaze up at the sky, where the constellations twinkle brightly, nearly turning night into day. Belle wonders which star is Astrid.

DOWN
THE
RIVER

"WE'RE STILL SLAVES, FOLKS. Our owners just removed the chains from our legs and wrapped them around our minds," Anselmo Washington said, careful to temper his tone. A black Mississippian born and bred to the plantation, as he described himself, he stood on his steamy front porch, hat in hand, and spoke to the white folks before him. He told them how he came to Illinois and decided to buy this grand old slave house on the north bank of the Ohio River to offer tours and show Midwesterners their true history. "You never know your future till you understand your past," he liked to explain. But only six paying visitors showed up, and he needed seven to break even. Anselmo wondered if he and they had anything in common besides the maddening horseflies buzzing around them. He swiped at the pests with his hat and led the visitors into the former slave master's quarters.

"Five greenbacks, admission," Anselmo announced. There were times he considered charging more, but his aim was to tell things like they were, and he feared raising the price would turn folks off.

"I'm Ruth from Rockford," a blonde, middle-aged woman said. "Interior decorator. Wasn't this a free state before the Civil War?"

"Yes," Anselmo answered. "But a slave owner arrived in 1834 and built this lovely mansion, Greek Revival style. It was one of the most notorious slave houses in the U. S. A story of misery and the vile ways slaves were treated by the most violent slave driver in American history. John Crenshaw."

"Crane-shaw?"

"No, ma'am, Crenshaw, John H. See the gorgeous view he had?" Anselmo motioned to a steep verdant hill leading up from the River.

"Magnificent," Ruth agreed. "But I'm here to see the inside furnishings."

"That there's the hill niggers like me climbed every day, all the way to the mines. Note the pole with ball and chain attached."

Ruth looked up in surprise when Anselmo used the n-word. Without speaking, she turned to the master bedroom featuring flowery wallpaper and sturdy oaken ceiling beams. She studied several cabinets with vintage toiletries and bed linen neatly placed on shelves. Beside the cabinets stood a glass case displaying shackles, pockmarked hand weapons, and a sawed-off shotgun.

"Crenshaw became the wealthiest man in the state," Anselmo said to the other visitors. "So he built this dwelling. Constructed by intelligent black men. They scoured the South for the best slave craftsmen. Those colored masons anchored this house in eight foot of solid bedrock."

"Amazing construction work, but this Crenshaw guy, he got away with it? Practicing slavery in the North?" asked a tall, serious-looking senior, who introduced himself as George Johnson, a retired building contractor from Indiana. He addressed Anselmo earnestly while his wife, who walked with a cane, hobbled from room to room. "I've heard tell of this place, but never knew what to believe."

"Crenshaw made his fortune on the salt mines. The work was too hard for white men, so Crenshaw smuggled slaves from Kentucky. He kidnapped Northern blacks and forced them into the mines. We still got an old salt kiln outside," Anselmo said, pointing to the backyard. He, George, and a couple in their twenties, gazed out at the kiln. "This mansion made 250 thousand a year from sales of salt and paid half the taxes of the State in 1842. Crenshaw was so rich he bribed Illinois senators for the use of slaves."

After Ruth and George's wife returned to the room, Anselmo continued talking as he led the group up more stairs. The sixth visitor, a slender Latina with a baby cradled in a sling over her shoulder, appeared from the restroom below. "I'm Carmen. And this is my daughter, Maria. Sorry to lag behind, we're from Chicago, just wanted to see how other ethnics lived," she said while pressing a bill into Anselmo's hand. "Ten, for me and Maria." Anselmo was grateful for the extra cash but felt embarrassed accepting money for the child.

"Crenshaw ferried Kentucky slaves across the Ohio," he explained. "In bad weather he kept them overnight in a slave hut. Or on the third floor, up above."

"Even farther up?" George's wife asked and pointed at the stairway with her cane.

Anselmo nodded. "Steep, all right."

"Never you mind, we'll manage," the woman assured him. "Just you wait and see!"

"John Crenshaw treated blacks like animals," Anselmo replied with a contempt for the slave owner that defied his smile.

At the top of the second flight, Anselmo paused for the Johnsons to catch up. He ran his hand over a shiny mahogany post. "Know what this is?" he asked. He reckoned no one would answer, but Carmen raised her hand like an eager school kid.

"A whipping post," she said.

"Sure, like at Chiago's Cook County Jail, huh?" Anselmo replied, as if from experience.

"Hey, my man Eduardo did a stint there," Carmen explained. "He's from below the border."

"No Latinos here, but lots of black men's blood ran down

57

this post. The whites taught us backwards, in their language, forced us to learn their ways. Out on the slope, horses pulled them apart, limb from limb. Early in the twentieth century old ex-slaves hereabouts still recalled their agonized screams. What's the difference, folks, between killing us on the spot and making us follow their white ways?"

While Anselmo waited for a reply, Ruth offered a friendly smile. George shook his head. "Beats me," he mumbled. The young couple looked at each other until the woman answered, "Up north in Minnesota, we got nothing like this. We're Stan and Kristine, married grad students, traveling through. Stan hails from Paducah and he doesn't know about any of this either. Just tell us."

"On the spot is instantaneous," Anselmo explained.

When no one commented further, he led them through the second-floor. "Is this more like it?" he asked and showed them Crenshaw's sumptuous banquet hall. The dining table ran the length of the room, with chandeliers jangling above. The group ran their fingers along the shiny tabletop and talked among themselves, while Anselmo detailed the value of the household goods. When they re-assembled, he produced a pre-Civil War bill of sale from the mansion's files. It listed two mirrors for $1.50 each, a shotgun worth $5.00, a chair for $8.00, a slave woman priced at $500, and her daughter for $100.

Meanwhile, Ruth and the Minnesota couple inspected a mixture of items arrayed along the wall, including canning jars and a cream separator. Ruth pointed at a gaggle of bones hanging from a rod in the otherwise empty cloak room.

"A dead skeleton," George's wife said blankly.

"A man's," Carmen added. "I can tell. Like *Dia de los muertos.*"

"Yes," Anselmo agreed. "A dead slave found in a salt pit. Crenshaw left him there. Never bothered to dig a grave. Somebody hung him up for tourists."

George's wife put her cane down and leaned against the banquet table. Anselmo pulled out a chair as she gazed at the spectacle. "Lord, so hideous."

"Folks say that's Lincoln's seat," Anselmo explained. He made a point of telling every group of visitors about the chair. He'd grown used to the blank stares his comment often left on their faces, but Ruth, Carmen, George, and the young couple stood firm and watched him intently.

"Abe Lincoln, the liberator?" Carmen asked.

"He ventured this far south, imagine," Kristine said to Stan. "Just like us, from way up north, honey."

"Not what we learned in school about Lincoln," Carmen added.

"Oh, yes, in 1840 Honest Abe passed through here, ran for state office. John Crenshaw hosted him at this very table, even threw a fancy ball, with white men's quarters below and slave rooms above."

The Minnesotans gazed up as if they imagined rebellious feet stomping on the ceiling. "Hard to believe," Stan said.

"Cars with plenty different license plates been here," Anselmo agreed. "I've had people try to sleep in the slave's attic. White folk don't last a night."

"Because they realize what their ancestors did?" Carmen guessed.

"Their conscience can't bear it," George deduced.

"We're all brainwashed to the max, black and white alike," Anselmo explained kindly, sensing how this group caught his drift intuitively.

"Nowadays us slaves believe we are free," George mused.

"Here we are a hundred and sixty years later," Ruth said with a sigh. "If we really were free, we wouldn't be here now, would we?"

"Free?" Anselmo asked. "Free puts you on tricky ground. You never know. Crenshaw captured freed blacks and sold them back into slavery. He tricked them into boat rides on the Ohio and dumped them on the other side in chains. Underground railroad in reverse."

"Thus the expression sold down the river," Ruth surmised.

Anselmo smiled at the group's attentive feedback.

"But we can change that," Carmen said as though reading his mind. "Can't we?"

Anselmo turned and led the way up another staircase. He showed them a line of windowless rooms.

"Like for Mexican farmhands," Carmen commented.

"Notice, some rooms don't have bars," Anselmo explained. "Only women and children were locked up. Sixty to a hundred slaves, eight to ten people per room, in this heat and humidity, no bathroom, no water."

"Hideous," George's wife repeated. She and George had managed the steps well and now stood resolutely in the narrow hallway. Anselmo noticed how they cringed as if the third floor still smelled of sweat, urine, and tears.

"Tiny wood bunks, no ventilation or daylight, in 100-degree heat," Ruth lamented.

George wiped perspiration from his brow.

"What about the men?" Carmen asked. "Why no bars?"

"Didn't need them," Anselmo replied. "If they ran off, Crenshaw shackled them to that pole outside, as an example. But he had to be careful. If he beat them too bad, the scars remained and the slaves' value sank. The worst offenders went to the whipping post."

"Their value sank on the free market," George commented ironically.

"Supply and demand," Anselmo agreed. "See this last room? That was Uncle Bob's. Crenshaw kept him locked up in there for twenty years as a stud. Like a stallion. Fathered 300 slave children."

"And Abe Lincoln knew this?" Ruth asked incredulously. "He was here. Saw it? Heard it?"

"Your guess's as good as mine. Stories, you know," Anselmo answered. "This place operated till the 1860s. Crenshaw outlived the War. The property remained in private hands, for the salt, and later for tourists. I owned it a while, till the State bought it from me. Now they let me run it and I keep the cash."

"You believe that? About Uncle Bob?" George's wife asked.

"He lived to be a hundred. Ended up in a senior residence. Story was, he thought they were moving him to a new stud farm, at age 85."

"Spooky," Kristine said.

Maybe so, Anselmo thought.

The tour over, he showed them down the stairs and through the house till he stood before them once again, hat in hand, on the front veranda, in the familiar summer heat.

"Interesting, folks?" he asked.

"Yes, very much so," Ruth answered. "More ways than one."

The others nodded yes, but said nothing. They waited together, free to go, but going nowhere. They were sympathetic souls, Anselmo knew, who had not set out that day to spend their cash on bitter knowledge. Now here they were, struggling with the full import of what they'd seen and heard, as though something atavistic and horrific crawled inside their bones. Their faces begged for magical words to exorcise their nagging unrest or somehow make such human cruelty fathomable, but Anselmo turned as voiceless as they. Seven times five, he thought, that's what my working day's amounted to. Yet he also realized, as never before, that he could do more than just break even. He could make the truth heard, if the time was right, and the people, too.

SEPTEMBER
MIST

LUCAS MOREY HAD NEVER SEEN EVE, the atheist, fully clothed before, so he did a quick uie when he glimpsed her in a yellow dress at the corner of Oak and Sixteenth. "Where you been forever?" she asked him, as he stopped beside her on his ten-speed. "Not here, I hope." She waved dismissively at the stucco homes around them, as if to say this is where she still lived and hadn't left.

"Pure serendipity, again," Lucas answered. He had chanced upon Eve in that same neighborhood ten years earlier when he and his wife Janice lived on Oak Avenue. On a Sunday in July, the two of them were returning home from a Science Museum lecture on entropy and joking about it.

"It's easier to create complete chaos than maintain entropy," Lucas quoted the speaker.

"So, the present feels like orderly decline to you?" Janice had asked. "Compared to what?"

"The future. It's speeding madly away, like the universe."

"And here's the present. What do you make of this?" Janice interrupted in a serious voice. She pointed at a VW van perched at a crazy angle on the curb. A disheveled blonde woman was leaning against it. When Lucas pulled over, she ran to their car. "Can you call an ambulance? I'm having a seizure. I've got narcolepsy. Now epilepsy, too. Lost control."

Lucas had hurried across the street to knock at the nearest

house. A black teenager answered the door and yelled back inside, "Hey, Mother, can you call 911?"

The First Responders arrived just as Lucas saw Janice move over to the driver's seat of their car. While the officers calmed the stricken blonde, the boy's mother emerged from their house and sat on the front steps. She was wearing dirty cut-off jeans and a partly unbuttoned blouse. Her coal-black hair hung in disarray over her shoulders. Lucas looked down at her thin, straight legs and bare feet, trying to win precious seconds with this casually evocative woman, who wiggled her toes while peering at the Fire crew's rescue efforts.

"Eve," she said when he finally turned away.

"Luke," he replied and walked back to his car.

Barefoot Contessa, he thought every time he passed her house after that, until while out biking one lonely afternoon he screwed up his courage and knocked at the door. The same teenager answered. "Mom? At work. Her garden store down the street." Lucas found the store's work crew planting tomatoes, while Eve tugged at weeds in a rain-splashed raspberry patch. Her frown disappeared when she saw him. "I had a feeling," she said. She gave instructions to the employees and struggled to keep a strand of hair off her face. "My locks're kinda unruly," she said. "Or haven't you noticed?"

Lucas talked languidly to her about his studies in Civil Engineering and Janice's library job. They had once entertained big dreams, he explained. Janice trained as a concert pianist and he longed to paint, but both were destined to end up as faceless bureaucrats.

"That was her, that Sunday, behind the wheel?"

"My wife? Yes."

"Pretty."

Lucas nodded in agreement.

"I work Sundays," Eve explained. "That's why I was such a dirt ball when you knocked."

"Ignoring the Sabbath?"

"We're not believers. My husband Leon's a bureaucrat," she said with a smile. "In Oregon. He couldn't handle the Midwest. Left me and our son to tough it out on our own."

"So you're an atheist?"

She smiled as if his question was amusing, and irrelevant, too. "My son's called Ben."

Eve wiped dirt from her forehead. While doing so, she bent over so her blouse puffed out. Glimpsing her ample breasts, Lucas felt a visceral desire.

Eve showed no embarrassment, but quit weeding. "Walk me?" she asked.

And so well into late summer Lucas whiled away his afternoons with Eve at the Community Gardens and then walked her home. They chatted about the hot sidewalk on her feet and how he had approached, and then passed, a thousand miles on his bike odometer. Eve said she grew up in Seattle but moved to Minnesota with Leon.

"He's from here, wanted to move back after the Army," she explained.

"Till he remembered what winters are like?" Lucas guessed.

Eve had always wanted to be an organic gardener or a physical therapist, "nurturing the soil or kneading bodies."

Lucas asked her about the blonde woman and all her "-lepsies." Eve said she saw her only now and then. Lucas explained how he went to college for Art but met Janice in a Chemistry lab.

"Civil engineering, huh? So you'll be nurturing the environment, like me?" Eve asked.

He remembered how they once stopped and looked inquiringly at each other. Lucas brushed her cheek and tucked the errant tuft of hair behind her ear.

"The first black woman you ever touched?" she asked.

"So long," he replied and headed off to meet Janice.

That fall, Janice became pregnant with twins. Lucas finished his Masters and found work, so the next year they moved to the suburbs. Two years later he was the father of two daughters, Jennifer and Jessica, and a son, Michael. In time, the only physical vestige of that summer ten years ago was his ten-speed. To keep his waistline in check, he resolved to pedal seventy miles a week. Usually he headed out into the countryside, but today, on a lark, he made for the city. The odometer had just ticked off fifteen miles when he spied Eve in her colorful dress.

As Lucas sat on his Trek and remembered the long-ago meetings with Eve, he also studied her as she now was. Forty, he thought, against my thirty.

Lucas and Eve lingered at the crosswalk as the light changed from red to green and back again. He noticed the snug fit of her suit and the easy way she turned her frowns to smiles. She told of leaving Community Gardens and studying land surveying at trade school. She was on her way to work at the Department of Transportation. "The gardens were great till Leon left. I needed income during the wintertime, too."

"Leon? Still gone?"

"He shows up now and then. I won't file for divorce. Committed to my vows, you know."

Lucas thought about his own marriage. He and Janice had lasted a decade, even if their hopes had turned to routine. It happened gradually. Lucas had wearied of work. His managers' stultifying talk sapped him of any desire to advance. Promotions seemed only a doorway to higher-paid palaver. At times he longed to pull a Gaugin and escape to the South Seas to paint.

Janice, in turn, had changed to a stolid music cataloger. Where she once taught Lucas to worship Stravinsky's shock vibes or form homespun theories about Beethoven's shifting sensibilities, she now talked about the great masters' OCLC catalog numbers. In college they'd sat in 3.2 bars and laughed or smooched, but Jenn and Jess ended their carefree ways.

Lucas loved flirting with women he met biking or at reading circles, or occasionally with co-workers. Each lady had moxie and pleasing manners, yet when he observed them in their social circles he realized how affairs, like matrimony, could settle into daily flatbread. In time he came to believe that women, whom he romanticized from a distance, could be as dull as the male desk jockeys at his firm or the aging athletes on his slow-pitch softball team.

"It wasn't just the winters," Eve said, jerking Lucas back to their conversation. She spoke softly now, so the roar of traffic nearly drowned out her words. "Leon drank, he never let on before we married. He beat me, too."

"And you respect the vows? Still?"

"My business card," she said, and pushed the *WALK* button.

Lucas watched her hurry off before he glanced at the inscription. *E. V. Cross. Land Surveying. Gardening. Organizing.* The simple words suggested a tantalizing aura re-entering his life.

A month later Lucas guided his Saturday bike trip back to the city and spotted Eve in her backyard. He watched her brush back her hair, first with one hand and then the other. The insistent strand clouded her view, but a muffled bark gave away his approach. A golden retriever sniffed at Lucas and lifted its butt in play.

"Pharaoh, my new rescue. He doesn't bite," Eve explained.

She snapped a leash on the dog and they set off down the same sidewalk he remembered from a decade before. While Pharaoh ran ahead, Lucas told her about a young elkhound he'd seen jogging beside its owner earlier that morning. It tugged mightily at its leash. Eve's teeth shone gloriously as she laughed at his story, but he noticed a crease on her neck, which deepened, he remembered, when she became nervous.

"I garden as a hobby now," she explained and tilted her head back.

Lucas asked what the tilting gesture meant.

"Leon called," she answered. They were turning back toward her house when she spoke again. "He's sick. He's coming home."

"Ailing from Iraq?"

"He never fought, doesn't want to work, is all. Such a flunkey. Imagines I'll support him." As Eve led Pharaoh up to the house, she looked at each car on her street as if expecting the worst.

Other times Eve told how she stayed put in the neighborhood, without knowing why. Probably, she mused, it was her being drawn to the diverse people there or the small cafés where she sat and sifted through memories of growing up black in a white Seattle neighborhood.

"Tough?"

"No, just a feeling of being invisible. White folks knew we were there, but we didn't exist in their mental world."

"Better here?" He'd heard about Ferguson and other civilian atrocities, but growing up in an all-white town he'd never identified race as an everyday issue.

She smiled benignly, like she had when Lucas asked if she was an atheist. He wondered where her patience came from.

"I should've divorced Leon before he left," she continued in a wistful way, which left Lucas wondering if she was indifferent to her present status, or if she'd come to terms with it.

Lucas told Eve of a recent trip to a pizza parlor with his family, where Janice blew her top when Jenn and Jess threw pepperoni slices at their brother. Lucas said he wondered if his wife was, in truth, frustrated over his waning attention to her. Eve glanced at him sideways and once again her hair fell over her face, which left her peering at him out of one eye. She looked like a carefree sixteen-year-old, until she twitched with concern when she said, "I needed Leon to leave, but I shouldn't call him a flunkey. It only reflects on me."

Pharaoh lurched at a squirrel and Eve tossed her head back gleefully at the pooch's playfulness. As she turned Lucas's way, he cupped her face in his hands and felt the fervency of her kiss.

After that glorious but confusing day, Lucas struggled to focus. Following too many tortured and sleepless nights, he resolved to honor his own marriage vows, but Eve's lack of pretension distracted him the way he guessed Tahitian sensuality drew Gaugin. Her supple movements were a world apart from his Anglo upbringing.

One April day, as he biked to Eve's, an Alberta clipper grounded him in the city. Eve drove them to the Botanical Gardens, where they entered a stillness weighted in humidity. "I come here," she said, "and imagine the Ivory Coast, where my ancestors came from."

"As slaves."

"In chains."

"And mine were the slavers?"

"No, other Africans. Your people sailed the ships."

Lucas paused before a flowering yellow and purple orchid. Its perfume, combined with the sultry air, made him lightheaded. As Eve pointed at another orchid, a delicate white called September Mist, he leaned on her for support. She wiped the nervous sweat from his face and sat him down. They were silent until she asked, "Wanna see my house...inside?"

As she wove in and out of traffic back to Oak Avenue, Lucas noticed her slender fingers resting on the wheel and how effortlessly she eased into her driveway. She smiled and her expression asked an unspoken question. When he didn't answer, she reached for the remote and opened the garage door. It was past dinnertime when the wind finally died down. He exited her house and unlocked his bike.

While pedaling home, Lucas recalled how he and Janice learned to value economic achievement and social position, yet their marriage now seemed only a perpetuation of longstanding habit. He was falling for a workingwoman who'd put down roots among people who lived from paycheck-to-paycheck. True, he and Janice once lived in that neighborhood, but for them it was a steppingstone.

On the surface, Eve had hardly aged since their initial meeting all those years ago, and Lucas pretended now they were both in their twenties, but as he washed himself before dinner at home, he was shocked to spy his first gray hairs.

"Do you remember entropy?" he asked Janice at the dinner table.

"I never forgot. So you think a beginning racetrack's the sign of orderly decline?"

"I would have," he replied. "Once."

"My dear, men have always lost hair."

After Leon returned, Lucas and Eve went a month without meeting. They broke the hiatus at the Botanical Gardens. It was a weekday with few visitors, when a thunderstorm erupted. They retreated inside the pavilion. Eve couldn't hide her concern. She described the troubled relationship between Ben and Leon, who insisted his son follow rules, though they'd scarcely lived under the same roof since the boy was little.

One June day Lucas and Eve went to a restaurant and as the receptionist showed them to a table, an older white man looked intently at Lucas. Later, when Lucas and Eve were sharing a bottle of wine, she said reassuringly, "I'm used to it, you know."

"Glances like that guy's?"

"Yes, some places black folks don't go very often—not that we can't—we just don't."

Lucas weighed her words. Her expression seemed an unlikely mixture of internalized rage at the white privilege she inferred in the man's glance and the mellow comfort she took in drinking fine dry Bordeaux with Lucas. They sipped their drinks in silence, until Lucas declared, "I couldn't care less."

"Black people've encountered these situations all our lives," she interrupted. "What do you want out of this?"

"Out of what?"

"Us."

"What do you mean?"

"You know what I mean. Me seeing you. I'm black."

"I'm not."

"There'll be never-ending looks."

Before Eve, Lucas had never been close enough to a black woman to discuss anything remotely similar to racial matters.

"Black women get on their men for dating white girls, and here I am doing it the other way around. Taking you out of your world."

"I'm sick of my world."

"When we met maybe I imagined myself younger than I am."

"You want Leon?"

"No, but I promised."

"For better or worse?"

"Yes, so did you."

Luke watched as Eve cut a slice of ham and chewed one morsel at a time, so it seemed the pieces melted in her mouth. He ran his fork through a mixed salad and speared several apple slices and a blade of dark lettuce on his fork. He felt like a klutz as the muscles in his jaw flexed with his awkward grinding. Stone Age mastication, he thought.

Still bothered by Eve's comments about race, he couldn't help chuckling at the tiny ironies she made him aware of. She, a vegetable gardener who ate meat but dined with the natural grace of royalty; he, Lucas Morey, a Midwestern white guy in love with a black woman raised on Left Coast non-conformity. He longed to sweep her away and transcend their differences. Realizing he could dream such a dream meant life's tables had turned, and he never again would be as before.

"We're both married," she warned.

"To people we're not in love with," he countered.

"I can't see you anymore."

Lucas abided by her dictum, but occasionally he glimpsed her passing on a city bus or as he drove his son to school. After sending her countless texts, he received a reply: *Don't transfer your emotional life to me.*

For the Fourth he and Janice rented a lake cabin and whiled away their days fishing. They spent evenings on the porch talking about boats or how fast the kids were growing up. Other times they savored the import beer Janice found, to her surprise, at a country liquor store.

"So light," he said one evening as he raised his glass.

"Yes," she agreed. "Your favorite brand."

Lucas answered her thoughtfulness with a smile but avoided saying he was referring to the setting sun. He wished like a desperate child to reach out and halt the descent before it slipped below the horizon. Impossible, he thought, to stop even a slow decline.

"Except to savor it."

"Except?" Janice asked.

Lucas wanted to bolt. It seemed life, or his mismanagement of it, had left him wandering alone into an unknown future, which in youth he'd thought Janice and he would brave together. Now he longed to share that challenge with Eve, but knew they were doomed to meet in lonely parks or darkened corners. And so Lucas clung to the warmth of home and hearth, as it cooled beneath him, and longed to experience Eve's passion, while she withdrew her spontaneity.

Over Labor Day Weekend he and Janice took the kids
back to the lake, but the summer fun fizzled. Jenn and Jess
argued in the heat and Michael developed a nasty rash, so
Lucas took him to a doctor in the city. Later he dropped
the boy off to visit with a school chum. Lucas called Janice
to say he was staying in town. On Sunday he met Eve,
who wore a relaxed smile.

"Leon's leaving," she told him. "A new job."

"Can we meet?"

"Tomorrow. Lake Julian."

On Labor Day itself Lucas needed to check on
Michael and promised to call Janice, but did neither.
Instead, he biked around the lakes. En route his thoughts
wandered back to the peroxide blonde with the VW
van. It dawned on him that this episode occurred a
third of his life ago and it was the one time he, Janice,
and Eve converged on the same spot.

His mind awhirl, he swerved off the bike trail at Julian
Park, tearing a deep divot in the turf. To regain his balance,
he leaned against a lamppost and looked across the lawn.
He left his bike and sauntered toward the bandstand where
Eve promised she'd eventually arrive with Leon.

A Finnish folk concert was underway. Lucas stood
at the back listening to the lead player, who explained
his ten-stringed instrument in a staccato voice. "This in
Finnish is called the *kantele*, but you know it as a zither or
lap harp," he said as two other musicians joined him on
stage. They explained their origins in Karelia, a distant
land of forests, lakes, and epic songs. Lucas's soul was astir
with regret for meeting Eve and leaving Janice in the lurch,
but he listened, distractedly.

Among the pale audience he spotted Eve and Leon
taking their seats as an aged woman in a folk dress appeared
on stage. She said something indecipherable to the leader
who introduced her in English as Hanna and explained that
she played a five-stringed *kantele*.

"Nuka, Nuka," Hanna said and plucked contentedly at the instrument. Lucas understood she was playing a lullaby which she had just given the title of in Karelian. Her gentle singing and the unadorned diatonic key of her instrument blotted out the turmoil in Lucas's soul. He forgot his mad ride along the bike path and the holes he tore in the park lawn. The serene feeling lasted until the lullaby ended and Hanna sang a mournful wedding lament which glided into intermission.

During the break, Lucas stole up behind Eve and whispered a greeting.

"No, you can't!" she said in a startled voice. She glanced around, fearful Leon or the older ladies would notice, but they were merely part of the restroom rush. Lucas took her by the arm and led her behind a boathouse. "You're mad," she said, wrapping her arms around him until she eventually pushed him away. "Have you no shame?"

"Leon's leaving," he protested.

"We're both mad. Go!"

"You mean you don't love me," Lucas said.

She lowered her eyes and whispered, whether in desperation or surrender, he wasn't sure. "Come see me."

Following a morning fog, dappled leaves were swirling in a late September breeze as Lucas approached Eve's house. She sat on the step holding Pharaoh, who wagged hello. Lucas realized the dog had seen him coming and alerted Eve. She wiggled her toes in greeting.

"Indian summer," she said.

"Empty garden."

"Empty house."

They looked at each other till he sat down on the step, with the dog between them. He touched her arm and they intertwined hands. When Pharaoh ran off, Eve stood up. Lucas approached her and she leaned on his shoulder, as though the four weeks since the Finnish concert had stretched to years.

"You not here," she said.

He remembered the tactile tingling of her hand in his. He knew they were both wondering why each had to be married to someone else, and why they should remain so.

"Meeting in secret places," she whispered.

"We…"

"I'll be old and haggard when you're still in your best years," she interrupted.

"So?"

"What man tolerates old age in a woman?"

Even if their ages didn't bother him, Lucas often wondered how their lives might be in a society only half believing in post-racialism. Or he doubted they could continue seeing each other if the ties to his family limited his space. As he pondered those doubts, the breeze blew stronger. He saw the leaves struggle to settle in scattered clumps, as though seeking best friends to rest beside.

Pharaoh came back and snuggled between them, so the three formed a wall against the stiffening wind. Lucas and Eve shifted expressions from pensive worry to smiling frenzy as they talked about the future and how they might escape the need to meet in shabby rooms or kiss behind aged boat sheds. "A way must exist to be respectable and avoid deception or chaos," Eve said.

"Yes, and when we're old," Lucas answered gently after they had talked themselves into exhaustion, "we'll plant your garden together."

As their thoughts wandered, Lucas finally broke the silence by reminding Eve about a day the past summer when he found her working at a Department of Transportation survey site. She took the afternoon off and they spent it making love in a roadside hotel, far from town and prying eyes.

Eve listened while furrowing her brow. "Oh, yes, those

shabby rooms," she said at last with a comforting smile. "We'll live it down."

When she un-furrowed her brow, Lucas knew more than ever they were heading into a new and splendid life together, but as he watched the worry line return and deepen on her neck, he realized they still had a long, perilous trek ahead of them, and the most snarled and sinuous part was only just beginning.

RAIN
SHADOW

"SHOULDA DID IT WHEN I HAD A CHANCE," Raul lamented. He staunched a nosebleed with his Jiffy Joe's napkin and peered out the café's picture window at waves of college students rushing to class. It was March in Minneapolis, a bad time for ordinary folks longing for spring, even worse if you lacked a home. "*Arroyos secos* in every direction, drying my soul inside out. If you ever lived in Winnemucca like me, you'd know," Raul continued. He glanced at his buddies, Albert and Eddie, who hailed from at least as far away as he. They grimaced at his reddening napkin till he tossed it away.

Across the table, Albert, a doughty Norwegian and ex-Army grunt, took a sip of cold coffee and flattened his paper mug with a decisive *whap!* Next to Albert, scrunching down in his Cedar Lake Bowling jacket and clutching the *Daily Clarion*, sat Eddie, a Brooklyn Jew. Only Latoya, the new bag lady, seemed touched by Raul's words. She offered him a clean napkin and smiled as he thanked her.

"Why, heavens, where in the world?" she wondered.

"It's out West. The rain shadow desert," Albert bellowed. "By the thousandth go-through you'll know Raul's damned drivel by heart. Warm and sunny Nevada, wretched hole."

Taken aback at Albert's aggressive tone, Latoya scooted away from him and pressed a black garbage bag to her bosom.

"Or put more eloquently," Eddie added, weighing his words carefully, "it's close to California, one of those locales where greedy mountains grab moisture-laden winds from the ocean and leave the other side God-forsaken, high and dry."

"Piss poor farming country, for sure!" Albert exclaimed.

"Works lotsa ways," Raul agreed. He shook his head sadly. "I came here all the way from the Sierra Nevadas for this drizzly weather, hoping for the best, and how'd I turn out? Dry as a bone."

"Just like my old man, wasted his life on this treeless prairie," Albert added. "He gave up his fishing boat in Lofoten when the cod quit running and immigrated to Montana. Boozed in Bozeman, like I always said. Finally froze to death in a blizzard."

All three looked out the window again. The downtown skyline hid behind clouds and snow mixed with rain. No blizzard for sure, but the solemn scene took the spunk out of them and their surroundings. The men fiddled with their coffee mugs or day-old newspapers, momentarily ignoring each other. Latoya studied each one separately like she was wondering what made them tick.

These men, she surely decided, could have formed a seamless brotherhood had they not buried themselves in incessant rambling about nagging hardships. A sense of loss tugged at their spirits, and their moods changed like sunshine flitting in and out among shifting clouds, so their faith in life and memories of better days blended with a gnawing sense of having failed at all they touched. Self-absorption kept them from discussing the issues at heart, so they clung to one another in desperate need while struggling to move from shared vagabondage to nurturing friendship.

They watched as discarded food wrappers blew against Jiffy Joe's windowpanes and the stream of students dwindled when classes began. "A humongous university, all right," Eddie said, and he and his friends heaved a collective sigh. Eddie and Raul remembered their former student days. In addition, all three men had once felt at ease in the nooks and crannies of this City of Lakes until developers gentrified their hangouts and relegated them to local Welfare. "Now here we are, hanging on with leftover crumbs, and this horrendous schlock," Eddie continued, sneering at his mug of dark roast. "Our lengthening shadows stalk us back to the shelter."

***

Only lately had Latoya joined the crew on their vigils in the college's tolerant environs. She wore a sagging, ankle-length skirt that only partly concealed a pair of worn but sturdy boots. Covering her head was a long black-and-white scarf whose ends draped over her shoulders and complemented a dark overcoat. Where she came from or disappeared to at night was hard to know. No one had ever seen her in the local homeless shelters, and she carried no outward identifying signs except her puffy black garbage bag with yellow draw strings.

"Why, I been followin' you gents across the Mississippi for a good bit now," she chimed in to Eddie. "And I don't see no shadows."

"Yeah, before you wander off alone every night and leave us in the dust," Raul said. "Our own mystery lady. Where you come from anyway?"

"You wonder who I be?" she asked and smiled at him.

Albert sat tight-lipped and listened, till thoughts of where he himself came from returned. "When Pa was alive, we done harvesting all the way from Montana to the Dakotas. He loved the whistles and chugging motors."

"You, farming with steam engines? What century was that?" Eddie wondered.

"Infernal contraption, blew its top on us one day!" Albert answered heatedly. He stood up and limped around to work off his anger.

Eddie waited out Albert's tantrum. "That hitch in your giddy-up. Burns from harvesting, or an IED in Iraq?"

Albert hrmpphed at Eddie and stared at sparrows pecking at scraps of food on the sidewalk.

"Me? I verbalize," Eddie explained. He ran a hand through his graying hair.

"Oh, no, not this again, not for the zillionth time?" Albert complained. "You, a New York Jew, coming west to study Religion?"

"Brooklyn, I'll have you know, Brooklyn!" Eddie retorted in

frustration. "I tried hard till the university gave me the heave-ho. For no good reason."

"C'mon, gimme a break, you claimed you knew more Hebrew than the profs," Albert protested. "That was on you."

"No, sir, all on the gentiles, totally," Eddie countered with a mischievous smile. "They claimed I mauled a Chinese exchange student, for asking us Jews, 'Why you kill him? Why you kill Christ?'"

"Not the way we heard it," Albert ribbed. "Just a damned smartass, that's you."

"You had a tough rep to shake anyway, huh?" Raul asked Eddie.

"After the profs kicked me out of Religion, I hosted Yiddish folk music on the radio," Eddie continued. He reached for the *Clarion* and brandished its rolled-up pages like a Billy club, striking out into thin air with it.

"I been listening to you fellas since I come here, weeks n' weeks ago," Latoya butted in. "I be a street vendor. Hear lots a' smack on the street, but nothin' like you all's darned malarkey. Talk sense."

"You black folks, not like us, you got what it takes. Hardscrabble," Eddie complimented her. "Like you, braving the elements all year round."

"We tough," Latoya agreed. "I's peddlin' my trinkets everyday up in Midway an' Rondo, to my people an' Asian folks, till the Latinos come with their extortion. I work that street before they's born, but I bundle up and come here to the U, the only colored among all you honkies, but good folk." Nodding toward the white youth and working folks at Jiffy's counter, she clutched her garbage bag, then tugged its drawstring.

"What you carryin' around there, anyway?" Raul asked. He poked at a hole she'd torn in the bag while shrinking from Albert.

"That my affair!" Latoya teased him. "You be keepin' your hands to yourself, hear?"

"SoyouthinkI'manotherspicfromthestreets,huh?"Rauljoked.

"Why, I can tell you about streets," she assured him.

84

"And so can he," Eddie said, pointing to Raul.

Raul cleared his throat, pleased they'd turned his way again. "My pa was Basque," he began, as Albert and Eddie looked up in surprise. Latoya raised her eyebrows, realizing Raul had revealed something new. "He came from Galicia to herd sheep in the Sierra Nevada on the California side, but he got tired of it and him and Ma moved to Winnemucca. He got a job driving a truck and Ma nannied neighbor kids."

"Just like my people in the old country," Albert interrupted. "Never had a pot to…"

"I was the first of us could read and write," Raul continued, ignoring Albert. "But Pa said, eighth grade? *Basta.* No more. He got me a burro and a knapsack, even a crooked staff like shepherds in the Bible, and sent me up in the hills, but I sold the burro and bused dishes at a Basque restaurant, snuck into high school. Pa thought it was great I got a chance, but wouldn't admit it. Then the bottom fell out."

Eddie sighed. "Who didn't have it tough? Why, on Brooklyn streets I saw things, like…" He paused and searched for the word. "The vileness," he murmured at last. His gaze turned inward like he spied dire events from a silent movie or a forbidden war film that sent shudders down his spine.

Albert squirmed at his friend's circumspection. At last he leaned forward and roared, "Say it, man!"

"Like Buchenwald," Eddie whispered as a tear clouded his vision.

Albert sank back in his seat while the others looked with sympathy at Eddie. They knew the difference between Brooklyn and Buchenwald, but the horror from centuries of discrimination affected all Eddie's people wherever they were. Latoya gave him a napkin and he wiped his eye.

"Yes, I bet you did struggle, Raul," Eddie continued. "But at least you weren't wetbacks." He swatted at the air with his newspaper and dabbed again at his watery eye.

Raul smiled, acknowledging this as the worst time of day for Eddie, when the sun passed its zenith. "Eddie's zombies are ready to attack," he said.

"The shelter causes him fits," Albert answered. "He raves all night."

"Those stinking winos begging booze," Eddie said. He brandished the newspaper again, as if warding off a mortal blow.

"If you'd take your meds, *gut!*" Albert shouted and grabbed Eddie's *Clarion* mid-swipe.

"Don't call me *boy* in that peasant tongue, stupid Norskie. Why, I'll whip you to within an inch," Eddie snarled. Like he felt a fit coming on, he pulled Cedar Lake up so the sweater covered his head.

"If you'd listen to your doc!" Albert roared. He steered Eddie to the water cooler, where he produced a bottle of pills and dealt him a handful. Eddie's Adam's apple bobbed up and down as he swallowed them all.

***

"You keep talkin', hon," Latoya urged Raul with a wink.

Eddie had calmed down, but the noise of a busy lunch crowd increased. Raul hesitated when a group of students began laughing loudly. "Me? Talk over this racket?" he asked.

In make-believe anger, Eddie swiped at the students on his way back from the water cooler. They chuckled as he sat down. "Okay, out with it!" Eddie said to Raul, his former sardonic mood restored. "If you must."

Raul glanced at his new, slightly blood-stained napkin. "One day, some drunk plowed into Pa's delivery truck." Pausing, he tossed the napkin away. His lips quivered.

"Why, you cryin', dear?" Latoya asked.

"After that first crash a bus came up and smashed over Pa's truck. So they had two vehicles piled on top of his. Flattened everything. The cops came and took me to identify him. Ever see a body destroyed from the head down?"

"When our harvester blew the hell up, yes," Albert answered.

"No, no," Eddie corrected Albert. "He means from the top

down. Nobody blows anything down upwards. Crazy." Fuming at what he perceived as the imprecision of words, Eddie tugged at his collar like the winos were at his throat.

"It's getting drizzly out," Raul said, trying to derail the absurdity resulting from his serious description of his father's death.

Eddie continued fumbling with his collar. "Whadda you have to go and tell us that horrible story for? Your pa getting run over when it's no fault of his own? On a dreary day like this?"

"Why, chile, your own father," Latoya said to Raul. She stroked his upturned palm with a chubby hand.

"I know. That's when I started writing verse," Raul continued. "I got work in a stone quarry in the high desert. I wrote about sandblasters. Something I knew about. 120 degrees in the pits. Coughing up dust. My nose bled, like now, and I thought, don't be like these guys. They'll die by forty. I was starved for learning and supporting Ma while I planned for college."

"Dream on," Latoya said. "They don't let no poor boy like you in no college, not in whitey's world." She made a wide sweep of her hand toward campus.

"I applied for a scholarship and included my poems."

"Yeah, our next great wordsmith," Eddie added. "Some bleeding heart let you in the U? I can see it. Civil Rights, I bet."

"I wrote about guys I knew, lucky if they escaped miners' lung."

"Why come here, to the frozen north?" Latoya asked.

"Some Latino from California, willed money for a poor kid out West. That was me."

"Geez, boring," Eddie grouched. "C'mon, tell her what really happened." He pointed to Latoya.

The wind blew stronger and smashed rain against the panes. Raul removed his hand from Latoya's and rubbed his nose. Satisfied the bleeding had finally stopped, he continued his tale as Latoya eagerly leaned over her bag to listen.

"I aimed for Med School, but crashed. Not my thing. Mostly drunk on modern poetry."

"Only on poetry?" Eddie suggested.

"Yeah, I got English rhythms in my Basque brain. That's for real, I'm telling you. So I got a new major. Found this great advisor, a Shakespeare guy. You know him? The Bard?"

"Bard, who he?" Latoya asked.

"So there I was writing a dissertation. Concupiscent curds. *The Idea of Key West*, you know, making order out of chaos. It had me in its grip. Look." Raul motioned outside. The rain had turned to snow, mellow flakes melting and streaking the window, then rain again, drops blowing wildly in the wind.

Latoya reached for Raul's hand. "What you mean, sweetie, in its grip?"

"He chose chaos over order, that's what," Eddie explained.

"Yep, met this lady, Aritha," Raul admitted.

"She on the streets?" Latoya asked, knitting her brow.

"Where I met her. I was writing my synthesis but got stuck, couldn't get it right in prose. 120 was a breeze next to the worry of words. To clear my mind, I got to cruising downtown. You'd be surprised at all the horse. Bought junk from this dude and shared it with Aritha, but one morning I go out to my car and the dude puts a gun to my temple. Aritha, she owe us nine, he says. Nine what? I ask. Nine hundred, you dumb or something? he answers. So I cough up the dough for Aritha. I go bust and the IRS garnishes my wages."

The wrinkles deepened on Latoya's forehead. "You clean since?"

"Yeah," Raul assured her. "I got to teach a course once, even sent my Ma dough, then she up and dies. Broken heart, I figure, after my pa. *Dios bendiga.*"

"I have a man myself once and a son, Kamren," Latoya said. "He my baby. As a chile, he have a hole in his heart, just like you, but a different kinda hole. Not like you and your hole, that only you can fix. The docs fix his an' he join the Army."

"Holes and holes," Eddie replied.

"Iraq. He send me money. Till one day the Army write me." Latoya's eyes welled up. "My boy, my baby."

Raul stirred abruptly. "Dope, you crave it," he said. "Me and verses. They lost their meaning when I tried to explain them. What's the use when the meaning won't come back?"

He and Latoya exchanged looks that said both had lost irretrievable things, which in their absence bound the two in spirit.

***

Albert and Eddie watched the students spill out from their classes until Latoya wiped her eyes and stood up to leave. The men followed her to the sidewalk outside Jiffy Joe's, where she motioned to the right and asked, "This way?" They helped her across the intersection and headed for the River.

A row of classroom buildings lined the street, and they passed the cavernous edifices like humble penitents. Farther on, they squinted at clumps of student bicycle commuters who whizzed by and splashed water behind them as they came up on the Mississippi River bridge toward downtown. Heading toward the men's night hostel on the opposite side, the four wanderers trudged up to the bridge. Sleet pecked at the bridge's covered walkway on its east side, but the sky had brightened far off in the west.

"Homeless heading home," Raul said.

Latoya's scarf slipped, so Eddie lifted the dangling end and gently draped it back over her shoulder. As Albert joined Eddie and Latoya, Raul stood at the railing and stared at the roiling Mississippi far below, where it split the city in two between the University and business district. The River was in spring flood and two tugs struggled to secure a rebellious barge. As they slowly nudged it to safety, Albert, Eddie, and Latoya walked on, shepherding Raul with them.

Halfway across the bridge, Eddie stopped. "Look," he said, pointing at a poster. "This old Tom Stoppard play. *Rosenkrantz and Guildenstern*. They're reviving it."

"Saw it once," said Raul. "You understand it?"

Eddie hesitated.

"Didn't think you would, understand it, I mean, no more than I did," Raul said. "Strange story. No plot. Rambling talk leading nowhere."

"Pretty much our story," Eddie agreed. "Pissing away the days in our own blather, waiting for you to kill yourself. Just a matter of where and when."

"All I remember about death on stage is Willie Loman. Worth more dead than alive."

"Oh, Arthur Miller," Eddie replied. "His Willie was full of it."

"What if you're not good for anything?"

"Raul, you're not worth a damned thing dead!" Albert shouted so the passing students looked at him askance. "Who'd even bother to bury you?"

To keep her distance from Albert, Latoya led Raul toward the edge of the bridge and placed herself between him and the railing.

Eddie studied the poster announcements—Yoga Classes, Inter-Faith Worship—until a clap of thunder and an unlikely cloudburst hit and all four quickened their pace.

"You know I didn't get kicked out of grad school at all, I quit," Eddie admitted calmly and for no obvious reason. He ran a hand through his soaked hair as they walked on in what was now a drizzle.

"Lots quit," Raul said.

Eddie stood beside Raul. "That inter-faith sign reminded me of this instructor I had. Faithful Fred we called him. The other Religion profs were process guys. Faith and God are fluid. To Fred, our Lord was a rock. You had to devote your whole self to Him."

"Imposing order?"

"No, order was built in. Fred talked about the Everlasting and us. Then it went haywire. He backed off, like the rock crumbled."

Raul shook his head. "Not the first guy to experience doubt."

"A learned man, decades of knowledge."

"Knowledge isn't faith."

"I wondered, what if the guy that gives me faith loses his?"

"The center won't hold?" Raul asked.

Eddie looked at him nonplussed. "Once I was crossing this very bridge. I looked up and spotted Faithful Fred, wearing khaki pants and a gray scarf."

"Like Latoya's?" Albert butted in. "But a different color?"

Eddie shrugged. "Dressed like any old guy. People were hurrying along when Fred casually put down his briefcase, you know, run-of-the-mill stuff, like lighting a cigarette or tying his shoestrings."

Raul looked up in surprise.

"And..." Eddie began.

"And he jumped."

Eddie nodded yes. "Rushing river and a concrete parking lot below. Dull thud and there he lay. The cops finally showed up and snooped around till it dawned on them his briefcase was on the bridge. They opened it, expecting lecture papers or Scriptures. Suicide note maybe."

"So?" Raul asked.

"Empty."

Raul eyed him closely.

"I kept going to classes afterwards, but felt dry as a bone. Like you, I never finished," Eddie said.

They gazed down at deserted houses and a rusted grain silo on the far riverbank. Directly under them, a bike path wound its way past Faithful Fred's fateful parking lot, its cracked asphalt speckled with water puddles.

On an impulse, Raul embraced the iron railing and gazed out at the troubled sky. Sensing this was the spot, and without looking down, he dug one foot into the concrete walkway and readied himself for launching over the rail.

Several students wandered past unawares as Latoya gasped and Eddie, wanting to help, leaned forward on the railing. He looked intently at his companion but spoke softly. "Strange. Why couldn't a believer like Fred live?"

Raul climbed higher. With one leg he balanced on the guard rail's concrete abutment while dangling the other leg precariously over the edge. Sitting astraddle the railing, he needed only the slightest tilt to hurtle to his death.

"I been there myself," Eddie explained in a cajoling voice without making any unwary moves. He squinted out into the same thick air his friend now flirted with and threatened to leap into.

Below them, an ordinary scene played itself out. Water dripped from bridge girders and landed in parking lot puddles, while swallows swooped out from under the bridge and settled next to pairs of doves pecking at loose gravel on the asphalt.

"Jump, if you must," Eddie said. "Sixty, seventy feet down. Maybe a hundred. It's over in seconds."

Albert stepped uncertainly toward Raul. With his brute strength, he could have carried the man to safety, but didn't dare act. Seconds stretched into tense eternities before Raul looked pleadingly at Eddie, who struggled for words.

"Once in the air you can't turn back," he finally whispered to Raul.

Suddenly bright sunlight burst from the west and reflected off the River and the puddles below. As raindrops stopped pecking at the bridge's east side, a rainbow appeared in the sunlight and formed a perfect half circle between the River and downtown. Orange, yellow, purple, and green ran along its edges, golden tints in the center. As a dry, rain-shadowy Eden miraculously emerged with the bright band of colors, Raul reached out for the spectacle and a look of joy lit his face. Slowly he lifted himself back over the railing and slid down till he stood on both feet, smiling in relief. The others rushed forward and helped him to safety, thankful they still had him among them.

"You know, I've always wondered what went through Fred's mind," Eddie said as he clasped Raul firmly around the shoulders. He waited till the adrenalin settled before speaking again. "What motivates a guy? Did he believe he'd find something better on the other side? What'd *you* expect?" he asked Raul.

"Fred didn't live to tell," Raul answered vaguely.

"I've stood on the edge myself," Eddie agreed. "But can't do it. I'm afraid there's nothing over there."

"Not the same for me. Something happened."

Raul looked back the way they'd come, seemingly to retrace in thought their trek from Jiffy Joe's. Distractedly he rubbed his nose to be sure the bleeding had stopped, then he turned and moved on.

***

"C'mon, sweetie," Latoya urged Raul as they shuffled on across the Mississippi bridge. Behind them were the blustery streets of early morning, the hustle and bustle on the margins of campus, and a day of bad coffee and worse food. Ahead lay an uncertain night.

"That stuff I tried," Raul said. "Today's not the first time for any of us, maybe. Least I didn't shame my mother's memory."

"Only you could stop you," Latoya replied.

"And you did," Eddie added.

"Hard to explain, but magic," Raul replied. "I reached for the rainbow like I could cup it in my hands and imbibe the colors." He walked on in silence while shadows lengthened at ground level and the sun's rays faded from downtown skyscrapers. "Hard to imagine in this dim light, but I dreamed I wasn't this me any longer, not the me you know, but something more, what I used to dream of being and once was close to becoming."

The others looked confused about whether he was speaking into the approaching darkness to clarify his own experience or inviting them to reinvent themselves through the chimera he'd seen in today's late winter rainbow. At a loss how to answer, Eddie started joking again about the old days in Brooklyn and Albert threw away his flattened coffee mug. Only Latoya approached Raul. Her unassuming smile warmed him.

The homeless shelter was open when they arrived. Eddie and Albert waited in the doorway, while Raul and Latoya chatted on the pavement till she tenderly squeezed his arm. "You take care," she said and adjusted her hold on the bag.

The three men watched as she shuffled away down the darkening street, where to, nobody knew. Someday, Raul guessed, he'd learn what place she hailed from and where she laid her head at night, but his focus drifted from her to his own youthful move to this northern city, which earlier today had felt so tempting to abandon.

Then he remembered Jiffy Joe, who let him and his friends lounge all day on a single cup, and the congenial students, who kept a distance but shared their public space. More than all else, Raul remembered the glorious rainbow above the River, and as he looked at his friends, he thanked the sky for prolonging his stay among them.

BASIC
SKILLS

JAKE BECKENBAUER'S Jiffy Buy got stranded on a bad block. No essential services or decent parking, so the company hired Jake to bring in customers. Like always, he'd started his day shift in the early morning darkness. Now he was standing idly at the till looking out on the fading December day. The glow from speeding cars reflected off the storefront windows, while the few stragglers outside hurried on, bent over against the wind.

Across the street, Jake spotted a one-legged guy in Army fatigues. He scooted down the sidewalk in a rickety wheelchair, guiding it with a long, skinny leg and spinning the wheels by hand. At the corner, the fellow eased over the low curb and out into traffic, navigating between honking cars and freezing slush till he struggled across to Jake's side. He used his leg to maneuver up over the curb.

On the sidewalk, the guy looked up at Jiffy Buy's neon sign as snowflakes began to fall. They fluttered down, turning red and blue in the flashing light. Then he turned and studied a help-wanted sign Jake had just posted in the window. *Cashier Needed. Good Customer Service. Basic Math Skills. Ability to Stand for Long Periods.* He pushed the automatic door-opener button and wheeled in from the cold.

Jake studied the guy's stump and the pants leg folded underneath it, his hands calloused from spinning the wheels. "Whadda ya need, pal?"

"A job. I'm Al."

"Tough times? Pawned your prosthesis?" Jake asked.

Al nodded.

"Gulf War? Iraq?"

Al stroked his graying stubble. "No, 'Nam."

"Afghanistan here."

Al nodded again. "Figures."

"I was tempted, but hung onto mine," Jake said. He lifted his right arm and showed an artificial hand.

"I can work."

"We need somebody can walk."

Al glanced at the cash register. "You run that thing with one hand?"

"It's hard," Jake agreed, "but I can walk to it. You can't."

"Your sign says stand. All I need's a chance."

"Hours of standing. Can you?"

Al clucked his tongue.

"Meaning no," Jake guessed. He went on studying his shabby visitor and thought about their downtrodden block. "Go redeem your limb," Jake said and gave him a wad of cash. "Come back tomorrow."

"See you then."

The flakes pecked angrily at the windowpanes. Rush-hour traffic was still racing along the street, workers heading for better places, Jake thought. At eight he turned out the Jiffy Buy lights. The snow was sticking now, so he followed Al's wheel tracks. As Jake crossed the street, motorists slowed for him and nobody honked. Their car tires obliterated the trail Al had left in the deepening snow. Jake walked on, never looking back at his own tracks.

FORGETTING
SHE
FORGOT

ADDIE VOSS'S Michael was the one with asthma, but she learned to share it with him. He wheezed and hacked and Addie complained about his clogged-up tubes like they were her own. Looking for relief, the two fled Chicago and headed for sunny Albuquerque, but the desert air gave Michael nose bleeds. In Redding and Denver, it was the heat or the altitude that bugged him. For two decades nomading it here and there had been the go-around. Ever since their marriage, in fact, Michael had been searching and hoping for good health, the perfect job, and a place to call his home. Addie had faithfully internalized his wishes while also accustoming herself to repeated pain. Or trying her best, no matter what.

Today, she was fidgeting with her purse and waiting in confusion at San Francisco International for a plane to Minneapolis, their latest city. She had waved so-long to Michael and their four children only a couple days earlier. For Michael, jobs were plentiful in Minnesota, but breathing remained a chore. Winters were cold and summers humid. Addie guessed other things weren't going to get better either, now that their four kids were down to three.

Just imagine, I go off on a tiny vacation and this happens, she thought. "Struggling for air is bad enough," she said out loud to anyone who might be listening over the airport chatter, "but nothing's like this disease called not-knowing."

No one seated around her responded, which caused her to fidget even more and desperately long for company.

"With what kind of ease?" a jovial older man finally asked as they boarded the afternoon flight.

"Not ease," Addie said, noting how he cupped a hand behind his ear. "You know, dis-ease, same as discomfort, like never fitting into these gawd-awful airline seats. They get tinier every year. Or I get bigger."

The man waited patiently while she wedged herself in the middle spot and then he took his seat by the aisle. Addie looked up distractedly and introduced herself.

"Addie."

"I'm Al," he replied. "Old-timer. Retired guy."

A young man with red hair was already crammed in the window seat, but he was limber enough to stretch his legs. "Richard," he said. "From Rochester. Been visiting my girlfriend in Vegas. On vacation."

"I was just starting a vacation, too. My first ever," Addie responded. "Here I am, 42 and never had a week off. Ever."

"Is that right?" Al asked. He looked past Addie and addressed Richard, which caused her to wonder if anyone would listen to her when she got a chance to speak again.

"That's a college girl you were seeing in Vegas, is it?"

"No, card dealer," Richard answered with a smile. "She deals black jack."

"No kidding!" Addie replied. "That's my line, too. I do housekeeping at a casino."

"Right in the action, I bet," Al said with an interested wink.

"Well, it's really the casino hotel," she admitted.

"Like I said, you seen it all?"

Yes, I seen it all, Addie reflected in silence. Like the guy that left me a hundred-dollar tip and then...She paused mid-thought.

"I can see you're thinking it over," Al said. "My question hit home, huh?"

Addie glanced at him, her emotions all mixed up. She didn't mean to be harsh, but this friendly stranger asked impertinent questions, which hit home and worsened her anxieties. First she was scared about the sudden journey back to the Midwest and now folks expected her to talk serious about stuff they chose to pry out of her. Still, she needed people, not just warm bodies, and here she was with a fellow on either side.

"I'll let you in on a tale," she said, thinking it wouldn't hurt if a story slipped out in public. "We had this guest, a hulking guy with a ten-gallon hat, a big talker. He checked in one Friday night, gambled away the family farm, then killed hisself. I'm the lady found him, bright and early on a Sunday morning. My boss said, 'You done plenty of this walking into rooms and finding people with their brains blown out. Take some time off. Go visit your folks.' And that's what I was doing, just this weekend."

"You were in Vegas, too," Richard interrupted.

"No, Redding. California."

Richard shrugged, while Al nodded knowingly.

"I lived in Redding once," Al announced.

"Yeah, me, too," Addie said. "Not this time, though."

"When then?" the older man insisted.

Addie wanted to talk but not about her first time in Redding, so she fell silent until Al's expectant look persuaded her to answer. "My first two kids were born there. It was like any other burgh in the middle of nowhere, with a freeway running through it. We lasted over two years. Russell, that's my hubby's brother, got wind from an old Army buddy that said guys could catch on as prison guards thereabouts. So Michael went for it. Great pay and all, till we discovered the jailbirds hung around after their release and raised hell with the good folks in town. Break-ins galore. Michael quit the guard job and we moved to a part of town called Poverty Flats."

"Ah, yes, remember it well," Al said.

"Hot as blazes all summer. I sat days on end in a ramshackle apartment with the AC blasting and my babies screaming. Gained 30 pounds and never got rid of it." She squirmed in her seat to emphasize the tight squeeze. "I told Michael we gotta get outta here, but he found another job right off and stayed."

"Doing what? A living wage is hard to find in those parts," Al continued in surprise.

"He hooked on as a dermatology medical biller. No experience, but what the devil, he used to say. They wanted him to peddle skin cream then post bills and collect 'em, too, driving around on those steamy roads digging up guys with faces the sun burned to a crisp. Trouble was Michael had to multi-task, which he was lousy at, and be gone all day, which didn't suit him once the asthma laid him low, not only once but then twice more."

"So you got outta there?" Al asked.

"Yeah, but Michael's dad warned him, looking all over for a perfect place means you gotta drag yourself with you. Russell was already long gone from Redding and my folks pulled up stakes in L. A. and retired to Redding. They're still there, but Michael finally decided to fly the coop in a big rush. So we hit the road. Everything was screwed up and I started wondering if I mattered or whether I was just along for the ride," she continued and then paused. "Like that's what gals do, you know, stand by their man, you know that song?"

When neither fellow responded, she realized Al was too old to have noticed it and Richard too young.

"And I had the kids," she continued with a sigh.

That was then, this is now. Or *was* now, Addie reflected. Now could be hard to define. For this Redding trip to visit her parents, her bus departed Minneapolis on Friday morning and she rode it till Monday night. Hours of starts and stops and strange characters, who might have been bearable to know about at some level but taken together they only seemed tawdry, some verging on illegal. That trip began only days ago, but it felt like a meteor of compressed time already speeding into a distant past.

Nevertheless, she loosened up and told Al and Richard about a few other incidents. Like the teenage girl from Oklahoma, who made her way up north alone and boarded Addie's bus in the Dakotas carrying a pink blanket and a pet squirrel she fed from a baby's bottle. Then there was the drunk who pawed at a thirteen-year-old girl across the aisle from Addie, while the mother slept and the girl squealed for the driver to intercede until Addie ran the guy off. People like that mixed together with ordinary folk quietly riding toward the California coast.

"Worst of all, was the thumpety-thump-thump of bus tires on pockmarked roads," she said. "The landscape was unchanging. Then we crossed the mountains at night. I slept feeling the bus climb higher and the curves get sharper and sharper, like daggers in my ribs."

Richard seemed to lose interest in her tale. Soon he was gazing out at cumulous clouds as Al strained to follow along. First, he thought she meant real daggers or knife fights on the bus, but gradually her words got through to him. Like talking to her father in recent years, she had to think as much about how clearly she spoke to Al as what she said. She was certain some folks took him for a caricature of his once youthful self, but she found his comments made good sense when he stayed on track.

"I see, like our plane ascending," Al added. "I thought that was a stabbing sensation on takeoff."

"Whatever," Addie replied. "Like I said, it was my first time away from the family. Never before this. So missing the kids caused my pain. I sent our twelve, fourteen, and eighteen-year-olds to visit my hubby's folks and left Eddie with his dad. He's my youngest, only six. I forgot my cell, so no contact all the way West. With nobody."

"You weren't concerned?" Al asked.

Addie squirmed once more and again it felt like the the past few days melded together. Richard turned her way, and with both men looking at her, she nervously forgot the order of events.

"I like riding the bus," she remarked in monotone. "Especially when we drove down out of the mountains. For some reason we got to Monterey first. Then we changed buses northward again," she continued. "The closer we got to Redding the more I felt the heat."

Addie fanned herself and waited.

"It seemed more desert-like. Soon as I got off the bus, everything was weird. The wind hit me like a wave and nobody was there to meet me. Finally, my father arrived and said my Eddie's dead. No more. He said it matter-of-fact, Eddie's dead."

"Just like that?" Richard asked in surprise. "Those're his very words?"

Addie nodded yes and leaned forward to catch her breath. Only slowly did she settle back into her seat.

"Something fell on him and killed him," she replied.

"That's too bad," Al commented soothingly without cupping his hand. "Is he all right now?"

"No, he died," Addie repeated.

Al leaned back and considered the ceiling, which made it unclear whether he couldn't understand or still hadn't heard. The plane was now in cruising mode and after saying 'he died,' like she was admitting it to herself for the first time and out loud too, Addie felt she was being rocked to sleep. Richard gazed out the window again. In a calm voice, the pilot announced they were flying over the Rockies. A storm was brewing, he explained, but it probably wouldn't hit before Rapid City, not to worry, they'd avoid it. Like most of the passengers, Addie dozed off. A little later she woke up thinking about storm clouds.

"I like riding the bus," she repeated in a distracted voice while glancing past Richard and out the window. "I like flying, too, but the plane costs too much. My dad bought me this ticket for $600. They call it a bereavement fee."

"You're right. Believe me," Al agreed, aroused from his daydreaming.

"I didn't even have time to stop in Redding. Dad wanted me on the first best plane back east. I had to get up at four to get from my folks' place to San Fran. Then I missed the early flight. They didn't give me time to get across the airport. I'd never been there before, and they ought to give us time to walk all that way."

Al nodded in agreement. Maybe he understood her, maybe not.

"They should give us more time in that terminal," Addie repeated. She brushed back her blond hair and dried a tear that inched its way down her cheek. More followed so she produced a tissue to dab them away, a smooth motion that matched the mid-afternoon stillness, which only the pilot broke. He announced he was veering south. Unless he did, they'd surely experience turbulence or even collide with the storm.

"Collisions are no fun," Addie said. "The time we left Denver, that was three moves after Redding, it was blizzardy and Russell—that's my hubby's brother, remember? He came from Tennessee to help drive us up north, a real cakewalk, he said. They had scads of bad weather in Nashville, that's as far north as you can get and still be in the Deep South, plus he had a new job driving semis. Michael used to drive truck, too, so they knew everything there was to know about those Northern roads. Like Russell said…"

"A real cakewalk, huh?" Richard interrupted.

"You better believe, Russell swore. He was driving our VW van, not my hubby, who was at the wheel of the other car. Russell got behind a couple semis and the snow was blowing so we couldn't see around 'em. Russell got on his cell phone to Michael and said if we stayed there we were goners for sure, froze tight in our tracks, so our only chance was the left lane, but the van was so loaded it stood still, kinda like it was suspended there. That's when I knew we were done for, but that ol' crate kept chuggin' on till it inched past both those humongous trucks."

"You were saved!" Richard exclaimed.

"Yes, but when Russell pulled off later, we skidded 360 degrees on glare ice and dove into a ditch. We crawled out in the drifts, okay, but it took us forever to get that van towed to town. Cold as blazes that day, I tell you."

"So you got it repaired, the whole rig?" Richard asked.

"Yes. We hunkered down in a flophouse motel and waited near a week. Russell had taken us all the way to Illinois and was gonna turn north toward Minnesota. Me and Michael ran away from Illinois years and years ago, and here I am, gonna cash in my chips back in that god-forsaken hole? No way, I keep thinking. You're the real truck driver, I tell my hubby, why can't you decide what road we take? But he just wheezed away and didn't answer. I never trusted that Russell again."

"That's living, I figure, always a lesson to be learned," Al added.

"Life's one huge collision waiting to happen." Addie bit the fingernails on her right hand, pausing after each finger to study how close she'd come to the quick. Realizing her actions looked unsettled, she rested her hands on her lap. "It's like, I could land this plane if I had to," she continued, "and get us outta big storm trouble. My dad was a licensed pilot. That was in southern Cal. He had a Piper Cub and showed me how they land and balance planes in the wind. I wonder where we are?"

She peeked out and saw ominous clouds towering higher by the minute. When she leaned back, Al craned his neck to see. "That's South Dakota down below," he explained.

"Oh, will we have to cross Illinois, too?" Addie asked.

"The Prairie State, your old stomping grounds?"

"Heavens no, not me, I only married a truck driver from there. That's my Michael, except he gave that up for sheet metal. Always something new."

"Well, anyway. Minnesota's next," Al assured her. "Not Illinois."

Addie closed her eyes and rocked back and forth. The flight attendants walked the aisle collecting throwaways, so she hummed a chant-like melody to calm her nerves.

"I don't like landings. Will we fly around the storm?" she asked.

"Yes," Al answered, "but what we see now aren't storm caps. Just rising clouds."

Addie lifted her frayed right hand and inspected her cuticles. Soon after, she began to bite the nails on her left hand.

"The real storm clouds are on the other side," Al reassured her.

Relieved at the news, she ceased nibbling her nails and rummaged in her purse instead.

"I lived in Wisconsin," she explained. "I grew up in L. A., but I notice how all the cheese they sell to tourists in California is made in Wisconsin."

"What in the world?" Al asked.

"I think about my Eddie," she confessed with a sob. "How hard it'll be to get home and him not be there. He was starting to get asthma, too. Lotsa times I could tell where he was in the house by his cough. He had toys and clothes in his room. His puppy slept with him. We named her Emma."

"What breed?" Richard asked.

"Oh, just a mutt. Black and white. Eddie wanted a boy-dog but when I took him to the pound there was this furry mongrel staring up at him. A girl-dog but it was love at first sight; they had to have each other, those two."

Al smiled kindly at her words. His willingness to listen so closely despite his faulty hearing struck her as coming from a genuine wish to nurture people—and surely animals, too. Addie wished Michael was as attentive. He could've taught their youngest to train the pooch and also nurtured the older kids in similar ways as they grew into teenagers. She had accepted him as her life partner and followed his path around the country, always giving him her back, but she had long been aware his fruitless search for better health or a dream job was a ploy to escape the duller duties of home and hearth. After Desert Storm he struggled to find himself, Michael's dad always said. She leaned back once more and closed her eyes.

In the silence that followed the plane began its long and slow descent toward the Twin Cities. The flight attendants made a final check down the aisles and took Addie's teary tissue. They handed her a new packet which led her to repeat the tale of Eddie's death, or what little she knew of it.

"What fell on him?" Al asked.

"They didn't say. Just that Michael and Russell will be waiting for me at the airport. My father-in-law, too. I still remember when we lived as newlyweds with Michael's mom and dad in that stinking hole, Joliet in Illinois, so close to Chicago. On warm winter mornings the fog'd settle and mix with cold air from the melting snow. The river canals were so oily they never froze, so this soupy slime rose off the water and mixed with exhaust fumes from all the trucks. Even the ducks stayed away. But not us. We slogged around in that mess till Michael caught asthma—and Eddie got it from him, later on."

"Is asthma inherited, I mean genetic?" Al asked.

"The docs said something but I never understood it. All I know is, Michael was once the picture of health. We met when he was with the Marines in Carolina and I was passing through. Before Desert Storm. Then he came home from Arabia and moved to Joliet, his home town. He caught that junk there, I mean the shortness of breath and wheezing. Russell says it was in Arabia he got asthma, but I know Michael wasn't that way before Illinois."

"So your kids have asthma as well," Al ventured.

Addie saw he was about to question her on the kids' ages, just to double check, when the pilot interrupted and told the attendants to prepare for landing. To acknowledge he wouldn't ask any more questions, Al nodded as they fastened their seat belts, and the coach lights dimmed.

"Anyway, asthma bonded us together, me and Michael," Addie explained. With him making all the decisions, she thought. But often it seemed things just happened with no plan, like layoffs and broke-down cars. That thought hit home as fears of the landing continued bothering her and she wondered, what if life's just like this? We sit in a plane the same way we go on living every day, our lives in the pilot's hands or nobody's hands, figuring everything's normal, or not normal at all, but we get used to normal or not-normal and take it all for granted. Then something really big happens we can't predict, like asthma, getting fired, or something falling out of nowhere and hitting Eddie on the head. Maybe it's time somebody takes control, for good.

As the plane began to circle, the pilot explained they were holding in a line of incoming flights. Rain splattered against the windows.

"Will we have to fly through the rain clouds to land?" Addie asked.

"Yes," Al answered. "We'll beat the worst of them."

"I decided, enough's enough!" She spoke loudly until she realized more than her seatmates might be listening. "Michael obsesses, thinks he'll smother to death, in his sleep probably, so I've comforted him all along by complaining, too. Then we had Eddie, the love of my life. I wonder, what has Michael done since I left? Anything, at all?"

When the plane finally landed, she glanced out at the late summer evening and saw the storm disintegrating to a steady drizzle. Somewhere behind them a woman announced the landing on her cell. "Carousel four. Meet you there. Love you, sweetie."

Other passengers were gathering their gear when Addie spoke up again. "I forgot it—my phone, I mean. I coulda called my baby if I had it." In dismay, she turned to her seatmates and beseeched them, "But my hubby? Where was he? Was it my fault for leaving?" Her voice was shrill and she felt her words rising from the depths of suppressed anguish, but nothing she uttered elicited any reply. Richard was briskly gathering his belongings, and she realized Al couldn't hear her over the de-boarding ruckus.

"Love you, too, honey," the female passenger concluded on her cell and moved down the aisle.

Addie was among the terminal crowd when she resumed talking, repeating how great it was that the pilot flew around Illinois, she could *not* have stood seeing Joliet one more time. "Not even inhalers help you there," she declared. At the top of the stairs leading to Baggage Claim, she paused and looked imploringly at Al and Richard.

"We named him after me, you know."

"How's that?" Al asked.

"You know, like me and him. Addie and Eddie."

"Oh, yes," Al said with a comforting smile. "Eddie and Addie."

With that, the two men chose the escalator down while Addie stayed one flight up, looking out over the crowd. Having no luggage to pick up, she finally walked down the steps and passed the carousels. All around her was the steady flow of passengers, and she watched Al and Richard, luggage in hand, disappear among them. Then she looked for her family.

When Michael emerged from the crowd, she hugged him until her father-in-law appeared, followed by Russell, in a Volunteers t-shirt. She embraced all three at once till they broke off to assess each other's thoughts. The hardest part is how we'll ever repay Dad for my plane ticket, Addie wanted to say, knowing Michael, given the chance, would conveniently ignore it. All she finally uttered was, "Who's been feeding Emma?"

Her men smiled sheepishly without answering.

"Okay, let's go home," Addie said decisively as they started the long, silent trek toward Short Term Parking. She knew the men were in denial about Eddie's death and couldn't talk, but someday she'd help them find a voice. Meanwhile, she walked ahead and counted what was waiting for her. Three lonesome kids. One empty boy's room. A hungry dog. Her idle cell phone. She knew she'd never forget she forgot it, but for now she needed to create something newer and happier for her children—and the men around her, too, if they could endure it.

IAGO

NICK MEIER HAD just fenced some canned fruit at Jolly Jim's for three teens of crack. That was enough to start a high with, so he revved his pickup and tooled out onto Lake Street. Off work tomorrow, he reminded himself, savoring how great it sounded. Still, he would've felt better if a couple things didn't bug him. First was Char calling him a dope addict, second was him knowing she got it right.

Char had every reason to fume at him for falling off the wagon, or whatever they called it in the crack world. Nick hadn't always been like that. He was a hard worker and a real brain, who knew the value of his dough. The only splurge he ever went on was his truck, which he'd bought brand new four years ago. To get the best bang for his buck, he spent weeks reading consumer mags before finally deciding on a Honda. Now here he was, sliding downhill faster than ever before after blowing the rest of his savings on junk. To console himself, he reached out the window and patted the side of his pickup affectionately.

In the past, he often asked himself how he ended up like this and the only answer was boredom. After his student days digging Paul Bowles and Heavy Metal, he caught on as an instructor of freshman comp at a downtown Vo-Tech. Frustrated with spouting grammar rules at welding majors and land surveyors, he started tooling down Lake Street—just like now—to enjoy the sights, mostly high-heeled ladies leaning against decaying buildings or nefarious figures scooting through back alleys. One time he barely dodged big trouble when his fender brushed a shirtless guy holding a 12-pack of beer in one hand and a naked infant in the other. The sun beat down mercilessly on the child while the man ignored Nick's frantic honking and ambled awkwardly across the street. "Hey, whitey, watch yourself," someone yelled his way.

When sleep wouldn't come in the wee hours of the morning, Nick drove aimlessly back and forth. Regular street people along the drag recognized his truck and gathered around hoping to peddle bad stuff or unload stolen goods on him. They rambled on about Mr. Jones, which was their code name for the big dealers. If they crowded in too tight, the cops pulled up behind Nick's Honda. They knew white guys were usually looking for women, but the only gals that approached Nick were whore chasers, who offered to go find a Mr. Jones for him. Since Nick always said no, the fuzz let him be.

Anybody who'd been on the street knew it was dumb to ask questions about crack, especially why. Deep down, Nick believed he was meant to be a writer or an adventurer seeking truth and excitement, which he always imagined existed on the dark side. And that's when Anita popped up and showed him the way. My Anita, Nick called her, a skinny white girl he first laid eyes on in a back-alley bar as she performed strip routines on the countertop. To his surprise, she sat down beside him during her break one night. She talked inner-city lingo and claimed she had a kid with some street dude. From the get-go, Anita understood Nick was off the charts different from the usual barflies or macho men that occupied her world. Clear as a bell, she said, he was tuned in to dope more than booze or sex. Nick was a sucker for cool lines, so when she skipped her next bar-top dance, he followed her to a neighborhood house and stayed the weekend. After that, crack houses became a steady part of his life, far from the excitement he once longed for. Crack just *is*, he discovered.

No wonder Char moved out on him after witnessing what he'd turned into and how he hung around with a low-life like Anita, but after knowing Char for three years, he could tell it like it was with her, too. She was black and had suffered scads of abuse. After her husband ran out, she moved in with a drug dealer, inhaled tons of coke, and went back and forth to Mazatlan with him, doing what Nick never knew. She almost lost her kids when a tough social worker took over her case. That was the thing about Char, though. She was a strong sister and never doubted her ability to get back on track.

About himself Nick wasn't so sure. He didn't know if he had it in him to get his teaching job back. Or if he even wanted to. Even so, he remembered the good parts of the old days both in and out of the classroom. After the working week, he could enjoy a weekend in the sun. He'd bump into friends or feel overjoyed to see folks walking with their kids and laughing. Feeling surprisingly good a few months ago, he called his school office about possible reinstatement on the faculty, but they never answered, and he soon dropped the idea altogether.

Some guys said crack was like a siren song, forever singing its irresistible refrain. To Nick, it was a false friend. An Iago, who wouldn't let him be, so he no longer smiled much. The only job he found was laying sod. Hard as the work was, the landscaper paid good, so Nick got salaried every two weeks. This evening, in addition to the teens, which were cubes the size of a thumb and short-term confidence-givers, he could feel a check for a few hundred bucks burning his pocket.

Yeah, bad enough, but could be worse, he decided, and cruised past a row of 3.2 joints and a Total Mart specializing in stolen firearms. A block ahead stood a check cashing business. Nick eased up under its neon sign and read *No One Denied*. He spotted Anita on the sidewalk, with a grizzled drunk pestering her. When he honked, Anita walked around the guy and crawled into the truck. Nick smelled her pungent odor, a sign she'd been on the street for days.

"Any moulah, hon?" she asked.

"On my way in," Nick answered.

He piled out, with Anita at his heels.

Close the door! Don't open the windows! a handwritten sign screamed inside the check cashing office. Nick crossed the sparse, gray room to a worn writing desk, fished out a pen, and signed his check. Anita lingered by an old-fashioned rotary pay phone, which bore an additional warning: *Calls no longer than three minutes! Three Minutes!*

"Signed on the back? ID?" a grizzled cashier commanded. He deducted a fee, counted out a bunch of twenties, and slid them under the bullet-proof glass, careful not to touch their hands. Anita grabbed the bills greedily and gave them to Nick, who finally smiled.

***

Anita said the cops kept a stake-out on Lake Street, so she insisted Nick take 28th to Somerset. 28th was a dark road with no glitzy businesses but stop signs galore, which Nick hated. Still, he followed the lady's wishes. The first thing he spotted at the crack house in Somerset was a lazy wrap-around veranda. Somebody had painted the window casings a bright red and chimes tinkled on the porch. From outside, the place looked so lovely Nick thought he could almost live there, but on the scraggly lawn dust rose up from under his feet as he crossed its countless bare patches.

"Needs sodding," he said to Anita.

"Wanna give me a hit?" she asked, and kicked at the grass, like this was her territory. "We get teens here for twenty. Lotsa base some nights. The family sells it're real cool, if they're around. They tell me when I've had enough. This other dude, though."

"A dealer? What about him?"

"Big on power trips. He'll make you beg for it, eat shit, you name it."

Nick shook his head and hid his money, and his teens. No, no hit for Anita. Offering to share, even with his best buddies, only meant they'd take it all.

Without bothering to knock, Anita opened the front door

and Nick followed her in. In a darkened room he saw a collection of sullen figures slouched on kitchen chairs by the walls. He flipped a light switch, but the electricity was off. A filthy, miserable dump, he decided, but sat down on the floor anyway, where he started smoking alone. When one teen wore off, he fired up the next.

After his euphoria vanished, Nick felt an emptiness no words could describe. He gazed dully at the deadheads along the wall and saw in them images of himself, waiting, waiting, waiting. Unable to banish crack from their minds, they schemed to get ahold of stuff. Any stuff. Their desperation deepened when no dealer arrived, not even the evil bastard Anita mentioned, who loved to march in and force them to demean themselves in their own faeces and laugh when they did so. In their frenzy, the crack heads quit giving a damn about anyone else or even what happened to their own money. Nick heard them jabbering to each other, till they slowly divided into tiny cliques and tried figuring out how to get a fix. Any old way would do.

"I play in a band," a black girl with long flowing hair and a perfectly chiselled face said to an older, heavy-set African-American woman sitting beside her. "Bass fiddle. Live with my lady partner, but I been gone from home two days now."

The older woman tried to fondle the girl's breasts and leaned in for a kiss. When the girl didn't respond and grew frazzled, the woman produced a tiny morsel of crack, barely more than a pinhead, and offered it to her for a pickup. "What your name, dear?"

"Jaynelle," the girl mumbled. "What if my partner finds out?" In crack-induced bliss, she snuggled up to the older woman, who held her tightly, and glanced around at the same time for a chance to snatch a hit or grab somebody's purse.

Across the room Nick saw a young couple standing in the candle-lit living room frantically discussing a lead on some stuff. They rushed in and out, banging doors behind them, until they finally collapsed in a corner. The guy whispered hoarsely to his companion, who nodded and slowly crawled over to Nick.

"When that Spanish guy comes in here, tell him we're gone, okay?" she begged.

"What guy?"

"Follow me," she said. She took Nick by the shirtsleeve and led him into the empty room next door. "See that hombre, over there? Tell him we never came in this room—never—me and him, the guy I left back in the other room, okay? This Spanish dude's got stuff hid in a closet, somewhere in the house."

Nick agreed and returned to his spot on the floor. A bearded bruiser sidled up to him and muttered in his left ear, "That couple, over there whispering?"

"What about 'em?"

"If they ask, say I never kept no junk in no closet. Besides, I got something for you in my car. Come on outside with me. *Veng conmigo.*"

Nick made a move to follow him but heard another voice in his right ear. "Give something? To the pot?"

Nick saw the lesbian women—Jaynelle and the older one—with their hands extended. "We got great stuff comin'. A real bazooka. Chip in an' we'll share. Everybody get some."

Confused and needing a fix, Nick took out his wallet and stuffed a wad of twenties in the heavy woman's hand. She clutched the bills and sneered when Jaynelle begged for half.

"My partner'll kick me out if I ain't got any dough or crack when I get home," Jaynelle wailed.

"Or sees you here with that fat bitch," the whisperer in the far corner barked across the room.

Nick listened in silence, his own paranoia mounting. Even on the drive to Somerset, he'd been thinking how stupid it all was. He had pockets full of cash but nothing to spend it on, and sure as hell no dealer with any brains was gonna waltz into this shithole. With cops circling around everywhere, the smart ones were too wary and the minor peddlers had already hightailed it off the streets or were sitting in the slammer. But Nick was getting to that time of night when Iagos popped up everywhere and spooked him like mad. He knew the clinker was hell, but nothing to match crack jail. Crack became its own prison but without walls, said guys who'd been there. Nick felt pinned in by dope peddlers. If he left the house, he'd hear a street lamp ask him if he wanted crack, and he'd answer 'yes' and fish out rolls of dough on the spot, for a stupid lamp post, like a Mr. Jones, sure as hell.

"How long you been on this stuff?" another voice asked.

A young guy plopped down next to him, whose question made Nick realize he'd been talking to himself out loud. Nick shrugged. How long? Another dumb question, like asking why. He answered by repeating the question. "How long for you?" The newcomer was thirty, maybe. Old enough to know better than be here. Seeing his white shirt and tie, Nick judged the guy worked in an office. He sported a wedding band.

"A year," the fellow replied, "about. But I've got it under control. Al, that's me."

Nick nodded at his newfound buddy as they sat together. Waiting, like their fellow squatters. There wasn't any build-up or climax to this idiocy, not like the plot of a Dickens novel or the contents of textbooks Nick used to teach from, with chapters that said sensible things and led to ideas. Here the regulars hung for an hour or a day or a week or, who knows, a couple months, and sometimes even longer, in these broken-down digs in what remained of a once decent neighborhood. Waiting for whatever stuff they could lay their hands on. Begging to spend their hard-earned cash for the smallest snippet. Willing to eat shit for it.

"That's me," Al repeated. "I've got it under control. Pay all my bills, the rent, the whole schmeer. I've got it under control."

"Better stop, now or never," Nick said. "Three years and it'll be too late. Little by little you'll stop paying your bills. Then the rent. Finally, you won't even bother to show up for work."

"My job's..."

"Just like me last week," Nick continued. "I ruined a whole day of business for my boss. You might keep your morals, all right, but you won't obey 'em."

"What?"

"My boss gave me his company credit card to buy lawn materials. I knew better, but I charged dope to it."

"What you need is help. Big-time."

"I've still got it here, his card," Nick continued. He dug deep in his pocket to show Al the plastic, but discovered it was gone, along with his car keys. "Damn! Where's Anita?" he asked in a panic. "She took my truck!"

"The skinny gal?" Jaynelle answered from her corner. "I seen 'er. She left, with some dude."

"In my Honda?"

The others met his question with silence, so he grabbed his phone to text Char and get help finding his truck. Not knowing the exact address, he wrote *Somerset, your old neighborhood* and leaned back. Feeling more and more desperate, he listened with half his brain as Al told him he'd come there straight from work.

"Like I said, my job's secure," Al explained. "Didn't even call my wife and tell her where I was going."

With the other half of his brain, Nick remembered how Anita had offered him a taste of life on the other side. If there's any why to crack, that's it, for sure, seeing the other side, he reminded himself. But God, it's a rocky ride. And not over yet.

"You know, I met this character," Nick told Al. "Tough guy, did twenty years at Joliet State Pen in Illinois. Got himself off the dope all alone, with no help, after seven years. Kicked it. Kaput. He'd been in a lot of prisons, but none as bad as..." Nick paused, realizing he'd already told that story, but to himself, or somebody else? "Crack prison, it won't let you go," he said.

"What about your car keys?" Al asked.

"I can see how far crack's made me travel by how people distance themselves from me. I locked myself out from home one night, so I went to my old buddy Will's. He let me sleep on his couch, but 'back off, buddy' he told me later. Maybe it's his wife."

Al nodded in agreement, which made Nick feel for the umpteenth time how stupid everything was. He explained how junkies stole and lied not because they were mean but were afraid of dying, but Nick had already faced death, like the time two dealers stuck a revolver to his head and demanded five hundred for Anita stealing their dope. "Yer dough or yer dead," they threatened him. No, Nick had already thought about death. It didn't scare him, not anymore.

"I just don't wanna go wrong in other ways," he said to Al. "Know what I mean?"

"No, not really."

Nick thought he was talking sense, but he got distracted when Jaylene and the fat lesbian snuggled up to each other again. Jaylene was mumbling melancholy stuff about her band performances and how being on stage got her higher than any dope, which rubbed Nick the wrong way. For some reason that he struggled to explain his blood boiled at seeing such a looker in another woman's arms, and not his. Crazy, I'm not even here for women, he thought. But seeing the two in what he could only perceive as rapture, he angrily realized the ecstasy enfolding them was something he no longer had a go at, what with Char being so pissed at him. What's more he wasn't likely ever to know any overwhelming visceral desire again as long as crack kept him in its grip.

It hit him like a bolt. He was locked out. Locked in this house, but out of happiness and fulfilment. They're not gonna reach into the pot and give me my money back or go out and get me some crack, he thought in a rage. These creeps don't give a damn about anything or anybody, only themselves. What about me?

"What's up, liars?" he shouted and charged at everybody in his way, fists doubled up. "You already been out to get stuff for yourselves, using the money I pitched in. Now you're about to split with the rest of my hard-earned dough. And my pal's, too. We'll get you! *I'll* get you!"

In the midst of Nick's ruckus, people kept coming and going, misfit after misfit claiming to head out for groceries or smokes, or lying that they'd caught whiff of a dealer and would go get some dope for everybody, which only convinced Nick even more they were full of it, he'd heard their bullshit before. Inside his head their voices registered in tandem, like hollow echoes of each other, until he lost track of who was who, or who was clutching whose dough, or which of their words were true, if any. And, worse still, if he could even tell the difference.

Losing his balance, he sank down in the middle of the floor and struggled to grasp where he was. At long last the unbearable crack-house confusion compressed into one solitary thought, "I've had enough, dammit!" A climax of anger and repressed fear forced him to his feet as he raged and shouted at Jaylene and the fat woman, "I want my money back!" Hearing no response, he lurched toward them. "It belongs to Char, a hardworking black sister, like you two," he lied, screaming so he spat in their faces. "She loaned it to me. It's hers!"

They continued to ignore him, so he grabbed their car keys off a table close by and stuffed them in his pants pocket, along with their I-phone. Or was it his? He couldn't remember. His failing memory rooted him to the spot. Dumbfounded, he stared at the women.

Still not a word. Nothing. Then he grabbed Jaylene's house keys from her pants pocket. "Char, she's a black sister, like you," he repeated. "I'm out of here, that's final."

He headed out the door, but at the edge of the porch he stumbled on the steps and hit the ground. Where am I going? Anita took my truck! He thought, then turned and yelled at the women. "The money! It's mine!"

When he saw them coming, it should've petrified him, or forced him to get up and prepare for a fight, or something—anything—but he started inner-monologuing instead. Crack, you've started a war inside me, almost got me killed and robbed me, too. It's in your nature, you do this to me logically, he told himself, just as the fat woman grabbed his hair and pulled him back. She cursed and yanked at his hair till gobs of it tore free. Nick wailed in pain at the same time Jaylene spotted her keys bulging from his pocket and jumped him from behind.

He struggled with both women till a third person leapt from behind and punched him in the gut. Doubled over in pain, Nick waited till he caught a second wind, then wrenched loose and tried to flee across the yard. In confusion he found himself back on the porch instead, panting and frantically doubling up his fists. He realized how fast his strength had faded when the fat woman grabbed his pants and ripped the rear clean off. Jaylene stepped up, seized her keys and tore gashes down his leg with them.

Leaving the leg of his pants in the fat woman's hand, Nick jumped off the porch and stumbled across the lawn, till he tripped on a tuft of grass and spread-eagled in the dust. The fat woman tore at his shirt as she hunted for her keys.

"I threw 'em in the hedgerow," Nick yelled to distract her.

She looked in the hedge, then searched his other pants pocket. Unable to find her keys, she held up Nick's wallet and his missing credit card, which he realized she, not Anita, had taken earlier.

Nick collapsed and bit the dust, on the very spot he'd said most needed sodding.

What follows the climax in a good book? was all that remained of his garbled thoughts.

***

When Nick regained his senses, he hacked and spat out dirt. Rolling over, he tried to brush himself off, only to remember one of his pants legs was missing. His shirt was torn and his sleeves hung by threads. He fought back sobs until he could think straight again.

"Under control?" Al asked.

Nick heard him but the pain in his ribs told him to stay still.

"They coulda killed you."

Not so strange, Nick thought, two spaced-out druggies trying to kill me over a car key. Maybe they've been strung out to the max fifty or five hundred times before, so it started feeling like fifty hundred multiplied by five hundred. In their

addled crack-brains they were getting even with me for
snitching fifty thousand keys.

"Besides," Nick said, "Jaylene was afraid she'd lose her
home. Anything but that."

"And the fat lady wanted Jaylene? She was jealous?"
Al asked. "C'mon."

Al offered a hand and pulled Nick up. They were standing
side by side when Jaylene and the other lady showed up again.
"You lied to her," Jaylene spat.

"About what?" Nick asked.

"The hedgerow. And that black sister."

"No way," Al said. "He just needs his billfold and IDs."

"What if I did," Nick offered. "Your friend, she had
it coming."

Jaylene stared at him while her older companion sulked
and stomped around the others. Protectively she put an
arm around Jaylene, who jerked out of her reach in a fury.
"Stay away, bitch!"

"Get off it," Nick argued, "I need my ID's to drive."

"When that chippie drove off in your truck?" the older
woman chided him. "What *you* gonna drive?"

"Let's bargain," Nick pleaded.

"No way in hell."

Nick and the women stood their ground till Al stepped in.
"Look, an even deal."

"My ass," Jaylene shouted.

"You give him his things. You get your keys back," Al said.
"Fifty-fifty. Simple as that."

Nick shifted weight to keep his ribs from aching while eyeing
the two women, who both glanced sideways, suddenly as wary
of the other as they were of him. He couldn't remember if he'd
returned their keys or they'd taken them from him. What was
all this about exchanges, anyway? Confused, he stared at the
faint morning glow and wondered what time it was. Maybe
there'd been more crack than he remembered. Or he'd slept
the night away somewhere. Or Char had looked for him all
night, only to give up. Nick glanced at Al, who strode over to

the fat woman and calmly reached for the wallet and card. The woman yielded to him and handed them over.

"You got your stuff?" Al asked her.

The fat lady looked in Jaylene's direction and nodded yes.

"Like you said, simple as that," Nick commented.

He watched the women turn and walk back toward the house. "He lied," Nick heard one of them complaining. He guessed they were willing to wait. And then wait some more.

***

With no truck, Nick plodded along till he spotted an apartment building and stretched out in its manicured yard, breathing in the scent of new-mown grass. He searched for his wallet, but soon remembered he had no vehicle and didn't need his ID. Instead, he tried to work up some guilt over his treatment of Jaylene and the other black woman or shame at his derelict state. Failing at both, he thought about Anita, and why she, more than Char, had such a hold on him. Where had she gone with his truck, and which bum had she spent the night with? Forty-two, he reflected, I'm too old for this shit.

Nick was wondering why Lake Street appeared so temptingly depraved when Char's Prius silently glided to the curb. He got in, apologized for where he'd been, and tried to think of something to say.

"How'd you find me?"

"It's Somerset. I grew up here, remember?"

He didn't answer, so they rode in silence till Char stopped for a traffic light. "You're a grown-up. Tell me which way from here," she demanded perfunctorily. "Lake Street or 28th?"

As the sun peeked over the horizon, the traffic light turned from red to green and back to red. The Prius idled patiently, while Nick's face grew crimson from the shame he finally felt consuming him. He looked at his tattered trousers, the torn shirt, and a totally ticked-off Char, who stared unblinking into the morning haze. Desperately, he willed himself to make the right decision before the light turned green again.

LOVING SØREN

THE FIRST STEP TO PURITY OF HEART...Karen Engberg read for the zillionth time...*is to will one thing.* That was a line from Kierkegaard. It felt strange to her coming from a lone-wolf like him, who figured he knew everything about life without ever experiencing it. She closed her copy of *Either/Or* and decided she'd done enough for a Friday afternoon. Not bad for a kid from South High. Assignments for Monday finished, both parents away for the weekend, and only a confused big brother to hold the fort. Boyfriend Eddie's coming over, so maybe it'll be both/and tonight, she thought, making her own small parody of the author's title. Realizing how silly it sounded and nobody but her would understand, and maybe not even her 100%, she tried her best to forget about Kierkegaard.

Karen was weary of this Dane in a Daze, as she called him. His books weren't the usual stuff for teenagers, but her College Prep class had a few bright bulbs in it, so they'd been reading selections from Kierkegaard, which their teacher, Mr. Hansen, assigned. The Dane wrote about giving up cozy sentimental illusions about life and explained how going steady with a guy or girl will kill your love forever. I opened my eyes and saw the real world and began to laugh, Kierkegaard added.

That stuff sounded like gobbledeegook, except *to will one thing*, which rang like an insistent refrain Karen couldn't get out of her mind. *The first step to purity of heart is to will one thing.* For starters she thought she'd will herself to walk out the door. That particular step might open up something significant, like purity or seduction. She wasn't sure any such thoughts made sense, or if the two were even opposites. You never knew with Kierkegaard. Maybe they were the same in his mind, but maybe not. How was she supposed to know what went on in that weird, whacko head of his?

She entered her room, changed clothes, and headed for the front door.

"Hi, sis, where you off to?" Josh asked, as she turned the knob.

"Out."

"Where to?"

"You know. Like it's Friday. Date tonight. With Eddie."

"You look tired."

"Yeah."

"From what?"

With a shrug, she sauntered back to her room. She returned with a dog-eared copy of *Either/Or* and tossed it to him with an accompanying sigh. "This."

Josh looked puzzled about whether she was expressing admiration or frustration for the author, and Karen wondered as much herself. Mr. Hansen had talked all week about Søren K, the lifelong bachelor, who finally got himself engaged only to seal his engagement ring in an envelope and return it to his betrothed. I'm not the marrying type, he explained to her, you wouldn't like me, I've got a disease of the spine, or some made-up junk like that. While Regine, the jilted girl, threatened suicide, Søren hunkered down and devoted his life to art. Art alone, meaning his writing. Even so, Regine "infused every page he ever wrote." Or so said Mr. Hansen, who loved that weirdo and was soon to be married himself. Mr. Hansen was part Dane and young and cool as well, so Søren must've been cool in some obscure way Karen had yet to figure out.

Mr. Hansen said you had to decide to make something of yourself and choose to believe, even if, according to Kierkegaard, doing so made no sense. This all sounded way cool, but the texts Mr. Hansen had his students read were tough sledding. And what if I don't know that much about myself? What do I decide then? Karen leaned on the door uncertainly and stepped back into the living room.

After leafing through a few pages of *Either/Or*, Josh looked up to study her closely, like he didn't know much making about life decisions either, even if he'd faced plenty since starting college. Getting close to Josh was like wading into a turgid creek whose tricky undercurrent might drag Karen down, not close to drowning, but deep enough to feel rock bottom. She suspected Josh had struggled in those depths and surfaced again, full of renewed desire yet suspecting the world of folly. Kinda the way Søren sounded.

"What're you reading this for anyway?" Josh finally asked. "A class?"

"English lit."

"And this guy's English?"

"We do world stuff, too," Karen explained. "In English."

"I see. For perspective?"

Impatiently she glanced at the half-open door, her competing impulses holding her in and yet urging her out. Any time her parents confronted her on touchy subjects, she tensely assumed an ambiguous stance, but since they were away visiting relatives she took her time and wondered if she was more ticked off at Kierkegaard for writing such long-winded nonsense, which she kind of liked despite herself, or at Josh for acting like a substitute grown-up. Maybe he'd been in on a lot, sure, but he was still just a college guy home on spring break, and her brother besides. At least he's not making a fool of himself on some drunken beach at South Padre like last year, she thought. There'd been trouble about that, but kinda hush-hush. Reckless driving. Their dad hired a lawyer.

"Blank," Josh said when she didn't answer his question.

"What?" she replied, jerked out of her silent pondering about Josh and the Dane.

"Your face. What's behind the mask? Something ill-conceived?"

"I hide my opinions."

"Fat chance," he chided her.

"You coulda gone to state college. Like any normal human. Least you're not a private college snob," she joked back. Private college, yes, she thought to herself. Snob, no. "Not yet, anyway."

"Look, I know all about it," he answered.

"Really? You get it all, about life and that other stuff? Like Kierkegaard?"

"Yeah, kinda. I read a book by him once. *Diary of a Seducer.* For Philosophy. Or Psych, maybe. Don't remember."

"Yeah, it's part of *Either/Or*," Karen replied. "My class didn't read it, but I did."

"Silly stuff."

"At least it had a plot," she said and thought disgustedly about denser parts of *Either/Or.* "This guy, Johannes, plans to hit on some girl, just to see if he can do it. He keeps a diary about it, step by step. Strange, though. It works."

"Like Trump getting women to vote for him?"

"Whadda you mean?"

"I mean Johannes is like a lotta self-absorbed guys? In it for himself. Seducing others so they go against their own best interests. Like getting folks to vote for their oppressor."

"Maybe seduction *was* this girl's best interest. Johannes kept at it till she seduced him. Ever think of that?" she asked, aware she'd invented that idea on the spur of the moment just to sound chic and impress her big brother.

She shifted her weight from foot to foot. Any moment now, Eddie would bomb up to the curb outside, honking impatiently and fuming in that crazy crate of his, like he had some place impressive to get to that couldn't wait. She knew the car had a nickname, but he wouldn't tell her. Probably more info than she needed.

Karen inched her way farther back into the room, expecting Josh to offer more college boy pearls of wisdom. When he didn't, she remembered their mother explaining he'd decided to come home for the break instead of returning to South Padre, ostensibly to study but mainly so he could think about the Deke-something-or-other fraternity that invited him to join up. Pledge, they called it. At first the offer didn't sound half bad to Karen, but after gathering details, she wondered, why *those* Deke-jerks? She learned reports had trickled in for weeks about a wild-ass frat boy from Josh's college. He was a Deke, accused of raping girls with ruffies. Now the papers were saying the judge gave him a seven-year sentence, one of those rare cases where the guy got caught and had to pay for it. Too bad they didn't throw the key away, Karen thought.

Josh's girlfriend, Suzanne, threatened to break up with him when he couldn't decide whether to accept or decline the fraternity guys' invitation. In the macho world some of his buddies inhabited it was guys who called off relationships, not the girls. If that's what a relationship boiled down to in the end, it was essential to be a snubber, or at least appear to be a snubber, not the snubbed. So the Dekes' standing at the college and Suzanne's opinion of them could be decisive to her brother's self-worth, Karen understood, but she didn't know where Josh stood on an issue like that. Maybe *he* didn't know either, deep down, and that was really what he came home to figure out. According to their mother, he was checking to see if the Dekes were legit, on or off campus.

"So she's not a Trump fan?" Karen asked.

"Who?"

"Suzanne."

While Josh thought over her question, Karen sat down and smiled in patient frustration. She wondered some more about seduction and purity. Was it possible to experience the first and keep the second? Carry on like normal, afterward? Were other girls in the same boat with their boyfriends, only less willing to consider or discuss it? She'd tried bringing the topic up with some girls, but got nowhere, which tested her faith in them.

Then came the task of being mature with Eddie, tolerating all his beating around the bush, making sure they were on the same page so she didn't have to put on an act or play coy, and he wouldn't go off bragging about made-up macho fantasies to his pals. How did that work? Or am I just philosophizing like Søren, she wondered, about stuff that doesn't matter to other kids? They just do things, whatever they might be, and then get on with life? Was Søren really so much smarter than us, or a coward afraid to play the game?

"Well, Suzanne can't decide," Josh finally answered. "She's disgusted at date rape, but thinks this guy in the White House will be a good leader. Drives me nuts."

"Going batty, sorta like me with Eddie. What'd Søren do the rest of his life? After Regine?"

"He got away from people, holed up, and wrote. For human contact, he strolled the streets every morning, talking to people."

"Strangers?"

Josh nodded yes. "That's all he had or wanted. Holing up. That's what I'm doing now, except no streets or strangers."

"Yeah, hiding away, but only for a week. What about the other guy?" she asked.

"Johannes in *Diary of a Seducer*? He's just a type, our prof said. Part of Kierkegaard's aesthetic stage. You know, delving into sensory pleasures, maximizing them," Josh replied. "That's what it is."

"That's what what is?" Karen asked, incredulous. "Dumb guys doing dumb stuff?"

"Seeing what they can get away with. Why else would you put something in a girl's drink? Nothing ethical about it."

"No, I'm not that stupid. Ethical Eddie? Give me a break."

"Guys fight against boredom. We all go through it. So what's your problem?"

"Purity stuff. The first step is to will one thing. What's it mean? What thing?"

"You name it, I guess. Go for it."

"Any old thing'll give me purity of heart? Long as I decide on it, mental or physical?"

"You read too much into it. Philosophy's just common sense."

"Meaning?"

"Choose something. Anything. One step at a time."

"Like Eddie?"

Josh nodded but didn't answer, like he was thinking, what's to say about Eddie? He laid down *Either/Or* and left Karen with her thoughts. She got up and waited by the door, holding the knob, deciding whether to go out or stay in. Weird, she thought for the umpteenth time, reading a 24-year-old philosopher, who left his fiancée in the lurch and walked the streets of Copenhagen thinking dumb thoughts and talking to even dumber people about still dumber things, all to get advice on boys. Whacko, for sure.

"As if Søren knew more than anybody else," she said anxiously, remembering something else Mr. Hansen said about Kierkegaard's ideas. Boredom. Anxiety. Despair. All life's problems in just three words.

When Josh still didn't respond, Karen thought how nuts everything was. Her parents leaving her alone. Josh in the clutches of rich frat freaks. Her dates with Eddie, who only loved action. First, a blockbuster movie with high-speed chases and gunslinging ruffians. Then more action of a different kind, alone with her. "Accelerating," he said when she asked him what he liked about the movies and their time together.

She knew he meant exhilarating, but she was weary of acting understanding. Correcting him was even worse. He'd refuse to say it right. Just being his age. Seeking sensory pleasures. Or was he? It occurred to her—here I am, convinced I know more than him.

"The same way Søren thought he knew more than us," she said to Josh.

He looked up in confusion.

"Meaning?"

Lots of stuff'll seduce you, she thought. Guys. Words. Ideas. Desire.

"I'll will to make things better," she said with determination.

"Or accept what you can't change," Josh replied. "The way I'm learning to do."

He waited for a response, which she didn't provide. Or couldn't, because she didn't really understand what he meant.

Instead, she listened as Eddie drove up and leaned on his dual-trumpet car horn twice. Then twice again. She waited, nodded at Josh, and closed the door behind her. As she walked out to the car, she prayed for Eddie to stop the racket, but he hit three more rapid blasts. She flinched at the sound and willed herself to keep calm. Refusing to fall for any dumb tricks, she looked around, opened her eyes wide to what was before her and laughed out loud. So I'm gaining purity of heart, she thought, and wondered if this was her first step to loving Søren.

BURNT
POTATOES

AFTER STAYING UP ALL NIGHT, Rolf Quello was so set on some tasty carcinogens he didn't see the blonde woman in designer eyeglasses till they nearly collided outside Al's Breakfast. Once inside, the two stood awkwardly together waiting for separate seats. When a lone customer got up by the window, they eyed each other until a bleary-eyed Rolf dashed the length of the diner and grabbed the spot for himself. Embarrassed at his own rudeness, he leaned forward over the counter and pretended to study the menu as she quietly took a newly vacant seat beside him and ordered two coffees. "One for him, too," she told the waiter.

In her words, Rolf detected a wry humor and understanding, so he went ahead and ordered himself the same breakfast as every Tuesday. "#2, over easy, bacon and hash browns." He didn't object when Al, the owner, patiently took the menu from him and placed it back in the counter rack.

Al repeated Rolf's order to the cook. "And burnt black, if you will."

"Sorry about my behavior," Rolf said to the woman as Al offered refills along the counter. After the second cup, Rolf woke from his morning blahs and continued. "I'm famished, you know."

"Late night or early morning?" she asked.

"Both."

"Doing what?"

"Proofreading, copy editing," Rolf answered. "At a neighborhood newspaper. All night, every Monday. For free."

When the #2 came, he attacked the hash browns with vigor, but after a few bites turned and thanked her abashedly for the coffee, hoping the second apology didn't sound like an even worse afterthought than the first.

"Meg," she replied, extending a hand, which he shook, noting her firm grip. "Margareta in full. Margareta Gradén. You know, *e* with an accent."

"Rolf here."

"That name! You're Swedish, like me!" she exclaimed and removed the Silhouette glasses to mark her surprise. The square rimless frame had made her visage seem angular and coldly professional, like her handshake, but without the glasses she looked mellow, her cheeks soft and her eyes a bright blue. "And you hell-bent on cancer? Ugh."

"Only one day a week," Rolf answered with a chuckle. He watched her until a glow showed in her eye. He finished the bacon and eggs as Al arrived with a refill, and he sipped at the warm dark brew while listening to Meg, who added cream to her coffee.

"I was born here in Minnesota but have lived all over," she explained. "Never abroad. You, though, intriguing. You add those burnt potatoes to top off the acid prose you correct all night?" She tucked the glasses away in her purse.

Rolf considered a clever reply but decided against bantering away his morning hours. He had another job this afternoon and needed at least an hour's catnap between now and then. Still, he recalled a vague feeling that someone was tagging behind him while out on the sidewalk, and now in the café Meg's manner suggested a mixture of sly mischief and careful reserve. Her erect stance as she waited for a seat and now the firm outline of her breasts under a cotton blouse aroused a visceral sensation. Had she chosen him, while passing on the street, as a likely candidate? If so, for what? Sex and romance? Talk?

"Something surely. But what then?" he asked, mostly to himself.

"At least it won't be today," she answered, her reply as vague as his question. "You can't develop cancer in a day, it takes years. But what about you? Are you from there?"

"What? The old country, as they call it?" he asked with a serious look, squelching his visceral response to her. "Yes, in fact, but only sort of. My folks came here from Gothenburg, as a young couple, to sell imported Volvos. Mom was already pregnant, so I was born in the U. S., but this Swedish name fits my reticence, they say." Her question was a clear invitation for him to ask about her, but instead it triggered his mind to consider his own origins, more than he was accustomed to, which brought on his serious expression. "As a child I spent summers at my grandparents' country cottages in Bohuslän. It was fun, but as a youth I got wound up in the urban scene here and refused to go back across the pond. The excitement was here around Uptown in Minneapolis, and I felt the beat, you might say. Then my parents were killed in a boating accident on the St. Croix River. After that my interest in their homeland and Uptown faded, pretty much together."

He looked at Meg and wondered if she'd been listening. She was forming her lips in a circle, "Bo…"

"Bohuslän. It's an area around Gothenburg. I went to their funeral there, but I've never been back to visit the graves. Before they died, they felt like strangers to me, money grubbing. 'The welfare state. You can't get rich in Sweden any more, they'd tell people, that's why we came to the States,' but I was already heading another direction. Psychology. Civil rights. LGBT. That stuff. I write an advice column for urban youth, the gender-bent mainly, along with proofreading."

"My dad's family came from Sweden, too," Meg announced. "South of Stockholm. They weren't farmers, like the rest who arrived here back in the old days. Dad went to college to become a doctor but ended up a Lutheran pastor. We moved from church to church. I once went to eight schools in seven years. You straight? Married?"

Rolf shook his head. "Was. Once. Married, I mean." He stopped himself from telling her about that youthful passion which had ended in disaster, but thankfully, no children. His ex-wife had gone on to trade in grain and cattle futures on the Kansas City market. She's like a man, his friends said, but in reality the most feminine of women. Their marriage ended more in dissonance over political views than long, drawn-out confrontations. He had since met other women, some of whom tantalizingly appeared online. He was disappointed every time their profiles failed to match their present situation in life, which made him wonder if he unintentionally misled others with his own self-descriptions. He had formed lasting friendships but experienced none of the chemistry so much ballyhooed on dating sites.

When he looked up at Meg, she was smiling, more through him than at him, or so he felt. He noticed the same smile as when she first ordered coffee, as though she held her next comment at the ready long before she uttered it. "I'm very good at guessing other people's ages," she began.

Rolf saw her staring at his graying temples, which he was sure she'd noticed from the outset but was now re-evaluating. He figured she might guess 42. He himself had never been greatly bothered about how people showed their age. He reckoned any grown-up, say 25 or above, had to be his peer, or, in the work place, an equal colleague, an assumption he sometimes came to rue. Nevertheless, he expected Meg at any moment to place him in a firm category based on his perceived virility, insightfulness, or plain old listening skills. He wondered if she judged all men this way, and, if so, why.

"But nobody can guess mine," she continued, to his surprise. "I'm 32, but I can easily pass for 23." She offered this assertively, indicating she not only could, but *did* move comfortably in different age groups.

"Sounds like an anagram. Transposing the 3 and the 2?"

"But I can do it," she protested.

"And you do, too? I mean, get confused for a 23-year-old?" Rolf asked.

"Most always," she replied with pride.

We should all be so lucky, he began, but her upbeat attitude beat him to it, which felt just as well, given the cynicism, albeit gentle, imbedded in his own mixed memories of being that age. Instead, he concentrated on Meg's looks. They were softly exceptional, punctuated by her smile, which actually seemed like only a half-smile promising untold love and empathy beneath the surface. Yet only time might tell if her physical and mental beauty would meld in unison.

Whatever the scenario, Meg's physical beauty was likely to grow over time. He wasn't sure whether to tell her, so he took the indirect path by sticking to anagrams. "Reminds me of George Orwell's *1984*. I read that he wrote the book as an allegory about the horrors of Post-War Europe in 1948, so he switched the 4 and the 8 to avoid being deemed too blatantly critical of controversial issues in his own time."

Meg stopped to sip her coffee. Realizing it was now cold, she stirred vigorously to remix the coffee and cream before emptying the cup with a single swallow. "And you're guessing that approach applies to me? Skipping around, concealing my issues?" she asked.

"I don't know your issues," Rolf admitted.

Watching her place the cup back down, he noticed her careful attention to detail, combined with a slight twitch of her lips, suggesting a sense of vulnerability not noticeable in her previous self-confident glance. He wondered if his intellectualizing about Orwell unnerved her or if she had prepared to approach him on topics she'd never before discussed with strangers, or anyone else, and he'd foreseen her intended move and beat her to the punch.

"With me it's all about love," she said. "Love. Every time I get in a relationship that makes me happy I feel I'm moving ahead in life, am giving something to the world and my partner. I want to accomplish something. Seventh heaven and all that. But when it fails, I'm crushed. I just want to leave."

"*When* it fails? Not if?" Rolf asked.

"It's never if, always when. When it happens, I want to get out of wherever I'm living and move on. Blow this pop stand."

"Once and for all?"

"Yes, like in that old movie, *Charlie Bubbles*. Starring Albert Finney, you know?"

Rolf shook his head. "Tell me," he urged.

"It's from way back, the sixties, saw it on a movie channel. Charlie Bubbles is a sales rep in England or somewhere similar, divorced, at a loss in life. One day a hot-air balloon lands in a field and Charlie shrugs and climbs aboard and floats off—like on a cloud, into the blue—away from his ex, his job, even his kids. I've been on lots of hot air balloons. Moved around. L. A., then Philly, Boston, western Mass, Dallas, Chicago."

"And now back here? Your folks, whadda they say?"

"Nothing like yours would. They're not materialists. They never give me any of that go-get-a-job junk. Dad coulda made big bucks in medicine, but chose the clergy. He says all a doc can do is keep you at the status quo and avoid death. Pastors can help you find life."

"So why come back here?"

"To make something of myself. Maybe?"

"Trying to move ahead in life, without love?"

"With or without. I'm going to the U."

"To do what? The clergy? Like your dad? Save lives?"

Meg looked down and smiled demurely. "I've always dreamed of writing screenplays, but not like *Charlie*

Bubbles. It's way too anti-climactic. The guy just flies off. I'm about love, remember? What is it really and where do people find it? How to keep it."

"And so, at present?"

"Love's on hold."

"But not failed?"

"How d'you know that?"

"Obvious, you don't seem to be fleeing."

She looked him straight in the eye as if to say this is my life, it's serious, I need to talk about it, but instead she gazed around Al's tiny café, with its mingling of displaced street people, bright-eyed college students, and fond couples, all oblivious to the drama embroiling Meg's inner self. Rolf looked around with her. Out through the only window they could see workers rushing off on their daily business. Only Al—tall, lean, and unshaven—looked Rolf and Meg's way, offering them yet more coffee, which they refused, and himself seeming bemused by the human comedy. Rolf guessed conversations like theirs had played themselves out within his earshot untold times.

"I'm in a relationship now." She took out her glasses and fiddled with the frame but didn't put them on, which meant she chose against the business look.

With relish, Rolf attacked the last of his hash browns, now long since cold like his undrunk coffee. Reduced by flames to a charcoaly essence, they tasted delicious, even if science said they came up short on sustenance. After finishing the meal, he glanced up at Meg and said, with a slight tinge of impatience, "Go on."

"But it's on hold," she continued.

"Love, that is. Like you said?"

She nodded. "I was taking a course, The Modern Novel, and met this guy in class. Jamie. We start talking one day during break, kinda bump into each other, but not like you and me." She motioned toward the door, then gave a wiggle like she was imitating Rolf subtly bumping her at the

147

entrance, which made him wonder if he actually had done so. "I mean with Jamie and me it was by design. We'd been eyeing each other for a while. His comments during class discussions were always out in left field, but interesting anyway. They caught my attention, like he thinks Hemingway was gay, so I totally laughed, but, you know, we started meeting privately and he came up with passages from *For Whom the Bell Tolls.* You know, that part about a wounded soldier in an Army hospital, being cared for by this horny nurse. The guy does it with her but he's latent, if you get my drift. That kinda made sense to me."

"Latent homosexual, you mean?"

"Yeah, like, well, anyhow, fate or something led Jamie and me to each other out in the hallway during class break. When we were alone off campus, I kidded him about his ideas and then we started comparing notes for a paper we had due. By then we were reading Graham Greene and Jamie said he was considering writing on guilt and the Catholic mind, which I thought was way-out whacko till he said he was Catholic and had once studied at a priest seminary. Thought of spending his life hearing confessions. All these strangers' sins."

"And you'd never dated a Catholic before," Rolf surmised.

"Dated? Never really knew any."

"In all your 32 years, not even in Boston?"

"Well, maybe a few. Irishmen, pub crawlers, but back at the pass. Not long and then we're dating. Jamie's so soft and caring, sensitive. Never been with a guy like that before, so I started thinking maybe he was gay, not Hemingway. But he gave the lie to that in a rush. I never been held like that before, not by anyone. We fell in love."

"Just what you're looking for. Why put it on hold?"

"I'm not holding back. It's him. He's 24 and has someone back East, someone who lives there still. It's weeks before he tells me this."

A guy or a girl? Rolf wondered, before deciding it didn't

matter, though something must have bothered this Jamie. "No one stops a mad love affair in mid-stream, no matter what they've got back East," Rolf said.

Meg considered this, then waved her hand as if it was off-base or way-out whacko, like she'd say.

"Before long, Jamie decided he needed more time to think things over and now I haven't seen him for what feels like forever."

"Which is how long, in the real world?"

"A month-and-a-half."

"So you're thinking of leaving again?"

"No, but I'm eight years older than him and women mature faster. We were just doing college stuff together, light-hearted, but still he couldn't get over how advanced I was."

"Of course. What did you expect?" Rolf asked. Only natural, he thought to himself, considering your age, but he stopped when an alternative occurred to him. "You lied to him? About your age?"

"You know, me 23, him 24. Twenty-three's only a year younger than him," she replied.

"And Jamie thought you'd lived in all those different cities and were still college-age?"

"He said he wanted more time. I could live with that. He said it with tears in his eyes, sitting on the edge of his bed one night. Bawling. Can you believe it? A guy?"

"He never put the pieces together about you? And what about this other someone?"

"He never said."

"You never asked?"

Meg paused and wrinkled her brow, like trying to imagine a worthy rival for Jamie's affections.

"What did he tell you about her? Was it a her?"

"Maybe I wasn't listening."

Rolf glanced around the café again. Breakfasters filtered out and joined the pedestrians passing Al's window. He wondered if Meg also had some place to get to, which made him think that maybe they were not so unlike after all. She had possibly trailed him to the café and lived a lie with Jamie, the guy she professed to love, but Rolf himself had acted rudely towards her and had never been stunningly successful with romance in his own right. She runs from relationships, he reflected, while I bury myself in work to avoid them.

"Maybe I wasn't listening to what he said," she repeated. "I don't remember. I chose to forget, probably."

If the love interest back East was a her, Rolf thought—not because he cared—but because he wondered if Meg herself understood where Jamie's affections truly lay. He motioned to Meg that it was time for him to leave and took the check from Al. "Coffee's on me," he said, and paid at the till before opening the door for her.

"I'm parked down there," Rolf said, pointing to a ramp.

"What I can't forget is the tears," she continued, walking by Rolf's side. "It wouldn't have been anything if he'd just said it straight out, how he realized I developed faster. But while crying? I still can't deal with it."

"Deal with what? Losing him?"

"No, the tears. He loves me."

"But he loves somebody else even more?"

"Maybe."

The parking ramp was a block away so Rolf asked if she needed a ride. There was still time for her to say yes. He wouldn't have minded. It wasn't every day a lovely young woman singled him out.

"Like I said, a man turning away like that and crying. I expected more. I don't need this in my life."

"Need what?"

"Being a loser. I don't want young people thinking I'm just an old loser."

Look at me, Rolf wanted to reply. Unloved. Searching but never finding. But you're a man, it's different. He knew

150

that's how she'd answer, and he saw her point.

His weariness began to take hold. "You know, you have to have something before you can lose it," he finally said.

A moment of doubt flitted across her face. "By my reckoning, I feel 20 years younger than you."

"*Now* maybe," he agreed, "but in a few years you'll know it's only ten."

"What else do you do that makes you so tired?" she asked. "Besides proofing and bad food."

"Listening to people's problems. I'm a resident psychologist," he chuckled. "Where I'm headed now. I have to work this afternoon. At a hospital."

"And you meet a weirdo like me on your morning off?" she answered with a feigned gasp.

Weirdo or not, she retained an inviting twinkle in her eye as she teasingly tilted her head in his direction. Whether she did so as a practiced ploy or an unlearned natural body movement he didn't know. He only knew his physical desire returned as he saw how her breasts pushed against the cotton blouse causing him to wonder if she was wearing a bra. This Meg could seduce any man she wanted, he thought, and then desperately wait to lose him. Just as she might lose my company, and I hers, in our hesitancy. But good Scandinavians don't linger on city streets talking to strangers, he reminded himself. It was unbecoming. That was one lesson his parents had taught him long ago, and it stuck. Though wishing to say more, he stood before Meg and searched for words, while shifting his weight in weary uncertainty.

"Thanks for prying all that info out of me," she finally said.

A ready rejoinder failed him. "What info is that?"

"You know."

She seemed to consider her next sentence, but surrendered only a slight frown, letting the thought drift away, hot-air balloon-like and un-retrieved. "Maybe I'll float away again," she murmured.

Even if he had experienced or heard about most behaviors on his job, Rolf was perplexed by a woman so unguarded in expressing her feelings, yet equally apprehensive about where they might lead her.

"Remember Margareta Gradén," she said.

As she turned to leave, Rolf wondered if he *would* remember. He'd try, but the only thing he knew for certain was he'd be late for work. As for Margareta Gradén, she disappeared among the downtown throngs and he lacked the time to wait and see where she was bound. He wondered if she knew herself. Maybe she wasn't joking about Charlie Bubbles.

As he walked on toward the car, he wrestled in his tired brain with the future of her anagrams. 32 meets 23? Maybe that works, but what happens when 53 dates 35 and 73 falls for 37? Most young can't count beyond 30, Rolf's job taught him, and tight-fitting cotton begs for uplift way sooner than is fair.

So far Meg had lucked out on all those scores. Rolf wished her the best. Himself as well. We have stories aplenty, as he knew from Al's, to sustain us all.

HOPEFUL
MONSTERS

AN ALBERTA CLIPPER was blowing gales as Woody Wells pulled a lone letter from his Minneapolis mailbox. Angry snowflakes blotched the envelope, so he glanced quickly at the card inside it. *Out by April 1, 2016*, Oscar Chilblain's chary handwriting instructed him. Woody mumbled April Fool's but reminded himself it was already February 28 and his landlord never joked about rent. Nervously, he reached for a cigarette in his coat pocket, but remembered he quit smoking five years ago.

After a quick hello to his fellow lodger Dawrence, arriving at the adjacent box, Woody pulled his coat tight around him and climbed the icy stairs back to his second-story apartment. Once inside, he placed some leftover coffee on a burner and started the oven. As the stove warmed up, he glanced out at the flakes pecking against his window and spotted a forlorn dove alighting precariously on a maple branch.

The struggles infecting our lives, Woody thought. That was the common refrain among workers on his old job at Oracle Middle School in Rockville, Illinois, like how the average guy never knows, you're only a paycheck away from being out on the street. Back then, Woody was still in his twenties, Oracle's best maintenance engineer, and the savviest quail hunter on the prairie. He had no worries and never a clue voters would send nutcase politicians to Springfield. They peddled the state tollways to sneaky private operators, who upped the tolls but let the highways go to pot. Left without State funds, public education went bankrupt, or close to it. Oracle's maintenance crew shrank from three to one and Woody landed out in the cold, just like this afternoon at the mailbox.

Weary of freezing, he opened the oven door and luxuriated in its hot blast while sipping his resurrected coffee. The law stated power companies couldn't turn off a client's heat till April 15, but that didn't stop good ol' Oscar from beating the power moguls to the punch with evictions. He kicked guys out and bumped the rent up. Woody didn't know how Oscar got away with his slimy tricks. Neither did he understand the quirk of fate that led him north to such freaky weather and shady property owners. Not a quail in sight, he thought, but turkeys galore.

No matter, a guy had to live. Once again, he thought back to his Rockville days. Being a vet from Iraq, Woody argued his maintenance job was assured. The superintendent laid him off anyway and the town's only factory paid lousy. And so using the same determination that helped him brave blizzards or stomp up and downstairs to his Minneapolis mailbox, hoping for good news but receiving none, he marched the stubble corn fields of Illinois for months on end hoping in vain for decent work. He shot at quail and bagged his share.

When New Year's 2011 rolled around, Woody had a talk with himself and decided not only did he have to live, but preferably somewhere else. The decision led to rural Minnesota, where he'd been these recent years and finally kicked the Marlboro habit. Now it was this drafty city apartment. Out through the window, he watched the brave but frozen dove cling to its swaying branch. Lacking a mate, it was toughing out another winter, just like Woody.

***

On the first spring day of 2011, the phone rang and Woody dashed indoors to grab it. "Sustainable chicken farming's a high-energy hell," his uncle Erv Noreen complained on the other end, his voice edged with fatigue. "I'm up against it seven days a week. My head honcho skipped out on us. Here I am, over 60. It's still winter in Minnesota."

"Minnesota?" Woody replied in confusion.

"Yeah, the farm was goin' good till my heart went bust drivin' down the Interstate. Docs couldn't decide whether to rip the ticker out or just get me breathing better. They did neither, but I'm on my feet again. Have to take it easy. Need help, bad."

Uncle Erv and Aunt Beth had to be desperate to offer Woody a job on their chicken farm, called Erv's Eggs. He didn't know a fart about birds, except how to shoot 'em. Still, saying no to them wouldn't still his eternal need for a smoke. Only regular work did that, so he headed for central Minnesota as his aunt and uncle's main man. On a marvelous May day he drove his rusty Ford pickup to their farm. It had rained sufficient for lilacs to bloom but not enough to bring out the bugs in their billions.

Aunt Beth met him at the door but kept the screen closed. "We'll give you food and shelter," she announced to affirm their earlier phone conversation.

Woody nodded okay, so she unlatched the screen to let him in. "Mosquitos, you know," she remarked lamely.

As she served up coffee, Beth explained, "Yes, your uncle Erv had a little fender bender, but giving you this job's only to honor his dear sister, your late mother. Okay?"

Woody nodded again.

"Settled then," she said with a sigh. "Your pay's five hundred a month plus a little something when we make a sale."

The next day Woody stood ready and willing when Erv patiently explained the work. "We do layers," he said. "That means hens that lays eggs. You smart enough to figure that out? You're up at six every morning, when the new chicks or eggs come in. Get it?"

Woody nodded yet again while silently examining the poultry house. Not Oracle Middle School, but spacious enough. Clean, too.

"You're here to supervise our workers. Both of 'em. Manuel and Diego."

"Mexican guys?"

"Yeah, father and son. They talk real to us, but plenty slow, only Beth tries on our end," Erv attempted to explain. He paused, while Woody wondered what's up. Why did Erv hire Mexicans if he didn't like them? Was his uncle really that old and sick or just disgusted because no Anglo guys would do this dirty work?

"They need lotsa warmth," Erv finally added, nodding toward the chicks so Woody knew who he meant. Erv showed him the chicken coops before retreating to the house, where Woody was also to sleep, in a well-furnished
but dank basement room.

The next morning Woody introduced himself to Manuel and Diego and found both spoke English. Diego went to community college but came every day to help with egg collection and deliveries. The two men explained the importance of keeping the creatures warm and their eggs safe. Woody watched Manuel sweep the floor before giving the chicks and hens food and water. At noon, Diego went off to class and Manuel stayed till dusk. Once Manuel left, Woody's task was turning up the heat against the evening's chill.

After the new chicks' first week, the men didn't need to monitor the temperature so carefully, but a few birds could die of exposure if the cruelest winter cold crept in. The older birds handled the chill, and the stronger the hens got, the bigger their appetite. Then came immunizations. Erv emerged from the house and described the process, but Manuel showed Woody how to do it. A poor job affected the birds' feeding and chicks' survival. Layers matured at five or six months, so Woody came to understand Beth's concerns about cash. It was vital the chicks grew strong and produced a ton of eggs.

"Every day," Erv drilled home to Woody.

As weeks of everydays mounted, Woody noticed the hens' personalities. He let them out to roam, which showed their pecking order. The small ones recognized the biggest hens and gave way at feeding. Some were shy, but grew more spirited and enjoyed being handled. Others were curious about their surroundings and independent.

Manuel and Diego loaded cartons while Beth and Woody counted eggs, one by one. Some were small, or cracked, and their shells appeared thinner than the Grade As or AAs Woody recalled from grocery stores. Modern automated egg collection worked faster than Beth and Erv's hands-on system, which was sustainable but only with persistence. The narrow financial margins Woody guessed at weren't because of lousy bookkeeping at Erv's Eggs. Every morning he saw Beth sitting over coffee and meticulously calculating who owed them what.

"The only problem's Erv's delivery truck. On the fritz," she told Woody once. Days later it still stood idle and eventually weeds inched up over the running boards. And so Woody's pickup became the delivery vehicle. Diego taught him the route and the names of customers, mostly bakeries or institutional food services.

"That's because all these eggs are Grade B," Diego explained during a run to the local hospital dining service. "Perfectly nutritious, but they rate lower in appearance."

"So fancy restaurants and supermarkets don't want ' em?" Woody guessed.

"They're your scrambled eggs at the old folks' home and school cafeterias. The yokes aren't as firm as As and AAs."

"So you're eating Erv's eggs at your college caf?"

Diego winked. "Like I said."

"Equally nutritious," Woody repeated with a smile. "They slide down your gullet as slick as Uncle Erv retreats to the house every morning?"

"By the way, d'you ever notice Dolly?" Diego asked another morning when rain splattered the windshields and talk was hard to come by. "She's my dad's favorite hen. He likes chickens better'n people."

"I noticed, but what's he see in her? She's just big and red."

"She's smart. She seeks him out every time she lays an egg, just to say it's ready for collection. That's something, man."

***

Hoping to witness what was up with Dolly, Woody watched her closely. The hen strutted to Manuel, clucked, flapped her wings, or scratched in the dirt to get his attention. One day Manuel was sick, so the hen snuck up on Woody and pecked at his heels till he followed her to the egg. Woody wondered if this was a sign of animal intelligence or whatever learned folks called it.

The next day he and Diego left on deliveries, their last stop a mom 'n pop hash house called B & B's, run by Bert and Bonnie. Bonnie was really named Bua, an outgoing Asian woman from somewhere strange, Woody guessed, who'd married Bert and moved to the States without losing her strong accent or infectious friendliness.

While Diego was unloading crates, she told Woody about Erv. "He never be the same since his accident. He drive on a light pole."

"Pretty near killed him," Bert added.

"We love them both," Bonnie continued. "But they getting old. Manuel, too. Your uncle, he not talk any more, and Manuel hangs with the hens. Loves 'em. Like family."

Bert went to his kitchen, but Bonnie lingered. Woody could tell she had something on her mind, just like he did, but he doubted she'd understand his question, so he listened instead.

"It's D got the smarts. He run that poultry house, you know. Without that boy, zip." Bonnie made a slashing motion across her neck, then went back to work, happy with her Grade Bs.

D's Diego, Woody realized, and he's the one running things, not Beth?

To give himself space for thought, Woody let Diego drive on the way back. His uncle and aunt's flagging energy was obvious. That left himself, Manuel, and Diego, the youth in his driver's seat, to manage the farm. With a feeling he hardly knew the origins of, Woody posed the question he'd wanted to ask Bonnie, "What's so special about hens? Why does your dad love 'em so much?"

Diego glanced sideways like he'd sensed the question coming, or had wondered the same thing himself, once upon a time. "Pa doesn't know either, he just likes 'em. When nothing was going right for him, they were his only friends. My ma died, low wages. Know what I mean?"

Without replying, Woody stared ahead. He remembered Bonnie's words about Erv and Beth, their problems, and Manuel's, too. Woody wondered where his own life was heading. Not the kind of stuff he'd considered in Iraq or at Oracle. In Iraq, he and the other grunts struggled to merely live another day. At Oracle he was surrounded by folks who didn't reflect, period. They just did, as long as tasks were clear and never-changing. Woody wondered when folk got beyond living for the moment.

"I took Bio at school," Diego continued. "The prof told us about birds—like Dolly. They're dinos."

Surprised out of his reverie, Woody turned in his seat. "Dinosaurs?"

"Yeah, no kidding. It was like some dinos started growing feathers. I mean way back, eons ago. Nobody knows why, feathers were no use to 'em, dinos weighed way too much. Couldn't lift off the ground, you know? But some dinos got smaller and grew wings, kinda. Scientists called 'em hopeful monsters, like they could almost fly, but not quite."

"They tried but failed? They were that smart? Hopeful?"

"No, no, not them, I mean the science guys. In white robes. They were hopeful *for* them. You know, like rooting for dinos in secret, in fossil form in the lab, to lift off and fly. Some scientists believe in sudden change. Like evolution sometimes takes big leaps forward and skips the gradual route. It just happens. Pow!"

"So a bunch of monster dinos shrank down and grew wings and learned to fly? Then they became chickens?"

"No, not chickens per se, but birds, chickens are birds. Barnyard birds, get it?"

"How many centuries?"

"Did it take, you mean?"

"Yeah."

Woody flashed Diego a sly smile which also conveyed a kernel of doubt. He'd heard his share of dumbass talk in Army barracks and guessed colleges could be full of fools as well, but Diego's story was just incredible enough to fire Woody's imagination. He'd hunted enough animals to know they weren't stupid.

"Like millions. Eons, like I said. In reality, there wasn't any hopeful leap at all, or so said other scientists. They figure dinos, like Tyrannosaurus, developed into birds, but it took millions of years, one little bone and a slimy scale at a time. A steady march down, from huge to small."

"From the ground to the air?"

"Yeah, well, sorta, and they changed form, too. You know, dinos had snouts. Look at Dolly, she's got a beak. That's like a dinosaur snout that changed, it became longer and narrower. Dolly doesn't chew stuff but pecks at it. The way she pecks at your leg."

"And you told your dad that?"

"He liked the hopeful idea best. It's like when you got the odds against you, you can turn them your way. To your favor. Maybe it gives Pa hope, how dinos changed so much."

"Hopeful for you or for him?" Woody asked.

Woody thought about some of the poor boys he knew, who desperately longed for a chance in life. Unlike them, Diego relaxed and draped one hand over the steering wheel, as if he owned the vehicle. Owned the world, too, Woody thought. He was like the few soldiers in Iraq, the exceptions that had schooling. They never talked about who they were or what they aimed to gain in life. With quiet pride, they took the future for granted. Beyond all doubt, it would be theirs.

"When life and society should be against them," Woody remarked. He realized he was talking to himself.

Diego nodded in acknowledgement, though he surely was guessing at Woody's thoughts. He pointed ahead with his index finger while turning in to Beth and Erv's.

"See what's ahead of us?" he said, meaning the farmstead. "Dinos aren't extinct."

***

"Back in the Stone Age," Diego loved to say. "A million years working with the same flint knives, nothing changing till some guy finally pops up and figures out how to sharpen the points different."

"That's how slow you think life moves at Erv's Eggs?" Woody replied.

"Yes, but your aunt and uncle're game for a change. Dad, too. I know 'em."

And so it was. The hoped-for future taking shape. With Diego explaining the technical stuff and Woody arguing the case to improve business, the two convinced Beth and Erv to give up on eggs and let the chickens live outdoors.

"Easy as pie," Diego said. "Change the poultry house to a processing building. We'll raise meat chickens for sale."

Erv listened dourly. "Off-layers?" he asked.

As a vet, Woody got a loan from the bank and Beth reconciled her schedule and check book so they could meet new customers' demand for promptness. The men set up a processing area. They rinsed tubs and tanks and filled them with fresh water and ice, scrubbing like mad to keep them sterile. The new plan also meant killing chickens at six weeks rather than raising them to adulthood. Woody and Diego fed and watered them daily and moved the field pens when necessary. On Mondays and Tuesdays, they readied chicks for restaurants. Diego helped load the pickup and carry the crates into the processing building. Woody killed the birds, dunked them in the scald pot, and plucked each animal, while Diego eviscerated them.

Manuel grew moody as he watched his downy chicks rendered to saleable meat. It was all for the best, Diego consoled his father. "Quick and easy quality control."

Erv warned about the dangers of feral dogs and wild pigs, but Diego didn't worry. "Plus where do you find critters like that in these parts?" he asked. "The biggest threat's foxes. They won't take many."

He knew his stuff, so he asked his father to guard the outdoor pens. Manuel kept the predators at bay and the team processed chicks on the farm, instead of sending them on long, stress-filled trips for processing in distant towns. Unwanted deaths sank to a minimum.

Erv's Eggs kept its name, but trod a new and different path. Diego collected the mail in town before class, while Buena paid the bills and cashed customers' checks for ever-increasing amounts. In time Erv, Beth, Woody, Diego, and Manuel put their heads together and bought a computer, which only Diego and Woody knew how to use. After a few months Beth developed a knack for it, too, and set up an electronic billing system. For Woody, life was on track again, like those early days back at Oracle. Money no worry. A place of his own soon.

One cheery March morning Woody was proudly reminding himself he hadn't touched a Marlboro for three years, when the sky darkened, a sudden storm blew up, and Erv's ticker quit ticking. Woody watched as the old man, trudging back to the house, tumbled into a deepening snow drift and lay there snoring his last. A few days later came the funeral. At the gravesite, mortuary guys used a backhoe to cut through the frozen crust of earth and a handful of locals attested to the stuff they liked about Erv. Bonnie talked longest. "Cranky and honorable," she concluded with a tear.

As she spoke, it dawned on Woody that his uncle's passing didn't point, as it should have, toward better times at Erv's Eggs, with younger folk at the helm. Instead, his death marked the beginning of its end. In vain Woody sought to explain that feeling. "We're stuck," was all he said in the end. He wondered what that meant and why he thought it.

***

As for apartment living, nothing got under Woody's skin like all the everyday thises and thats, topped off by fiddling with an ancient microwave, which stood in idle grandeur atop his

China cabinet in Minneapolis. Both items came from Beth, and the microwave desperately needed repairs. I've never tried that before, he thought, so I should definitely be able to do it, a line he remembered from some silly kid's book.

He began fiddling with the microwave but looked out the window when he got bored. Yesterday's clipper had slowed to uncertain gusts, but the snow continued to fall. It reminded him when Erv died and Beth entered a nursing home only a month later. Not a year passed before she, too, was gone. As neighbors attested at her funeral, she'd sorrowed Erv to the end. Sorrowed, Woody thought, a word that solemnly lingered on mourners' tongues and expressed an old folks' longing.

Despite Diego's new ideas, Erv's Eggs carried on in a familiar fashion after the oldsters died. Erv and Beth's friends described how the old man, in his seeming do-nothing state, and Beth, with her attention to facts and figures, held the farm together as long as they could. With Beth gone, Woody and Diego ran the business while Manuel cared for the chicks. Erv's grumpy insistence on doing things right vanished and so did the strict attention to cleanliness. Woody's maintenance skills would have helped around the poultry house, but he spent his time repairing the ever decaying pickup and keeping Diego balanced between school and work.

Woody paused from such thoughts and turned back to the broken microwave. Maybe I'll sling it, he thought while cranking up the stove, but what would be left? As the kitchen warmed, he remembered Dolly. Fleeing a fox one frigid night, she ran into a space heater and broke a wing. Manuel put her to sleep but came out of the experience more shaken than the hen. Tired of seeing chicks and hens die before his eyes, he took early retirement.

When a nearby state college rewarded Diego with a sparkling diploma, he took a job in the suburbs whereupon the work force at Erv's Eggs dwindled from three to one. This time Woody was the guy left with a job, but no money. He tried to refinance, but the bank said no dice and put the business up for auction.

Financial pantry as bare as my apartment kitchen, he thought, as new storm winds battered his window.

***

"I keep checking the darned mail for jobs," Woody's neighbor Dawrence complained the day after the Alberta Clipper. "Never a nibble."

Woody and Dawrence's girlfriend Anna waited till Dawrence finished probing his empty mailbox. He said he was laid off from construction for the winter, and Woody told them he hadn't worked full-time since moving to the city from Erv's Eggs. He wanted a maintenance job, but the schools weren't hiring. Anna explained she was a waitress. "One that actually has a job," she said coyly to the men. With that comment, she retreated indoors to get ready for work.

Left alone on the porch, Woody and Dawrence shuffled their feet and looked out at the yard's enormous cottonwood. From the grey clouds, a sleek crow swooped down onto a middle branch. A second crow settled on a lower limb. They balanced deftly as the branches swayed, gobs of snow falling and settling in the drifts below. On the maple tree, the dove remained encrusted in a death-like shroud of yesterday's snow.

"March 1," Woody announced and shuffled some more. "You two out of here next month, too?"

"May be a crummy place, but we need it." Dawrence gestured at the door to his and Anna's tiny efficiency. "Bugs creep in the cracks."

Fondly, Woody thought back on his musty room at Beth and Erv's. In time he began to fix dinner for all three of them and lounged in their living room through the evenings, which is why Beth left him the China chest and microwave. Now he was living bare bones in Minneapolis, but fancy quarters were out of sight expensive.

"I need work, too," Woody repeated with a nod at the mailbox. "Got a laptop for applying, but I write letters by hand as well."

"I used to apply online, from a coffee shop," Dawrence replied, "till their manager unplugged the computer."

Woody's thoughts drifted again to his aunt and uncle. Strange. Erv's Eggs managed okay old-fashioned but failed after going electronic. He reached for a Marlboro, which wasn't there.

"That's what they oughta do on Chilblain," Dawrence continued. "Pull the plug."

"The other way around, way I see it. He's pulling it on us."

"You know what he does? Takes our damage deposit, and then won't improve the place. One guy took him to small claims, but Oscar's got friends at City Hall."

"So the big shots kicked the renter out and kept Chilblain?" Woody wondered.

"Something like."

"They toss us out and rob us, too?"

"Illegal's been legal for years. Maybe they forgot to tell you?"

"But the Landlord-Tenant Laws. Oscar showed 'em to me."

"Sure he did. That's how he gets around 'em. Knowing his stuff. Fights fire with fire," Dawrence argued.

The men gazed out across the neighborhood. Stucco homes with fading paint stood against the newest winter onslaught as blankets of snow whizzed between buildings. Wistfully, Woody told Dawrence about his quail hunting days in Illinois, how the dogs stalked the birds and him and his buddies fired together. Then he told of his years with Manuel and Diego, that nutty story, how dinos gained clout by sprouting wings.

"Fire with fire, huh," he said after Dawrence quit listening.

"The good guys caught up with him. Us building unity and strategy pays off, like you hunting with your pals."

"Fat chance."

"Oscar's no saint, but we're not alone. We joined up against him."

Woody looked inquiringly at his companion, who refused to back down.

"Honest, there's a class action suit against Chilblain. Anna heard about it. He bought scads of apartment buildings from a slumlord called Flaskberg, who the City barred from renting property. Flaskberg had housing violations up the wazoo, but worse still Oscar unlawfully sold half the properties back to Flaskberg and lied to officials about it. The class is seeking damages."

"The class?" Woody asked. He stared in confusion at Dawrence, who averted his glance when Anna rejoined them for a smoke.

"Us tenants. There's three right here, you and us," she explained. "Over 5,000 folks that've rented from Chilblain, just since we been here. How long's that, hon?"

"A while," Dawrence said with a sigh.

He took Anna's cigarette and inhaled deeply. Woody watched them pass it back and forth. He'd been so long from the habit the nervous grabbing for a cig ruled his brain more than any immediate need for nicotine.

"Fifty million coming to us," Anna continued. "What's more, courts could rule for damages, my boss said, five to ten times more."

"Ten times fifty?" Dawrence asked without waiting for answers.

Five hundred million bucks, Woody thought. He imagined five thousand angry Chilblain renters across the city straining to believe their luck.

"But we have to go sign for it," Anna added. "They won't come looking for us, not for that kinda cash."

"Lotsa dough," Woody agreed.

"We're only a paycheck from…," Dawrence began.

"Sounds like things're goin' our way," Woody interrupted, "about time."

"Yeah, can you believe it?" Anna chimed in.

"Remember, us three, together," Dawrence said as he and Anna snuffed out their cig and turned to go.

***

As Woody ascended the outside stairs, the crows started up a raucous cawing, which faded like shredded missives tossed to the freezing wind. The class action euphoria slowly deserted him. Courts take forever. Appeals, too. Chilblain, he thought with a shudder.

From atop the stairway, he hoped to see the tardy mailman arrive. Instead, he paused to gaze at the moribund dove. Miraculously, it ruffled its feathers, spread its wings with a flap, and headed aloft into the teeth of the storm, never swerving. Thin and silent, it continued higher and higher in perfect flight, till it soared above the tallest tree tops.

Watching it disappear, Woody reminded himself of the things he knew. He'd never forget the guys in Iraq. Diego's smarts were off the charts. April 1 was no joke. And his fifth summer up North was on its way. All he wanted was an honest job with decent benefits. He sensed the first step toward that future lay in finding a purpose. For now, it was fixing Beth's microwave, simple enough. He went to his kitchen to turn up the oven and plan some more. After all, he reasoned, if dinosaurs could grow wings and dead doves fly, so can I!

SIXTEEN

ASHIR'S FEET SMELLED WITHOUT SOCKS, but he walked across Waterville in his outsized clogs anyway and clambered up the steps to Swede's white frame house. Seeing nobody around, he knocked softly and peeked in through the screen door. As usual, Lena, the furry yellow dog, was lazing on a sofa which she knew to stay off of, but never obeyed. *Big as a lion*, Ashir was thinking, when Swede, a scraggly oldster with faded tattoos, entered the room. He gave a gruff command to the dog, who yawned but didn't stir.

Swede turned to the door and nodded, so Ashir let himself in.

"Little Ashir, good to see you."

"I'm big Ashir, remember? Little Ashir's my brother. He's older than me, but I'm bigger."

Swede motioned at him with one hand and jerked his head brusquely. "C'mon, make yourself at home. You've trudged a good ways," he said. Ashir grabbed a wicker chair and waited for the next move, which came pretty much like always. Swede sat down beside Lena, who muzzled him till she broke wind. Irritated, the old man nudged her off the sofa, so she plopped down on a fake afghan and let out a frustrated sigh. She blinked up at Ashir, who hesitated in fear. *The lions came before the hyenas. They were mangy and starving. We knew to keep away.*

"Ok to pet her?" Ashir asked after screwing up his courage. Without waiting for an answer, he scratched the pooch's head, stroked her back, and whispered to her in Somali, mostly to soothe himself. Ashir knew her needs were simple like his, except for one thing, a new phone. He needed a Galaxy Emerge something awful. "Listen, watch, and game!" an excited voice on TV commercials told him about the J3 Emerge. "Just the thing for YOU!"

"Yeah, Lena's friendly," Swede finally answered. Talking about the dog was his way of greeting folks, and Ashir told himself any canine letting an uncertain Somali boy approach wasn't about to bite. As Ashir petted Lena, he waited for the right moment to turn the talk his way, unless Swede beat him to it.

"So what is it?" Swede asked, beating him to it. "You here to do the yard work?"

Ashir didn't know how to reply. Adults talked different than kids at school, and all he caught from Swede was 'work.' Searching for an answer put Ashir's mind in a jumble.

"My dad doesn't work here," he said. "He had a job but they let him go 'cause his car break and we got no transportation. Ten miles from where we live to there."

"Where's there?"

"There he work," Ashir replied, getting more confused. "Worked, I mean."

Ashir watched a sad smile spread across Swede's face and knew he'd misunderstood and answered wrong. It wasn't just that Swede was a grownup. He didn't talk like other people in Minnesota; his sentences went up and down like he was singing a song. Ashir's father said that's how folks sounded in Swede's country. They had a strange melody and you had to get used to it. Swede had lived in America for thirty years, or maybe more, who knew how long? Put that against Ashir's two years, and their wires could get crossed, just like now.

"So your dad has a job now or he had one before? Which?" Swede insisted.

Ashir didn't answer. Instead, he thought of Lena, which brought a smile to his face. The silly pooch patiently listened to him mumbling in Somali and Swede barking commands in his own tongue, and she understood Americans, too.

"So does that make her smarter than all of us?" Ashir asked with a sly smile.

"What?" Swede wondered.

"Never mind," Ashir answered, his thoughts returning to Swede's original question. "Back in Somalia, you mean?"

"Either way," Swede replied with a note of impatience.

"Back home, my dad drove truck and cut hair, but this is our home now."

"So you still live way down the street from here, same apartment as before?"

"Yeah, it got cold till we learned about the heat."

"How to turn it on or that you even had any?" Swede wondered.

"Both. Our neighbor come over and showed dad the thermostat. Then we got heat." *But nothing like summer in Tieglow and Baidoa. The soles of our feet burned when we ran out of sandals. Then we had to stay inside. Only came out when the sun was gone. Or in Kenya. We played soccer with coconuts in the boiling sand, barefoot. Next the rains came, then stopped, for good. The grass died and the earth cracked right under our feet.*

"So what does your dad do these days?" Swede asked.

"He work at a company putting things together, but he's laid off 'cause of the car. He was a farmer till our cows starved to death. We took them down to the river, but it quit flowing. Then he drive a truck."

"Like you said."

"He's looking to be a barber here, but he needs a certificate. Where does he get that?"

Swede shook his head and raised an eyebrow toward his wife in the kitchen. "No idea. She cuts my hair these days," he explained.

"At the refugee place in Kenya, guys came to our tent or sat outside while my dad trimmed their hair."

"Tough times, like where I came from, way back when," Swede said with a slow shake of his head.

***

The room fell silent except for a long, drawn-out "Ja" from Swede, which meant he was trying to think of something else to say. When Lena fell asleep on the rug, Ashir got up and sauntered around the room, eventually stopping in front of an ancient desktop computer. He tried to boot it up and saw a quick flicker but no display on the screen.

"Do you want this?" Ashir asked.

"It's hers," Swede answered. He looked over his shoulder toward his wife. "Dagmar, do you want this PC?"

A heavy, harsh-looking woman stuck her head around the doorpost and spoke in a surprisingly mellow tone, "Why, heavens, no. That old thing? Does it even work?"

"Mr. Foster, my shop teacher, can fix it. He makes this kinda stuff work," Ashir said as he stared at the dusty black screen.

Swede listened but only shrugged wearily. He used to have an important railroad job, flagging and guiding locomotives, but he was too old for that now and saw no need for electronics. "Damn doodads for kids, of all ages," Ashir remembered him saying on his last visit there. Ashir's dad said Swede still lived in yesterday, when they switched engines with hand signals, like some remote places he remembered in Africa. *We heard about trains in Somalia and our grandparents talked of seeing them in Mogadishu when they were little. We imagined they were dusty and hauled freight across the desert. But the trains disappeared. Supplies arrive on trucks now, big wheelers. Armed guards sitting on top of the freight. They looked mean and never talked. We didn't know if they were government troupes or belonged to chieftains, who Dad said ran the clans. They held rifles, like they'd grown from their skin, and stuck out like rhino horns. Little Ashir told me, steer clear, don't speak. They'll think you want to steal food.*

Swede liked to fiddle with his hands, which was why Ashir enjoyed his visits. He helped out around the house, but never had to get in a hurry about it. Most of all he feasted on stuff Swede owned that he'd never use again and had probably had forgotten about, like the PC or an air pump in the garage that

Little Ashir wanted for his bike. Being good to Lena always helped, Ashir knew, even though his brother told him to "beware of the dog," the way lawn signs around town warned folks. Little Ashir knew who to trust.

"Can I have it?" Ashir asked and pointed at the computer. "It helps me."

"How's that?" Swede wanted to know. He raised an eyebrow in wonder.

"Mr. Foster'll get it working, I know he can, for me to watch TV on. That's how I learn English. *Red Dead*. It's about America. I love America."

Ashir waited. He noted something was clicking in Swede's head, like maybe a distant memory of *his* America, suddenly awakened.

"*Red Dead*," Ashir repeated, eagerly nodding yes as if that would trigger recognition in Swede. "You know, the way they talk tough, like 'there ain't no civilization here'."

"A video game?" Swede asked.

"Yeah, you make your own morality. You get rewarded for doing good stuff. Or bad. You decide yourself. Like saving somebody from being kidnapped, or kidnapping them yourself. I know 'cause my buddy saved a lady from a gang of carjackers, on his own."

"No videos in my day. Me, I learned the lingo honest-like," Swede said. "The railroad section gang was all mixed. You know, burrheads and bohunks, so I talked English to the bosses. They were born here."

"Where you born?"

Ashir caught Swede studying him, until he replied simply, "The Old Country. Way off, across the sea."

"What sea was that?"

Swede sucked in air, which wasn't a word, but a sound he made if he meant 'yes' or 'give me a minute, that surprised me.'

"Two weeks it took," the old guy finally said without naming the sea. Ashir watched Swede retreat within himself, like he was reliving those fourteen days in private.

"Back in the day, huh?" Ashir asked, like kids at school said.

Getting no response, Ashir resumed his seat beside Lena. His mind was set on the computer more than the Galaxy now, but Swede would insist it belonged to Dagmar, like he did every time Ashir or his brother asked for something. The old man didn't want to be bugged about clutter, so he always nodded his wife's way. She gladly gave the boys whatever they wanted, but only after Swede gave the final okay. The ritual could take forever, but this time Dagmar hustled out the door to go shopping, thus leaving Ashir and Swede to face off.

Every few seconds Ashir glanced up at the skinny man, who had nicotine fingers on one hand, like the foreign aid workers in Kenya. Somewhere, Ashir guessed, there was an ocean wide enough to separate Swede's mysterious country from his own sandy desert. Yet there was something else about him that was even harder to understand. Like what made this wiry guy act so gruff and grouchy on the surface when he was so soft and gentle inside. Here he and Swede were, halfway around the world from where they started out, with only a drowsy dog between them, who knew them only through her nose and worried not a minute about where they came from or how they got there. Ashir wiggled his toes. Lena sniffed them and licked his smelly feet.

***

"So how you got across that sea in two weeks?" Ashir asked. The dog's rough tongue tickled his feet as Swede slowly emerged from his secret thoughts.

"Cargo ship. Carrying Swedish steel. Icebergs like mountains. Cold. And you?"

"Airplane. From Nairobi."

We started in Tieglow and walked for days. Barefoot, to keep us from wearing out our boots. Me and Little Ashir tied the laces together so they hung around our necks and down our backs. Mom walked with big sister Axado. Her name means Sunday, the day she was born. Dad carried little Hani, "the happy girl."

The first truck in Baidoa wasn't the grand ride uncle Abdi ordered. It smelled like garbage and was weighted down with people. They said it was a dirt loader that would dump us, but it let us off at a crossroad. We waited in the sun till our water ran out. Lots more people came. They whispered about lions. Nothing scared us, not the heat or the dirt or having no place to sleep, except the lions, hungrier than starving babies. They came out of the bush. One guy said our smell attracted them. Others figured it was their hunger driving them on until they discovered us. The men and boys threw rocks at them, but desperation drew them closer. Then came the hyenas.

We got even more scared at night, our bellies emptier. Then another truck showed up. It had side guards and a canopy, more like the kind Abdi and Dad paid for. The road led west and was full of people walking to Kenya. They slowed the trucks down, women with small kids, no food. Most went naked because they gave everything to bandits just to stay alive.

"Bandits came after our truck, but the driver floored it. Then he picked up women with tiny kids who'd been running from hyenas day and night. They were too tired to walk and sat by the road waiting to die," Ashir blurted out.

Swede listened without blinking. Only slowly did his expression change and show he understood Ashir was talking about a journey long before Nairobi.

"Surely some didn't make it," Swede replied.

"No, the hyenas wanted to eat them. It was like they were laughing at people. I can still hear them cackle. They went for the smallest or weakest, but the women said they stuck together and surrounded the little ones. 'We were like mother elephants,' one lady said. 'We kept the hyenas away.'

"So you made it to Kenya, you were refugees there," Swede guessed.

"Our driver gave the ladies water so they wouldn't die. Then we found another truck to Dadaab—that's in Kenya," Ashir continued. "Next year I can drive, I'll be sixteen."

With his thoughts back in Minnesota, Ashir got up and stood by the computer, pushing the power button in and out. "I have to read the driver's manual at school, I got nothing to read it from at home." He paused to eye Swede, who seemed sunk in thought again like he was recalling his own trip across the sea or figuring out what to say about the computer. "If I only had a PC and could drive, too," Ashir repeated.

"Yeah, you wish for your heart's desire. Don't we all?" Swede interrupted, partly talking to himself. "The north Atlantic in December, waves higher'n a skyscraper." Swede clucked his tongue at the horror of it, but swiftly returned to his senses. "Leaves. You here to work or not?" he asked Ashir. "Ten dollars an hour?"

"You bet," Ashir answered. "I'm ready."

With a computer I could study the driver's manual at home, he repeated to himself. *But still. A Galaxy! Gee!*

***

It was true, nothing had grown in Somalia for most of Ashir's lifetime, but he wasn't born yesterday. Three years at a refugee camp in Kenya and two in a lousy Minnesota apartment had taught him about heat, cold, and bedbugs. Helping Swede meant he also knew how green grass begged for mowing in summer and dead leaves needed bagging every fall. As Swede headed toward the garage, Ashir strode silently ahead of him and got out the rakes and a box of black garbage bags.

"Drawed string?" he said to Swede while holding up a bag in full view.

"You betcha," Swede replied. "Remember last time, cleaning roof gutters?" He jerked at the draw string and chuckled. "I sent you to Harry's Hardware three times for the right bags before you figured out what was up?" He waved a hand at the heaps of yellow, red, and blackened leaves on his lawn and then nodded toward the driveway. "That wants clearing. Let's do it," he grunted, trying his best to straighten a stiff back.

Knowing the routine, Ashir bent his own back to the job. First, he raked up a batch of leaves and stuffed them in a bag. Then, Swede stuck a foot in it and pressed the leaves down.

Ashir watched him remove his leg from each bag, careful not to punch a hole in it. When Swede judged it was full, Ashir pressed the leaves deeper still and added more till the bag was bursting. Then he yanked the yellow string and knotted it.

After a while, he handed a batch of bulging bags to Swede, one at a time. As the oldster stacked them in neat piles against the garage, he could maintain a feeling of being in charge, while Ashir's mind drifted back to the Galaxy Emerge. Unlike Swede's funky old PC, he couldn't get it for free, but every kid at school had one. All a Galaxy cost was forty bucks' student discount plus seven dollars a month. Five-inch display. Sixteen gigabyte memory. Instagram. Visual voicemail and Worldwide calling. Guys punched calls to Somalia, where every thatched hut had Wi-Fi. He'd help his mom talk to her ma in Tieglow.

As the sun got warmer and the stacks grew, Swede grew weary, so he wiped his brow and ambled to the porch. Shortly after, he returned with two bottles of water and Lena at his heels. She frolicked in the leaves, which meant they'd have to rake them again, but so what? Ashir and Swede slaked their thirst and Lena, now exhausted, plopped down between them on the lawn.

"Not good," Swede said to the dog in mock irritation. He turned to Ashir. "There's spiders. Terrible bites. They itch and burn for days."

Ashir swigged his mineral water, then jiggled what was left, careful not to waste any, though he knew water had no meaning here. It rained and puddles lay full and nobody paid any mind. *Kenya had water too. There was a faucet on the opposite side of the camp, but no containers to carry the water in. Like the other women, Mom made do with any flasks she could find. She walked to the faucet, three or four trips a day in the blazing sun. If she couldn't find any containers, she hoped other women would loan her some, which she knew they would, but it was still a bitter struggle, and she prayed the jugs wouldn't spring a leak. Then it'd be two families left out on the next walk for water, her family and the family of whoever loaned her the water jugs to begin with.*

"Lena gets spider bites from the leaves," Swede continued.

"Here, under her right shoulder. Feel that? It swole up, so they drained it. The Cephalexin cost me a mint."

Ashir pretended not to hear Swede but patted Lena by her right shoulder. "Mr. Foster says nobody values bottles here," he added. "He says plastic floats in oceans, like the one you crossed, and strangles whales. One had sixty bottles in its belly."

Swede tried to listen but nodded off in the sun, which reminded Ashir how time dragged in the refugee camp. *Three years of roaming tent city. Nothing to do but get in trouble. Like when I tripped over a coconut during soccer and ran a ballpoint in my pocket through my bladder. The camp docs removed the pen but put the catheter in wrong. I was infected for months.*

As if he could read Ashir's mind, Swede mumbled something in his own strange tongue and jerked awake.

"Was it hot?" he asked. "In the camp?"

"The sun," Ashir sighed and hesitated. He was unaccustomed to telling non-Somalis his stories but knew Swede came from far away, just like him, talked a language Americans didn't know, and never kicked his dog. All that helped Ashir relax.

"The camp had nothing," he continued, smiling sadly. "Dad said, just wait, we'll be in Dadaab before you know it. We saved the women and kids from hyenas, but all Dadaab had was lots of nothing and millions of people. My uncle Abdi had money. The millions had nothing."

"Just empty bellies?"

"Less than that. The camp ran out of tents so we cut down trees and stuck branches in the sand. When the branches bent toward each other, the men hung sheets across the poles for tent covers."

"So that's where you lived?"

"That's where our neighbor lost his boy. The guys said hyenas took him, but I knew better. It was lions."

"Nobody chased them away? Nobody cared?"

"Care all you want, it don't help. A big lion had the kid's head in his mouth. He was kicking while the lion chewed on him. Guys said, don't be a hero and try to help, the lions'll take you too, then who'll feed the rest of your family? It's true, I watched."

"My people were starving way back, too, but no lions," Swede said. He finished the water and wiped his mouth with a shirt sleeve. He said something to Lena, who rolled over and wiggled with joy. To the west, the autumn sun had begun tilting toward late afternoon, so Ashir followed Swede to get their bagging finished.

"My people came over here a hundred years ago, or more," Swede continued, as he tramped more leaves in a bag.

"Never had a pot to…"

Ashir watched a tear swell in Swede's eye, but he continued with his own tasks. This time he leaned the newly filled bags against the garage himself. He pulled at a yellow string on one. "Trawed string?" he asked.

Brushing away his tear, Swede corrected him.

"Traw string," Ashir repeated.

When Swede didn't answer, Ashir wondered if he'd pronounced it wrong again, or if Swede couldn't say it right either.

"Three years in Kenya felt like a hundred," Ashir said, as he heaved a new bag onto the pile.

"Imagine that, a lion swallowing your kid," Swede whispered, allowing a new tear to form. "A lot to lose."

Not one kid, but two. We named the next baby Hani, after our first Hani, who Dad carried across the desert and who never cried. Then first Hani was gone and so Mom had this second Hani. But tough stuff. Mom didn't know the second Hani was born dead and thought the European nurse was trying to steal her. An aid officer came but Mom screamed like crazy, grabbed him, and bit his arm. She wouldn't calm down and they arrested her. After that she got mad at Dad and smashed his phone on the floor, which got her a week in camp jail. We waited a year for her papers to clear. Two Hanis in two years.

"My uncle Abdi was gone by then, to Minnesota," Ashir announced.

Swede scratched himself under an arm, pretty much like Lena. Ashir realized the old man needed time to make sense of what he'd heard.

"Abdi sent us money and a letter saying we could come to America."

A breeze blew up and scattered more leaves across Swede's driveway. Ashir swept them up and waited.

"That's way more than two hours work for you," Swede said.

Ashir looked out over the lawn, where weeks of fallen leaves lay in deep mounds, some driven high against the garden wall. New leaves continued falling by the minute but Swede stuck to his driveway limit. Just as stubbornly, Ashir held onto the rake.

Breaking the impasse, Lena scooted up against Swede and then sat down at Ashir's feet. Swede glanced at her before studying the boy's sockless feet. Ashir guessed he wanted to ask why.

No socks? We went years without shoes. In Africa, spiders hid in the sand. We flew to America with the boots Abdi bought us. Once we got to Minnesota, Dad used relief money for clogs and bargained for our apartment in town. Seven people, one bedroom. Some guys showed Mom the dishwasher and garbage bin, but she'd never seen anything like it. Trash and cockroaches mounted up. Me and Little Ashir sleep on the kitchen floor with bugs, just like in Kenya.

"You don't smell trash when that's what you are," Ashir told Swede. He felt sad more than mad and longed for the gentle love the yellow dog understood by nature. He flashed a smile at Swede, knowing how few people had that love inside them.

Swede listened, but words mostly abandoned him. He lumbered across the driveway muttering only "C'mon," the way he'd done when Ashir arrived earlier. He stopped by a sturdy cottonwood.

"Needs trimming," Swede said.

He returned to the house, leaving Ashir to study the cottonwood while Lena lazed in its fallen leaves.

***

Ashir shed his clogs and approached the ancient tree. He snapped the lower limbs off cleanly and clambered up to twist and tear the middle branches before lopping them off. At the top he sawed and hacked awkwardly but managed to create an opening in the remaining leaves, through which he watched the blue sky deepen. The sun beat down as wispy clouds floated by. Eventually, Swede came out to inspect the fallen branches. He decided to burn them, but Ashir piled them by the curb instead.

"Mulch?" he said, unsure of the word. "The City'll grind 'em up for you."

Swede agreed but looked embarrassed that Ashir knew more about the City crews than he did. The work completed, they looked at each other steadily. Ashir felt money hanging in the air before him, almost like he could touch it.

"I got the computer inside. Still want it?" Swede asked.

Guys did that in Kenya, too, bargaining in the dust over how much a haircut cost or about trinkets up for trade, patient but determined. Abdi and Dad planned for months with guys in suits and ties where we'd go in America, knowing we needed somebody to wait for us there, wherever it was. In Minnesota the grownups gossiped how Mom had false papers, and others whispered about her biting aid workers. People worried she'd ruin things if she rambled on about workers stealing kids and selling them, like at the market in Djibouti.

Ashir didn't want the PC anymore, but here he was ready to bargain for forty bucks and a phone. He shifted his feet nervously but never took his eyes off Swede. "Where d'you get those tattoos?" he asked.

"I was a sailor. Merchant Marine," Swede answered. Relieved to avoid any talk of money, he showed Ashir the tattoos on each arm, one a three-masted sailing ship, the other a curved sword, like from Arabia.

From a school book Ashir knew Arabs sharpened the inner side of their curved swords, not the broad outer edge. "Ever kill anything with it?" he asked.

"We weren't pirates," Swede answered with a smile, making light of himself, but proud, too. "Got tattooed in ports. I jumped ship in New York and headed for here, after my troubles."

"What trouble?"

Swede shrugged, a sign to let it be. "Never owned a sword."

Me and Swede, Ashir thought. *Like mongrel dogs in Kenya. Everyone said they were dirty curs, but some found good people and hung around them. They barked at hyenas.*

"The computer's yours," Swede announced suddenly, beating Ashir to the subject again.

"Old PCs are junk," Ashir replied. "Mr. Foster said so."

"Two times ten dollars an hour then? We agreed on that," Swede answered. "Twenty bucks."

"I need forty," Ashir replied. *Now or never.*

"Twenty and the PC. I'll throw it in."

"I know what I need," Ashir answered.

"You're a kid," Swede hesitated. "Grown men work for less."

"I climbed your tree. Barefoot."

Swede looked up at the cottonwood and Ashir knew the old guy couldn't miss the opening he'd made in it. *In Somalia, the sky got dark and mean and blew in sand. Dad prayed each grain would turn to a drop of rain so the cattle could drink and not turn to skin and bones or die.*

Swede remained silent, so Ashir went and got the sawed-off tree limbs and awkwardly pounded several into the ground. He bent the branches together and draped empty garbage bags across the top, like a makeshift tent. Ashir glanced at Swede. "Could you sleep in there for three years?"

Swede placed a hand on the small structure and peered inside. "Out on the treeless prairie, my people lived in sod huts."

"Sawed huts?" Ashir asked. Confused, he waved the saw. "No trees, so what'd they saw?"

"No, no, sod, like dirt. They dried the sod and cut it into bricks."

Ashir nodded. "For houses?"

"You got it. If they went to town for lumber, loan sharks hooked them for 35-40 percent. Know what I mean?"

Ashir nodded again, still focused on the forty dollars. *The Kenya camps were like the ones in Red Dead. Some of us stole from the starving. Others had nothing but helped out best they could.*

"So your people never got to choose?" Ashir asked.

"Choose?" Swede asked. "Means anything you want it to."

Ashir lost the energy for quibbling. He needed a Galaxy. *With the right apps, I can do anything,* he thought, as Lena awoke from a new slumber and plopped down between them, yet again. Swede reached down to pet her but she scooted out of his reach toward Ashir. Looking ashamed, Swede stuffed a hand deep inside his overalls pocket and pulled the hand out again. No words. Two twenties.

***

Ashir made for the phone and appliance store. His gym pants didn't have any pockets, so he clasped the cash in a tight fist. He walked slow and measured, like men in Somalia. *Dad went ahead cradling little Hani. "My baby," he called her. She smiled up at him. Sun there was like water here. Too much or too little will kill you, like babies burning in the heat or starving mothers with no milk. The women we saved. Mother elephants, without tusks.*

Ashir knew his dad would want the forty bucks. He and Little Ashir had no good pants to wear. Axado needed new shoes for school. *Dad thought if he didn't look back at us when he carried Hani, we wouldn't see him crying. He slept on the ground in Kenya and gave Mom the cot. Swede said his folks were bad off, too. Funny, they sawed dirt?*

Through the store window, Ashir spotted tons of Galaxies. Far in the background flickered a video trailer of the new hit *Red Dead Redemption.* He wondered what redemption meant, something good probably, like Swede struggling through his troubles, whatever they were. Or Somali women braving the hyenas and living.

Reaching for the door handle, he noticed store lights brightening in the dusk, like the opening in Swede's cottonwood, which revealed the sun. *In Kenya, I laid for days with the ballpoint stuck in my gut, and the pain shooting through me like lightning, my folks there with me, minus two kids already, praying I wouldn't be the third.*

All that was then, he thought, *but so is this. Sometimes now feels like then.* Slowly he let go of the handle and turned away from the displays. He unfolded the twenties, then started to put them in his pants, but remembered he didn't have any pockets. He clutched the bills again, adjusted his clogs, and headed for home. No socks. Smelly feet. Sure of the way. *Almost sixteen.*

VICTORIA

"VALENCIA ISN'T IVY LEAGUE. It's better," Sylvia Glasgow remarked and immediately had second thoughts about her words. As an alum, she loved her college, but she'd been on the road recruiting for its Admissions Office over a year now, forever struggling to meet expectations. Today a delayed flight from Logan prevented her from reaching MSP ahead of time, so she was swiftly pulling up facts about Miss Larson, the day's first interviewee, while offering her the standard introduction. "We're recruiting serious students for a college with conscience."

Sylvia gathered her thoughts and studied the young woman, who'd emerged from Starbuck's noontime throng and introduced herself as "Victoria—Tori, for short." The first impression was of a thin-lipped and self-effacingly sly young woman, but on second take she seemed more calm and self-contained. Just like me, as an incoming freshman way back when, Sylvia thought. In those days at Valencia I kept quiet and let others label me as they wished.

"Sorry for the crowded setting," Sylvia continued as she filed her initial reactions away and wished desperately for the coffee she'd ordered. "My schedule's mad. Snowing in Boston. Snarled traffic in Minneapolis. But I so wanted to meet you."

Tori nodded. "You just flew in?"

"Yes. And you? Any trouble getting here?"

"I drove. From home."

"Which is where? Let's see."

Sylvia searched her info sheet for Tori's hometown, but as

on previous Twin Cities visits, she was dumbstruck figuring exactly where Minneapolis ended and St. Paul began. The two metropolises were adjacent to each other, of course, but the Mississippi wound in and out between them while hundreds of city lakes and waterways made directions hard to follow. Local maps seemed to perniciously obscure any and all city limits, not to mention bedroom communities with confusing names, which stretched outward across the prairie.

"It's the burbs," Tori replied, as if reading Sylvia's mind and wishing to keep things simple.

"Yes," Sylvia agreed. "You're from Golden Valley."

"No, Apple Valley."

"Right. To the southwest."

Tori's smile failed to confirm whether Sylvia was right or wrong. "Close enough," she replied, a comment Sylvia took to mean, you have to live here a while to know.

"So you're at Central High?" Sylvia asked. "Don't get many apps from there."

"Not hard to figure why," Tori explained. "Inner city hood, rubbing elbows with Latinos and blacks. Boat people, too. I had a boyfriend, once. Nice guy but one of *the other*, like people call them. My folks said no."

"No, to what? Him or Central?"

Tori nodded without saying which, so Sylvia assumed she meant both the boy and the school. At last a barista appeared and served a cappuccino to Sylvia, who nodded toward Tori. "Your turn. My treat," Sylvia said, relieved to skip the intricacies of Metro geography and ethnic attitudes in Minnesota.

"Light brew, tall," Tori ordered while looking steadily at Sylvia. "My father's company, Villospor, is close to my school. I used its location to argue for Central, going to classes near Dad's work place, you know."

"So your father's employed at Villospor?"

"Kinda owns it."

While Tori added cream to her light brew, Sylvia talked community service. "Valencia's moving from theory to awareness to engagement, all for the common good." She stirred her cappuccino, before locating a paper napkin and delicately wiping a smudge of spilled coffee from her cup. Tori observed her actions with a sight twist of her mouth, but a neutral expression.

"Sorry," Sylvia said, referring to her cup. "It's my germ phobia."

"Lots have 'em. I'm immune," Tori replied. She described her volunteer position at the Humane Society, where weird microbes flourished. Her job was caring for abandoned or feral cats. "The boss gave me that task. I didn't want it at first but learned to love the critters. They're wild, though I calm them down, eventually. I found four scrawny kittens dumped under some football bleachers. Tons of fleas and claws. They scratched me. See?"

"Heavens," Sylvia exclaimed. She applauded the rescue but was taken aback by the lengthy bandage on Tori's arm.

Tori lifted the gauze and fresh blood blotched her hand and slowly spread across her forearm. "Dear creatures," she said while partly wiping off the stain. "What you see in their eyes is what they have in their hearts. Sorry that sounds so dramatic, heard it in a movie the other day."

Sylvia glanced again at the girl's injured arm while fumbling for her high school transcript from Central. Her wish was to talk academics, but she was unable to locate the right papers. She put away the scattered school documents and decided to conduct the interview from what she recalled off-hand about Tori's record.

"Yes, yes," Sylvia said absentmindedly, looking for her notepad and encouraging Tori to continue. "About your coursework."

"My ex is a like a kitten. He woulda been in college now."

Sylvia squinted, trying to keep her mind on the girl's sequence of comments, but not knowing what to expect next.

"This ex, he was your boyfriend?"

"Name's Pancho. Long gone."

Sylvia puzzled over 'gone' but avoided prying. "I know you've got good grades," she observed. "Any exciting classes?"

"Spanish. Our teacher's TexMex. Señor Gonzalez. Gonzo. Speech is great, too. Learning to get ideas across."

"Fantastic. Valencia's new curriculum emphasizes communication across boundaries. Demographics are shifting," Sylvia explained, avoiding the apparent anomaly of Valencia reaching out to the poor while recruiting the rich.

"I took a mini-course on digital literacy and fake news," Tori replied, as she nodded yes to a refill from the barista, who proceeded to spill a tiny squib. Tori swiped at the spill and licked it from her finger with a flourish. Sylvia wasn't sure if the young woman's gesture hinted at an ease in her presence, or boredom with her questions.

"Sorry, me and my boyfriend had that habit," Tori explained. "Licking the cup. Real dumb, I know."

"At Valencia, we're taking theory and practice to the community," Sylvia continued while filing away the girl's words. "Explaining complex ideas in everyday language."

"Speaking well's a must," Tori agreed.

"We're located back East, on the Atlantic. Lotsa nor'easters. Some want palm trees."

"Cool and breezy here, too."

"Other schools on your agenda?"

"Hancock. In San Fran. Went there with my dad. He bought a cottage at Nob Hill. Least that's what he calls it. Not in your dreams is it a cottage, lots bigger. He says that to impress Midwesterners who wouldn't know the difference. We stayed there, Thanksgiving and Christmas."

"Yes, great campus, great city," Sylvia replied enthusiastically.

"Cal State's better."

"Which Cal State?"

"Dunno. One of the state colleges."

"Very different places."

"My ex, he was going to go there."

"Not Hancock, but Cal State?"

Tori nodded in affirmation.

Sylvia considered their differing sentiments about California universities—private and state sponsored—and thought again about Tori's 'gone' boyfriend. She guessed at disagreements between daughter and father. Did Tori prefer state universities because of their popular counter-culture reputation, or because the boyfriend rejected her father and his preference for well-heeled private institutions?

"Dad says Nob Hill to bowl people over," Tori repeated about her father and San Francisco. "The cottage is on a hill, all right, but no knob. Nob means a guy that thinks he's better than others. I looked it up. He makes a ton buying warehouses and storing stuff for big companies. Dreams of buying his way into uppity places."

"Valencia features study abroad. Interested?" Sylvia asked, seizing her chance to change the topic since the suggestion of hobnobbing with the ultra rich set her on edge. As often was evident at Valencia, her family's modest social standing contrasted to her own youthful decision to study at an established private college. However, the possibility Tori might perceive Sylvia as pretending to be something she wasn't faded quickly, so they turned their attention to the interview again.

"My family was in Biarritz. And a month in Tahiti. Mom even came along. French is lovely," Tori explained.

"I spent a year in Grenoble, as an exchange student," Sylvia said, happy to pick up the ball and continue the conversation. "The Alps and trips to Paris. Changed my life. My French prof always said the French are the most intelligent people on our planet."

"I liked their language better than the guys who spoke it. Way too grabby!"

When the barista offered Sylvia another refill, she answered, "Yes, gladly," and met Tori's tiny outburst about French-speaking men with an understanding smile. The coffee waited as Sylvia reached for her notepad. Wishing to comment on the applicant's academics, she jotted 'not your usual scholar' but could think of nothing to add. Her eagerness to speak eloquently about the great wide world and promote the chance to study at a prestigious college like Valencia gave Tori little impetus to explain her goals. Maybe, Sylvia pondered, she's already been there, done that. But at eighteen? And what would I know about such privilege? Me, an ex-scholarship girl, sent out by Valencia to rustle up students with big bucks, and hopefully brains to match?

"Let's be frank," Sylvia decided. "Generations of bookers have kept my college steeped in tradition. We're searching…" Whoa, wrong word, she caught herself thinking. "Actively seeking."

She stopped to consider if she was speaking about Valencia or herself. The prospective students and parents she used to meet came from old wealth and took their social standing for granted. Only lately had the new rich begun trickling in. Sylvia didn't seek out applicants of humble means, as she herself had once been, or those of strong social pathos, most commonly careerist young women striving for equal pay or objecting to male leaders' offensive opinions about women, but she enjoyed hearing their views and sympathized with them. Lacking a deep knowledge of economic theory, she wavered in judging the college's desire for financial upgrades.

"Seeking to further the common good," Sylvia added, even though she knew her words were repetitious and seemed barely believable to some in light of what Tori might have heard from various sources. Editorials had criticized Valencia's capital campaign as crass and self-serving, while defenders described it as the natural response to a bear market.

"I know, seeking something new," Tori interrupted. "I'm an intuitive learner." She paused as if intuitive learner was something she'd said before, or heard someone else say, without finding a concrete theme to pair it with. "Like your college, I'm looking for an answer." Tori waved her half-empty cup back and forth like a rhetorician placing her words in perspective. Nothing spilled.

Unable to locate any catchy nugget in Tori's words that Valencia's tuition-driven staff might find useful, Sylvia blurted, "Study habits? Any nook or cranny you visit to get school work done? To vent, in silence? Or cool it?"

A bemused smile flitted across Tori's face. Probably at my phrasing, Sylvia thought. *Chill* is what youngsters say nowadays, she remembered. Tori's reaction reminded Sylvia of her husband Michael's patient reaction when fielding their children's innocent questions at home.

"Not really. Like the testers say, I'm a creative learner," Tori answered.

Intuitive learners don't search out places to study, Sylvia realized, because they never study, at least not systematically, like the goal-oriented brains that Valencia's reputation rested on.

"Creative, meaning what?" she asked Tori, determined to continue.

"I hear the questions and put my label on them after they're in."

"So you wait for people to present their ideas and then decide if there is a question?"

"Kinda," Tori agreed as she ran a finger around the rim of her coffee-stained saucer, before she licked it once more. "Or if the question's worthy of attention."

"So if there is a serious question, you decide to study?"

"That's when I decide to look for better answers."

Tori watched the noon-hour lunch crowd filter out to work, while Sylvia sipped distractedly at her cappuccino. She jotted 'well-placed family' and 'extensive travel' in her notepad, but she was merely scribbling. Mostly she reflected on why the young woman reminded her of herself as she had been at eighteen. Maybe Tori's way of smiling from a distance at the bustling downtowners was an expression of sympathy, as if she imagined the office workers scurrying back to a demanding boss, not unlike her father. Sylvia remembered herself as a booker, though she'd never buried herself among the stacks of

Valencia's hallowed library. She read in cosy cafés and observed passers-by in the same thoughtful way Tori did, or at least as Tori was doing right now in the coffee shop.

"Sorry, not your usual interview, I know," Tori said softly, a half question and half apology, which interrupted Sylvia's wandering thoughts.

Interviewer and interviewee scrutinized each other, gradually rendering transparent the hazy filter that separated them. Sylvia asked in confidence, "Central High. Why?"

"I told you. Pancho."

"And his real name? C'mon."

Tori squirmed slightly after being found out for concealing her boyfriend's name. Sylvia felt equally uncomfortable asking about it. Calling out an applicant for a white lie wasn't a sin, she reflected, but not part of her job either. Nevertheless, Mr. Larson's social climbing, measured against his daughter's kitten rescue, suggested some discord in their family, however trivial it might seem. Sylvia guessed the relationship was grounded in a powerful bond between father and daughter, which nurtured Tori in the frequent absence of her mother, whose maladies the girl had alluded to in her application essay.

Sylvia guessed Mr. Larson's strength of will appeared in Tori after she enrolled at school, but in ways the father least expected. Tori had written of emptying her little brother's piggy bank as a ten-year-old and treating her friends to candy and pop because poor kids got no allowance at home. Yes, even in well-to-do suburbs the permanent underclass and unregistered immigrants were present, and Tori had clearly befriended them at an early age. In high school she joined an array of diversity groups, as her essay proudly detailed. If such extra-curriculars took the father by surprise, he tolerated them as youthful whims. Sylvia could only imagine the fall-out when Tori brought Pancho home to meet her parents.

"His real name's Chino," Tori admitted. "His family's from Guatemala. They've lived here since he was a baby. He taught me Spanish."

Images of Tori and Chino dallying at school and conversing in Spanish flitted through Sylvia's mind. Such scenes may well have troubled her father, and the visions gave Sylvia pause as well, but not because she judged the teenagers.

Before Sylvia could carry her thought any further, the baristas began clearing tables. She and Tori were the only customers left. "My next applicants are in Park Center, wherever that is," she announced.

"We were doing okay, me and my dad," Tori continued, seeming oblivious to Sylvia's words. "He wasn't happy about Pancho, but I handled it. Least till Dad voted for Trumpkopf. Now he's in the White House kicking Latinos out in the street."

Sylvia hesitated, unsure whether to break Office rules and discuss politics or say "Sorry" and move on to other interviews with her trusty GPS.

"You're looking for Oro Park plus Oro Center. That's Park Center for short. North Metro from here," Tori explained, once again appearing to read Sylvia's mind.

"So why call your boyfriend Pancho?" Sylvia asked.

"We met in Phy Ed tennis," Tori replied, unable to hide a blush. "He was *so* good, always hit the sweet spot. The teacher said some Latino named Pancho was this all-time tennis champ, so Chino became Pancho."

"They didn't get along, he and your father?"

"Yes. No. I mean nothing like that. Pancho's polite to his elders," Tori said intently. "Dad's a push-over, long as you toe his line. He looks the other way when hiring at Villospor. The feds are always checking on him. There were considerations."

"Meaning?" Sylvia asked.

"Meaning don't tread on Dad's space. He takes it personal."

Sylvia guessed a guy with Nob Hill on his brain found it unbearable to have the government interfere with his business or a Latino call the shots with his daughter. Mr. Larson could live with Pancho's family in the workplace, but nowhere else, which clearly weighed on Tori's mind. The more she discussed her seemingly vague college plans, the better Sylvia understood she was bending their conversation in a more pressing direction than her father's ideas about social standing.

"Dad didn't worry about Pancho," Tori continued. "Only the gangs. Knifings, drugs. Mexicans were meaner than Central Americans. He thought they'd go after Pancho."

"So what did he propose?"

"I insisted I could date who I wanted. Not under my roof, he said. Mom was already holed up in her sick-room, and Dad wasn't about to lose me, too. That's when the travel bug hit. For him, the lifelong workaholic, seeing the world was a dream, like another Nob Hill or Shangri-La, as long as he could keep me close. France and Tahiti were cakewalks, and we went to other places you wouldn't believe. Kangaroo Island, Kamchatka, Kiev. He took my brother shooting polar bears in Spitsbergen so I tagged along. You think Boston's rugged, try Goodyearbyen in their spring, so-called. Or Nuuk."

Tori realised her voice had risen, so she stopped in a hrmpph. "All this to make me forget a boy, which I was never about to do?"

Tori wasn't the first girl to be in that boat, as Sylvia recognized, even if she remembered it the other way around. She'd left for France over a decade earlier fearing a year abroad would cause Michael, then her college sweetheart, to forget her. She cried for days prior to departing and even now the memory produced a twinge of conscience even now. Unlike Tori, Sylvia didn't encounter any grabby French guys, but fell for Youssef, from Bahrain, who claimed to be a political refugee in France. They met at a foreign-student reception in Grenoble and made love in student digs, Alpine resorts, and leafy parks by gurgling streams. While Michael waited for her at home, Sylvia freed herself from what Youssef termed middle-class convention. In the long run, it was Sylvia who almost forgot Michael and would have if Youssef hadn't abandoned his studies and returned to Bahrain, despite being under the threat of imprisonment at home. After that disappointment, Sylvia's re-entry to Valencia hadn't been easy, but she and Michael reconciled and got married after graduation.

"So what do you want from our college?" Sylvia asked. Normally she used the final minutes of an interview to discuss the finer details of what the college and prospective student could offer each other, but this applicant's response remained so vague Sylvia narrowed the topic to Tori herself.

"Getting things right," she answered Sylvia. "I picked Valencia when I read about your school's financial problems. Dad gave in to me. I said I'd never forgive him unless he agreed."

"So you reconciled?"

"You have no clue," Tori continued. "Pancho took a year off after Central, so Dad employed him at Villospor as a stock boy, to see what he was made of. That's when Pancho applied to Cal State. He knew what he wanted."

Sylvia looked around the empty café. The silence liberated her from concerns about flight delays and scheduling. About Guatemala she knew only vague details. She once attended a lecture on indigenous Mayan weaving and dyeing, which gave her an admiration for the *huipils*, loose fitting tunics worn by Central-American women. In lovely hues of purple, red, and blue, the garments were produced small-scale until first-world production methods threatened to inundate traditional industries on the international market. Otherwise, Sylvia remembered only disturbing reports of brutal government attacks on Indian villages in Guatemala. She had no way of knowing if Pancho's family or relatives were among the injured and dead. Or were they the poor boys drafted into the Guatemalan police and taught to murder?

"But Pancho never made it to California?" Sylvia guessed.

"This country's hell. Latinos cower waiting for ICE to knock at the door and jerk them away, like Guatemala used to be."

"Trump says Latinos are 'bad hombres'," Sylvia replied, instantly realizing she'd very nearly ventured into partisan politics.

"Pancho's little brother went around screaming '*Trump es malo*. Why does he want to take my parents away?' His folks had to stop him from saying it at school, where you couldn't be sure who was listening."

Noting Tori's switch to the past tense, Sylvia patched together a sequence: First Pancho applied to college in California, then Tori began looking, too. That was when talk surfaced about building a wall on the border and word hurriedly spread. If ICE pounds at your door, don't open it. If ICE appears without a warrant, don't answer them. If ICE asks your name, don't give it.

"Even my dad's aghast at the madness," Tori continued. "Pancho's folks went for their annual immigration review, but ICE put them in detention. Pancho had to sit down in private with his uncle and figure out how to manage the household while his mom and dad were detained. Pancho got a second job to maintain the payments on their mortgage, and an aunt agreed to care for his little brother and sister. The authorities claimed the family had Indian blood, but they're from a town called Verapaz. They're descended from German immigrants, and Pancho's got blue eyes. Even if they were Indians, why build a wall to exclude the continent's original inhabitants?"

Sylvia felt uncomfortable fielding questions that contained their own answers. She searched for a sensible response while thinking about her next interviews and the even more chilling stories she might hear in Park Center, if Tori's was any foretaste of changing demographics.

"There's yet more?" she asked, perfectly aware her own question answered itself.

"ICE deported them, all three of them," Tori replied, her emotions visible for the first time. "Him and his parents. Gone. Pancho skyped me last night from Verapaz. Said the hardest part was that they took his parents 'away from their heart, their little children. It was the worst pain. Like they were dead.'"

Sylvia thought about Youssef. Immigration authorities in France had treated him fairly, but common people often looked askance at him. When Youssef left for Bahrain, Sylvia said she'd join him and naively imagined herself aiding his cause, which in truth she never understood. Looking back on her affair with Youssef now, she sometimes questioned if he indeed had a cause.

"Your dad? What does he say?" Sylvia asked, fishing to plug the temporary lull.

"He read up on research that revealed getting rid of immigrants would set our economy back 15%. That tipped the scales for Dad. One hope was having Pancho brought back to the U. S. on a foreign student visa, but Cal State hadn't even read his application. Plus, Immigration insists he's an *indio* and they won't let him return as a foreign student because he's not a foreigner. Next'll be his brother and sister, both born here."

"So what's the question you've sorted out?" Sylvia asked. "Cal State? Hancock?" she asked cautiously.

"No way, it's Valencia or Verapaz," Tori replied with a determined shake of her head.

Her composure made it unclear if she'd come to the interview determined to present that very ultimatum or if she'd invented it on the spot.

"Me below the border? Dad'd never dream of it," Tori said. "But if Pancho can't come back here, I'll go there, come hell or…" Tori paused. "I'm begging you."

"To step in where others have failed? Who am I?" Sylvia protested.

"Remember, a college with conscience?"

Sylvia considered the phrase, how it once sounded so full of verve and rolled off people's lips at Valencia with unparalleled optimism. Gradually, though, it drifted toward cliché as the college's drive for money took precedence, and here was Tori, a co-ed with cash, like so many others. If she *did* choose Valencia, was it truly possible to convince colleagues in Valencia's Administration, those with clout, to approach Immigration on Pancho's behalf? And if they did so for him, would they follow suit for others? Maybe, she allowed. A warehouse man's money was as good as anyone else's. But how would the college use it? Actions spoke louder than words.

The two women looked each other in the eye. Sylvia weighed what might have happened to her if she'd been as fiercely determined as Tori and followed Youssef back to

Bahrain. Or was his story of political exile only a ruse? Did he cunningly plan the end of their relationship to coincide with his departure from France?

"Using me till the time was right?" she asked before realizing she was talking to herself. In her mind's eye, Sylvia tried to reconstruct her youthful self. As a student she had been independent enough to ignore her parents' objections and study in France, her main wish being to escape the stifling conformity of small-town living, though in her late teens she would have found it impossible to explain specifically what it was that stifled her, if anyone had asked. Taking the safe path hadn't always been her forte; she could wilfully act against what seemed her best interests, if the temptation or potential reward felt enticing enough. Before meeting Youssef, she took it for granted Michael would wait an entire year for her, as she first assumed she'd do for him.

Chief among her shortcomings was the tendency to keep her own counsel; to family and friends she gave off as little personal info as possible. That left them to guess at her feelings, which were strong, especially about civil rights. Through the years she came to abhor the blithe acceptance of white privilege surrounding her at Valencia. She originally took the recruiting job hoping to make a difference with incoming students concerning gender and race. At present she seethed in private at the hatemongering and fear emanating from D. C., but learned to keep a low profile. She quickly realized her job was evaluating applicants' readiness for college, not judging their opinions, which differentiation, her Admissions chief explained, "could be a fine line to tread." In these troubled times she'd learned to strive for a conciliatory and subtle approach, knowing not everyone would be good with it. Anyway, she thought in moments of self-preservation, life has turned out good, for me.

"C'mon, time to go," Tori said impatiently. "How will you make Park Center alone at this rate? GPS?"

"You have a better answer?" Sylvia asked, awakened once again from her pondering.

"I'll drive. I made you late to start with."

"And my rental car?"

"Follow me in it."

"The answer to my prayers," Sylvia said. Arriving on time at Park Center would make catching her late flight home a cinch; Michael fared better with the kids when he knew she was en route.

Sylvia paid the cashier, and they walked to the car. "Sorry, but I need to find my own way," she uttered suddenly.

Tori halted. "They didn't name me Victoria for nothing," she said.

"You have an interesting application," Sylvia explained guardedly. "Don't know what more I can say."

"I won't be stopped."

Sylvia held her car door open, one foot in the driver's side, the other planted on the pavement. When Tori stubbornly leaned against the front fender, Sylvia sighed and stepped out. She compared herself with the younger woman, privileged in different ways yet equally involved in others' woes. Slowly Sylvia let her guard down and smiled, first in dismay at the world, then sympathetically toward Tori, who returned the gesture. Thus they stood locked in a not unfriendly standoff on the bleakest of winter days.

The weak sun was sliding toward mid-afternoon before they realized they were still silently studying each other and time was wasting. Sylvia checked her watch again. "Okay," she said. "Let's give it a try. Talk to your dad. I'll do my best back East. No promises. We're not Ivy League, you know."

"No, you're better," Tori answered.

Sylvia got in the car, zapped down her window electronically, and shook hands with Tori.

Driving off in a rush, she fell back on her independent streak and neglected the GPS. Before long she lost track of where she was and even forgot which city she needed to pass through, Minneapolis or St. Paul, in order to reach any suburb of the north Metro, or even where on the map Park Center actually was. No matter, she consoled herself, as she oftentimes did at confusing sites like the Twin Cities, every road eventually leads some place good, for somebody. As the sun sank lower and she drove on with only good sense to guide her, she wondered if good was always the same as right.

YESTERDAY'S STORMS

LAKESIDE BAR AND GRILL was an inglorious dump. The building stood placid and unpainted while muddy water lapped at the dock. Carmony Cernik knew the only thing that stood out was the waitresses' breasts, including her own. They were the bringer of generous tips and Lakeside's claim to fame among local bikers. "It's all right to have boobs, just don't show 'em to all your customers," bartender Ellen told Carmony on her first night. "You'll see off the bat who's interested."

That was that. Short shorts and loose necklines were the only solid rules, which Carmony liked to ignore. A friendly attitude was the cardinal virtue, but she was having trouble maintaining such a mood on this dull August afternoon. First she'd gotten her kids off to rec lessons late, causing bad memories of her childhood to surface. Afterward, she'd searched for enough dough to pay next month's rent while also trying to figure out why she ever gave up her easel and brush. Nothing helped, so she reported for work wearing a blah expression to match her knee-length shorts and well-buttoned blouse. She had donned them in protest, not against the bar but her occupation, which she took up when young and lacking in what folks called ambition.

She'd just seated two couples at a table by the dock, when three mid-lifers arrived. A tall guy in sunglasses led the way, followed by a shaggy man and a dark-haired woman, who had God on her mind. "I weeded the garden," she said to the shaggy guy, "and hit a rock. I realized then He made that rock just like us. With cells and life." Carmony pegged them as typical of the artists and intellectuals who occasionally wandered in. What lured them to Lakeside, apart from drinks, she'd yet to figure out. Their talk could be as turbid as the lake after violent storms swept in and churned up mud from the depths. The most recent cloudburst was yesterday, which meant the bar and grill had just now reopened its patio. The day's first customers were loud and thirsty construction workers.

Carmony saw the three newcomers had manners. The tall guy pointed politely at a sunlit table. When his friends hesitated, Carmony offered them seats in the shade. She waited with the menus while the guests talked. "Frida, I heard jabber like yours all week on vacation with my Bible-banger relatives," the shaggy man said. "Christians think God's made in their image and resembles a venerable patriarch. Aren't you a believer, too?"

"Yes, Norm, but you know I don't think God looks anything at all like you or me physically, or them either," the woman replied, waving out toward the other customers. "I feel some abstruse power. It infuses us."

After placing menus on their table, Carmony stepped back. The sun shone strong, so fish flopped in its brilliant light. She saw the tall fellow gaze at the splashing and study the gulls flapping out toward deeper water. They plopped down mid-lake and bobbed on its gentle waves.

"But don't you have to accept what the Bible says? I mean God's present and talks to us, in person?" Norm continued. "We hear Him but ignore all the horrible acts He incites."

Seeing they hadn't thought about ordering yet, Carmony stepped in and tried her luck at light chatter while picking up the menus and placing one before each of them. Frida and Norm frowned slightly at her interruption, so she backed off again, which made it harder to get their attention. Only the tall guy noticed the impatient twitch of her lips. She poured water, first for him and then the others. He took a sip and smiled. His companions eagerly looked at each other.

"You're talking primordial Old Testament," the tall guy said to Norm. He looked at Carmony while lowering his glass. "More and more churches are going over to New Testament stuff."

"But it's still blind faith, isn't it?" Norm wondered. "Like believing Jesus rose from the dead? Biologically impossible."

***

"I don't believe God's a bearded old guy in the sky, despite what you say I think," Frida continued after pausing to consider Norm's expression of doubt. "There's a spirit. An Oversoul. You know, like in Thoreau."

"Emerson, wasn't it?" the tall guy added. "The Transcendentalists."

"Yes, Ralph Waldo," Frida agreed. "Our Oversoul."

"Okay, but it's totally at odds with science," Norm continued. "I work in immunology. We do experiments. Science is about truth and testing hypotheses. You can't prove anything without evidence."

"You mean, if I can't touch it or feel it..." the tall guy butted in.

Yes, then it doesn't exist, Carmony thought, completing his sentence for herself. As she thought through his words, she could sense him studying her again. Earlier he'd glanced at the younger, slimmer waitresses from behind his dark glasses, but his steady look now fixed on her. She wondered what kind of guy he was, deep down, intellectual or biker?

Ellen called from the bar, so Carmony left to take an older couple's order. When she returned to the Philosophers, as she had begun to think of Frida and Norm, their enthusiasm roused her from the blahs. They made her wonder why she turned down the Art Institute's scholarship offer all those years ago. That was the one place she knew where people talked about stuff that mattered.

"So when we die, the lights go out?" Frida asked. "Here in life we're dependent on impermanent things that can be taken from us, like jobs or houses. You know we end up suffering if we only depend on stuff like that. We've got God and the soul."

"If God created us, who created God?" Carmony broke in when she knew she shouldn't, but she felt part of their conversation.

"Precisely," Norm agreed with Carmony. "It's mechanistic. There was a void and then something came up with a single thought in the nothingness and blackness."

"And whose thought was that?" Frida objected. "If not God's? Is He a something to you?"

Frida paused at the memory of her intangible Oversoul. Yet here she was giving it form. The next step would lead to her arguing for an old white-haired patriarch, which she'd already denied. She frowned at the dawning conundrum.

"Bang!" said the tall guy. He smiled at Frida.

"Yes, the Big Bang," Norm said. "Mechanistic world to a tee. The universe came into being from one single point, expanding outward forever and ever."

"But how did we get life out of expanding rocks if not for Him?" Frida asked. "And souls, too?"

"Way too abstract for me," Norm broke in. "If I can't experience it, it doesn't exist. We'll never know who thought up the universe or created consciousness."

The conversation so engrossed the three companions they appeared oblivious to everyone else. Carmony jostled to maintain her spot before them as new customers arrived and searched for tables. She reminded the tall guy of his menu and suggested the shrimp. He shook his head. "No meat for him," Frida whispered to Carmony. She and Norm opted for chicken.

The tall guy chose an anchovies pizza. "Medium or large? Which do I want?" he asked.

While Carmony wondered whether he thought of fish

as meat or not, Frida and Norm grew impatient, clearly thinking their tall friend was like a kid who needed grownups to find him something he didn't dislike.

"Large," Carmony said with a decisive nod. "I know you can handle a large serving."

"Okay by me," the man agreed. He nodded and removed his glasses. Rubbing his eyes revealed they were hazel, a match to his light brown hair. His faint smile showed a hint of emotional reserve.

Carmony placed their orders. As she gathered their silverware, she felt intrigued by this stranger, but even more enlivened when she thought about her own private observations. Driving to work or taking her kids for walks, she often recalled some of her customers, those who gave her new insights or acted unique. She wondered how they lived and thought. At the same time, she realized this humble tavern was a far cry from the hangouts of serious thinkers and the artistic life she'd dreamed of. In her paintings she tried to depict the intriguing worlds she glimpsed in other places or imagined visiting, but she feared she lacked the training, or insight, to capture them in their brilliance.

Carrying orders to her guests' table failed to distract her from those ponderings, so she had difficulty remembering which dish was Frida's or Norm's. The tall fellow began talking before she served up his pizza.

"What interests me most is, if we could exceed the speed of light, could we catch up with time?" he asked.

"You mean experience the past?" Norm asked. He looked ravenously at his meal, like he wished Carmony had served him faster so he could dig in sooner, which led her to wonder if he was only talking science and egging Frida on to kill time before filling his belly.

When the tall guy didn't respond to Norm, Carmony looked at him and pressed a tray across her chest. "If I could bother you, what's your ethnic group?" she asked.

Seeing her use the tray like a shield, the tall fellow chuckled. "Part this, part that. Norwegian and German. You?"

"You're not Czech?" she continued. "I thought by your chin and nose..."

"So you're Czech yourself?" he joked.

"Yes, my family. I'm Cernik now, was a Zahradnik."

Her three guests attacked their meal without commenting, so she produced a pitcher of beer in place of the bottles they ordered.

"On us, the house, my tab," she said.

"Will you have a glass with us?" Frida asked hesitantly.

"I can't, no. Not on the job, but I don't either, never nowadays, not even in private," Carmony answered nervously. "My family, though."

"They did, drink, you mean? Your Czechs?" the tall man asked cautiously.

"You'll never know how much."

He nodded sympathetically while Frida and Norm ate on. Norm was tearing off a drumstick when Carmony spoke again. "I just thought, your nose and jaw, they look Czech."

"Him? He's a star gazer, out in the blue," Norm interrupted with a laugh. "Nothing earthly about him."

"They drank, your folks?" the tall man enquired again.

"The whole clan. As a kid, I come home from school every afternoon and my ma and pa and brother, uncles, too, have been boozing all day. Vodka. That's when the fighting always started."

***

After that the three paused for a refill as Carmony checked on other tables. Two parties paid up and left, so Carmony returned to finish her family tale.

"Like I said, I come home from school and they set me down with a bottle. Next morning, I leave for classes with booze on my breath. It must say something in the Bible about that, huh?" she said and looked at Frida.

"How do you spell Zahradnik?" the tall guy interrupted.

"Yes, I'm sure it says something, somewhere," Frida started to answer, but Carmony turned away from her and looked to the tall man.

"Z-a-h-r-a-d-n-i-k," she spelled out. "Like it sounds."

With all three talking at once, they arrived at a verbal bottleneck. Carmony watched the tall guy sip his beer and run a finger around the rim of his glass. Interesting, yes, I'd like to know him, she thought, but not flirt, get to know him for *real*.

"That speed of light thing," he resumed. "If we could catch up with time, it'd be possible to meet…"

"Yeah, yeah, witness historic events back in the day," Norm butted in, "Still…"

"Not up your alley?" Carmony asked Norm, barely concealing her disappointment over not getting to hear the first guy out.

"Imagine, meeting all the greats," the tall man continued. "Talking to Shakespeare or watching Michelangelo paint the Sistine Chapel. Where does that genius come from? Painting majestic scenes on a wobbly scaffold."

"How do you know if it was wobbly?" Norm protested.

"We'd be there, see it and touch it, like your empiricism dictates."

Carmony listened closely until she walked around the table and faced them. "What's your professions?" she asked straight on, looking at the tall guy.

"Astronomer," he said.

"Student financial aid, that's me. He's a lab tech," Frida answered, pointing at Norm.

"You see wonderful things," Carmony announced, astonished. "Like everything around you's alive. Everybody around *me* is dead. My kids—11, 14 and 16—were lazing around the other night, phones on, connected but disconnected, you know? I unhooked and unplugged and yanked 'em outdoors. Lovely out, birds chirping, leaves rustling. I explained the glory of it, how light brings life.

We passed an apartment block. Three hundred units. In every window, the same electronic glow, silver and false. All those folks living with nature outside their window, but numb and dumb to it. I wanted to paint what my kids and the others couldn't see, emblazon it on their foreheads or buildings."

"And what was that?" Frida asked. "What they were missing?"

"The sun, moon, stars, translucent."

"Like Michelangelo?" the tall guy mused. "You'd hang from the scaffolding and reproduce nature on the wall of their building?"

"Yes. I was driving home the other day and you know what?"

She felt close to the gangly man, who seemed like a quiet visionary, the way he studied the people around him and the lake, or likened her to Michelangelo. "No, but tell us," he told her.

She glanced around the grill; some of the customers listened while others jousted raucously and lifted their beer mugs. The scene was okay in its place, but Carmony longed to transcend it, along with Frida's silly God-searches, and find an inner light. Putting that desire into words others would fathom vexed her, so she kept it short and simple.

"I had my pooch Junior with me on a ride when I realized everything's sentient. Junior's got two eyes, two ears, fears and joys. Animals squeal and cry. Trees and plants breathe and perspire."

The three guests wondered at her imagery, which she felt was bland like this weekday afternoon, and maybe not so different from Frida's after all. Eager to keep them interested, she quickly searched her phone for photos of murals she'd done.

"Here's what I'd make Lakeside into," she said and passed her phone around. The first photo showed a long row of whiskey barrels in a room with wooden floors and a log roof. At the far end, two large windows let bright sunlight illuminate the plank floors making the aged casks glow. The shaded barrels rested in sulking obscurity.

"What're whiskey barrels made of?" Norm asked.

"It's oak. The wood adds taste and aroma and soothes the contents. But this is vodka, from the days when I boozed," she continued.

"So vodka's distilled in whiskey barrels?"

"Yes, I dreamed of a bright light rescuing me from what my family started me on. Some of the booze evaporates and is lost to the heavens. It's called angels' share. I'd turn Lakeside's face to the sky."

"If you could?" the tall guy asked.

Carmony darted a nervous look at him and then at his friends.

Satisfied they'd learned enough about distilling, Frida and Norm passed the phone to the tall man.

"This photo shows your painting hanging above tables under large ceiling lights. Do you have it displayed in a restaurant?" he asked.

"Yes, the light's to inspire diners. Without it, they'd only see the barrels as an invitation to booze."

"No ambiguity?" the tall guy asked with a grin.

"Is that the world you live in?" she asked while studying his sly look. "Nobody uses words like that here. Folks have feelings, sure, but they struggle to explain them."

***

The tall guy didn't reply and nibbled his anchovies like he was wondering how those rare morsels made their way so far from the sea. Frida and Norm had long since finished their chicken and put God to rest. When they asked for the bill, Carmony produced it and left them to settle their payment.

"Harder than understanding God," Norm joked. "Do we pay separate or together?"

"On me," the tall guy replied.

Carmony rang up the charge for him, without a peep from his friends.

"I figure you paint and let the picture tell viewers what they don't have words for," he said, looking at Carmony.

"Gerome, I love you," she responded. She'd learned his name from the charge card, but felt puzzled by her own words. They were what her kids said to youngsters they took a sudden liking to. Here she was quick as a cloudburst herself, but born back in 1973 and hardly ready to fall head over heels for a stranger on the lakefront. "I'm 43," she added quickly.

Gerome sensed her reaction, verging on embarrassment, so he saved the moment by handing the phone back to her.

She hastily flipped through the apps till her favorite painting popped up, a mural she'd done in her youth at Hermosa Beach. Those were the days she dreamed West Coast sun and surf would inspire her as Gaugin imagined the South Seas alleviated European ennui. After three kids and a failed marriage in California, she'd returned to the Midwest with her tail between her legs, but not without bringing along photos of her art and some finished canvases.

"See this," she urged. "I called it *Sunset with Low Tide.* Later I got to thinking it was sunrise instead."

The mural showed craggy peaks seen from the ocean. Behind them the upper half of a brilliant sun shone on tidal pools. Whether the sun was descending into darkness or bursting forth at early morning was anybody's guess.

"You need to change the title then, establish clarity," Gerome said.

"Or keep everybody hanging."

"Sunset or sunrise," he countered. "You're torn between two things that aren't alike but illustrate the same thing."

"Which is?"

"Sun shining bright or burning out?"

"More like me, go off and paint or work here."

"That's what I mean, one is sunrise, the other sundown. What do you long for, your art or this dying joint?"

"Stuff with a bang. The whole world's my oyster. It's like Georgia O'Keefe going to the desert. I could move away and discover a new world. Colors. Faces. But I stay on. This is my job. I chose it," she said with a sweeping gesture to include all of Lakeside.

"You've got ideas, develop them."

She considered Gerome's words, which came to him easily like berries ripe for the plucking. Did talk like his limit creative work or was it, in truth, another form of inspiration?

"Where's the light?" she asked, without expecting an answer.

"You showed it in the mural, but you couldn't decide what to make of it yourself," he replied.

Carmony fiddled with her images. The brightness from her camera contrasted to the fading sunlight. She had done her best mural work at this time, as daylight failed. "Here's my cabaret scene," she said. "See, the old stars of stage and screen in half light. I saw them once in L. A. and imagined them visiting Lakeside. I painted this on the wall at Tomaso's downtown. Without a title."

The photo stared out at Carmony's guests. Around a long table with a checkered red-and-white tablecloth sat lifelike representations of James Dean, Elvis, and Dean Martin. The three kept a sullen distance from each other. Only an empty wine bottle connected them. Their down-turned faces suggested a losing struggle with stardom's illusory flame. Above them hovered a sunny-faced Marilyn. Her smiling visage should have spread inspiration. Instead, the jaded males could only interpret her as a temptress mocking them beyond their endurance.

"I know what you're thinking," Carmony admitted. "No stars'd ever set foot in this hole."

"A girl can have her imagination," Gerome said, like he knew the daily jousts with Lakeside dullness bumped against her drive to create. "Marilyn—your brush caressed her face tenderly," he continued. "She was never that angelic in life."

"It's a conflicted world," she agreed.

Carmony saw him nod in assent, but rather than linger in those thoughts, she produced another painting. Again, Gerome, Frida, and Norm passed the phone around. It showed a verdant scene in a match-stick forest. Some trees stood in clumps so thick they bent the sunrays at oblique angles. The forest floor, which should have glistened and produced tender shoots, suggested the dank abode of slimy crawlies and evil specters from ancient folk tales. Where the rays angled away from the clumps, light broke through in red and gold before exploding in brilliant sunbursts.

Carmony's spirits improved as she watched the others gaze at her colors, but in the end Norm squirmed in his seat before rising to go. Frida followed him. She placed a hand on Carmony's arm. "Marvelous how you visualize doubt and hope," she said. "Art is where we find God."

If art it is, Carmony thought.

For his part, Gerome calmly eyed the lake. "How clever," he said.

"What?" she asked.

"Your transitions. The subtlety between receding dark and conquering light. You must feel it."

"I haven't felt anything for years," Carmony admitted. She spoke while watching a group of departing customers.

"Drinkers all of them," she noted, perplexed at her own utterance. She wondered if she was still haunted by an unconscious desire to revert to the bottle and join the crowd.

"Why not feel?" Gerome asked. "You have to feel to paint."

"I haven't painted either."

Gerome looked out at the water, then up to the sky. His fixation spoke of an enduring search for meaning.

"I can't think of anything to paint," she said.

At a loss, she cleared the vacated tables and gathered her tips.

***

After checking out, Carmony found Gerome still alone. "Join you?"

"Why not?" he asked, showing he appreciated her return and remembered their words.

"Why not paint?" she asked. "That's what you wondered." She made a dismissive motion toward the bar and grill. "Plagued, like I told you. I imagine images painted on a surface, then fading into nothingness. The drive to create should override my fear of paint pealing from an abandoned old wall."

Gerome looked her way, like he and Carmony had a choice, similar to the gulls. "Get up and do something. Or slosh in our own mire," he announced.

Carmony noticed his slight frown. It suggested regrets over what might have been, which aroused a feeling of affinity. She was sure both had missed out on something valuable, she for forsaking art school, he for some unknown sin of omission.

"We," he began before cutting himself short.

The pause made her wonder if he intended his thoughts for humanity in general or the two of them in tandem. In either case, his *we* cheered her.

"Why are we given so much and others so little?"he asked.

"You mean we might emerge from this lakefront dive as changed souls?" she asked in her first attempt at fun.

"We're in a closed universe, self-contained like this lake," he answered with a gentle smile. "No Big Bang. Truth is the universe is beach-ball circular. It had no point of creation and isn't exploding outward either. It's encased. Within itself."

Carmony looked up at the evening sky with him, or what could be seen of it through Lakeside's overhead lamps.

"I study the light. You paint it. Beauty's its own reward," Gerome continued.

"That's my hope?" she asked, taken aback but not down in the dumps. "Because I paint pretty?"

"Better than most," he admitted with another chuckle.

They spoke no more. At dark, the last customers departed Lakeside's deck while the remaining wait staff bustled about clearing tables, their busts as prominent as ever. When the bar's lamps finally dimmed, a galactic stillness spread over the lake. Gerome turned his gaze back to the water and then up at the firmament, as though the view was its own reward. Carmony remained at his side. Like him, she looked up into the late summer night and marveled at the stars twinkling in their millions. Someday, she was sure, she'd paint this evening's sky with loving care and as she remembered it, most likely godless and a world neither shrinking nor growing, only begging to be embraced.

THE FIRST,
BEST BUS

LATOYA WASHINGTON'S Wednesday dawned different. With a jolt, she remembered this was June 5, the last date she ever knew her son alive. Poor Kamren, she thought, losing my baby just like that, if only I'd been there. Darned Iraq.

Hoping to keep the sadness at bay, Latoya grabbed her garbage bag, lumbered out the front door, and flagged a #22, the first, best city bus that came along. She boarded it and rode aimlessly through Minneapolis' snarled traffic, burying herself in bittersweet memories of happier times, like when Kamren learned to walk or ate his first solid food. Her reverie went on and on, until a heavenly aroma wafted in through the bus's open window. Latoya leaned back and inhaled the light fragrance of Kofi's Coffee.

Kofi had shops all around, so she felt comforted. When the bus driver pulled to a stop in front of a small neighborhood takeout, Latoya was thirsting for a *koficcino*. She stepped off the bus and dug in her bag for the needed change. Disappointed at not finding any, she searched for diversions. At the end of a sloping city street, she spotted a quiet lake glistening in the late morning sun.

The sight of calm water was soothing but it confused her, too. Inner city from birth, Latoya couldn't name the distant suburb #22 was destined for or imagine which silent residential neighborhood she had stumbled onto. Each weekday she herself moseyed out and caught a ride to downtown markets in Minneapolis or St. Paul, ten miles apart on either end of University Avenue. Moving among downtowners who were hustling off to work or lounging in crowded parks, she felt at home. She peddled second-hand doodads and trinkets in familiar haunts till late in the evening, when she packed her bag and trudged back to the basement room and kitchenette she now called home.

The thought of going back to her room felt like a long trek into nothingness, so she studied the nearest street sign and understood she was at the corner of 50th and Fairmont, wherever that was. Choosing Fairmont because it led to the attractive lake, she followed the sidewalk toward the water, which gently lapped against a stone barrier. She chose a bench nearby and settled in to watch the ripples. The angle of the sun showed late morning was gliding over into early afternoon. To the west she saw a guy struggling to steer his sailboat clear of a bathing beach. Nearby stood a low building she hoped would house a concession stand. If she could make it there and dig up the wished-for coffee money, things might be okay.

Judging by the neighborhood's mansions and swanky cars, Latoya reckoned this was white folks' territory, but the first people she met while setting off around the lake were a black couple with a tiny dog. She said hello. They returned her greeting but continued talking in a strange tongue. Walking on in the opposite direction from them, Latoya soon reached a wading area, which was empty except for a lone Latino family. The father, mother, and their teenage boy spread out on a beach towel playing cards, while their small daughter paddled out to deeper water. A nearby life guard warned the parents to keep an eye on her, but only the boy understood, so he shouted to the girl in Spanish before going out to guide her back in.

Latoya kept on thinking about Kamren, the light of her life. When he was little, they lived in the projects with their dear Walter, her man and Kamren's dad. On sunny days like this, she and Walter took the boy to Martin Luther

King Park to play. Walter pushed him so high on the swings Kamren shrieked with joy and Latoya trembled for fear the boy might fall. Walter tossed balls with him on the Little League field and joined the other dads bragging about how great their boys played. Latoya took snacks along and they ended their days sitting in the shade and munching on crackers or sipping pop. Those happy years lasted as long as Walter worked for the railroad, but he lost his pride after being laid off. Idle months living on unemployment turned him into easy prey for neighborhood no-goods, and his easy-going habits gave way to brooding when the lay-off proved permanent.

Gazing out over the lake, Latoya realized the closest she and Walter ever got to a glistening body of water like this was the Mighty but always murky Mississippi. She once showed her son the River from the city bus that crossed the rickety old High Bridge in St. Paul. He oohed and ahhed at the busy traffic of river boats and barges far below.

There were no such stunning sights at this particular lakeside except for towering oaks and cottonwoods. The land around the lake spread out wide and flat, which made it easy to walk around. Flocks of haughty Canada geese gathered in the grassy glades, ignoring Latoya and the occasional pooches straining at owners' leashes to chase them down. A west wind blew up and refreshed Latoya almost as much as Kofi's light brew or his *koficcino*, whenever she found the money to pay for one.

Farther on she followed a path to the west side of the lake and saw a sign with *Lake Nokomis* spelled out in slanted letters. She wondered about the meaning of *Nokomis*, but decided nothing; the world was so awash in offbeat names these days. As the afternoon progressed, the lakefront filled with people from every corner of the globe. Large groups from India and other distant lands picnicked at huge tables or played soccer on the lawns. Geese gave way to ordinary mallards, who waddled after Latoya hoping for handouts.

Prominent on the busy beach stood a sign with large black letters: DO NOT FEED THE BIRDS!

Latoya could see the message had no visible effect on such a beautiful summer's day. People acted both carefree and careless. When not swimming or eating, they entertained themselves by tossing food and sticky candy to the ducks and by example encouraging their children to do the same. A gang of youngsters, still dirty from playing in a sandbox, threw slices of white bread out from under the sign. Watching these people made Latoya think back to her days at Martin Luther King Park, when she still had Walter and Kamren. Folks came from places she'd never heard of before, like Liberia or Barbados, and people of color were the rule. One and all received an immediate welcome. On the playgrounds and public tennis courts black mixed with white while the women shared dishes, so Latoya learned their art and later found work as a short-order cook when Walter's unemployment payments ran out.

Here at Nokomis most frolickers kept a polite distance. Despite the hubbub they acted what Walter called civil. In race, religion, and language, every group still appeared to be strangers to every other, except those most comfortably dressed in American styles, who mixed, gorged themselves, and mindlessly pitched their leftovers, much to the ducks' delight. They scurried after each discarded tidbit and fought over it.

From a picnic table off to the side, a slim girl in her early teens got up and strode toward the sign. She wore a loose-fitting dress with a shawl and out from underneath her headscarf gleamed a pair of gun-metal Augusta eyeglasses. She wore a silver MyNameNecklace. When she faced the crowds, the girl started to speak but stopped and turned toward a woman at the picnic table she'd come from. The girl said what sounded like "um." At public markets where she did business, Latoya heard Muslim kids say that to their elders in tones of respect and assumed it meant 'mother.'

When the woman nodded in approval, the girl turned back to the picnickers and spoke to them loudly in English.

"Stop! We're not supposed to feed the birds." The girl waited for the throngs to quit throwing food to the ducks, but in the jabbering Babel they ignored her. Stubbornly she continued, "It says so on the sign. In plain English. Can't you read?"

Latoya watched as the girl gradually realized some of them couldn't read English, while those that could cared for little but an afternoon of boundless fun. A handful of Anglo boys dashed past her ready to plunge into an area marked Deep Water. They stopped short only when the life guard yelled a stern warning over her loudspeaker and a Park Patrol arrived to ensure the boys obeyed. The commotion distracted the majority of picnickers and sunbathers, which allowed the ducks to go about their business unbothered.

In irritation, the girl marched off. Sensing she and the youngster had something in common, Latoya got up to follow her. Though her and the girl's sad feelings were surely different, it seemed to Latoya their pain measured equal. Just as the Muslim girl might need consoling, so did she, the aging African American. Latoya thought: *She have her mother and her mother have her, but me and Kamren both miss each other.* The girl finally found a bench away from the crowds and Latoya sat down with her. She wondered what the girl's name might be in the language she spoke with her mother.

They remained on opposite ends of the bench, an awkwardly silent pair, with nothing of outward features in common that Latoya could see, neither age nor race nor dress. In a tenuous way, they shared only the park bench and their quaint and differing versions of English.

"Why, chile," Latoya dared utter after a while, putting out of mind the many things that separated them as well as the festive but rude masses they'd just turned their backs on, "what your name?"

"Inaya," the girl answered. In a pout, she darted a glance at Latoya, her lips only slowly softening into a slight smile. "In-ay-ah," she mouthed loudly, as if expecting her older seatmate to be hard of hearing or a non-native English speaker, pretty much like everybody else on this side of the lake.

"Inaya. Pretty name. La-toy-ah. That be me. What your name means, I wonder."

From over her shoulder Latoya heard a woman's voice call the girl's name, but the rest of the words were lost on her. She watched Inaya turn and flash a broad smile.

"This is my mom. She says to tell you my name means 'protection' or 'care' in Arabic. We're from Iraq."

Latoya moved her garbage bag to make room for Inaya's mom, who took a seat in the middle of the bench. Latoya offered the other woman a friendly smile, though she didn't fully know what to expect of her. She guessed Inaya's mother was younger than her, forty-something probably. She was thin like Inaya, though lacking her daughter's calm exterior. Similar to Muslim women Latoya saw at Twin Cities open-air markets, she wore a headscarf, but unlike them no face-veil. The mother seemed set in her ways, but nervous, too. She said nothing in English, not even her name, so they sat in silence, with Latoya glancing expectantly from mother to daughter, until Latoya broke the quiet once again.

"I followed my man here from Jackson, Mississippi, way back when. Why you here?" she asked.

"Here, in this park?" Inaya wondered.

"No, ma'am. This city. This state."

Inaya's mother looked at her daughter and showed a slight tic, a look that indicated she understood some of what Latoya and Inaya said to each other, even if, like lots of foreign ladies at the markets, she seldom spoke directly to people outside her own language group. Maybe she never exchanged a single word with folks from America at all, even if she lived in their midst, and brushed shoulders with them every day. But here was Latoya, a different American, brown-skinned and with no airs to give off. The mother relaxed and began talking in Arabic.

"We come to Nokomis for the green and the water. My husband Yani, Inaya's father, his name means peace," she began and looked at Inaya, who nodded in encouragement while translating her mother's words. "He fought with the Americans. In the past Yani's father, Inaya's grandfather, turned against Saddam when he made our lives unlivable, which is why we come here to the lake, for peace. Yani was side-by-side with the Americans in Iraq."

"Your man," Latoya said in a whisper.

"My dad, till he was killed," Inaya added. "They called it friendly fire. Caught between guys on the same side, Iraqis and Americans, all fighting for the same thing, Mom says, fighting for their lives."

Inaya and her mother grew quiet, so Latoya figured they were thinking about what Yani's death meant for them. At the same time, she wondered how the fates had dealt with her Walter in the many years since they last met. Maybe she'd never know.

"My mom says it's good in Minnesota, but hard, too," Inaya continued. "The government let us move here. I'm in eighth grade."

Latoya fingered her garbage bag. The sales trinkets within it were vital for her income. The dollar value from Social Security dwindled over time, so she peddled winter and summer to make ends meet. The bag offered solace, too. It became a buffer between her and the troubles life placed in her way, like her having a son, in Iraq, who was never coming back, dead like Yani. She struggled to explain her sorrow.

"My boy Kamren, he be your age when his pa left us," she announced to Inaya. "The cutest boy. Him and his pa was peas in a pod, till my Walter up and left. He said a man's not a man that can't support his own. We never seen him again. After that I raised the boy by my lonesome."

Inaya translated Latoya's words and exchanged glances with her mother, who responded in a halting but proud voice. "My mom says that's how she's raised me, here in Minnesota, too. By herself. She makes beds in a hotel while I'm at school. Picks me up every day at four and we go home together."

"I sell these," Latoya replied, releasing the drawstring on her black bag. Carefully she pulled out an assortment of key chains, bracelets, Minnesota Gopher mementos, boxes of greeting cards, and bandannas, which she spread out before the Iraqis. "My Kamren growed up with me in Housing. I was a cook, then work at a laundry in St. Paul, and see him through school. He the sweetest boy. Sickly as a chile, but grow up strong. I got so proud he could graduate high school. He run track and have a girlfriend."

"What was her name?" Inaya asked.

"Gudiva her name. Then Kamren up and join the Army. I feel so happy, him coming back home in uniform an' all to visit his poor ol' ma, an' me an' Gudiva on his arm out among folks in town. I fill with pride. Him on tour all over, like on tour of duty? Every week I get a letter. He write good, but I feel so alone. That's when I take to the street. You know, surrounded by folks? The crowds help me forget."

With extreme care Latoya flattened out a couple of bandannas on the bench till they looked newly ironed. "Yes, ma'am. Friendly souls. Like you all," she added with a broad smile. "My Kamren."

Once again, Inaya translated for her mother, who whispered to herself, then looked at Latoya sympathetically.

"Five years, five long years since that bitter day, my mother says."

"Yes, ma'am, that what I say, too. Five years ago, to this very day, the government write me and say my Kamren IEDed. A big, important Army man looked me up and say they bury him with the others, all of them just like him. Some place different. I never see my boy again. I thought I surely would die myself."

"We understand," Inaya said, as Latoya brushed a tear from her eye. "I was nine when Dad died. Five years ago, today. We come to the lake every year, to remember his life."

Finding people so different from her, yet so alike, too, felt like a miracle to Latoya. It offered a barrel of things to work through. She'd known and loved many Minnesotans, who'd all come and gone: Walter, the only man she ever loved, God bless him. He left home one day hoping to find work, destination unknown, and never came back. Kamren, at rest with his unnamed warrior buddies, buried who knew where. They came from all over and ended up in a mass grave in the burning sands, she guessed. And Raul, a kindly soul who wanted to jump from a bridge over the Mississippi, but changed his mind, with Latoya's help, and became her best friend out on the streets. For years she'd kept him on the right track.

Remembering them, she looked out over the water, beyond the swimmers and boaters, and saw wavelets dancing in the sunlight. A gaggle of geese winged its way from the south and skimmed the surface before pulling to a halt at a tiny inlet on the north end. After settling on a dead calm, they circled serenely until a paddle boat appeared and swerved to avoid them. It was mid-afternoon and the sun had halted at its highest point, seemingly fixed in place forever.

At long last, the sun began its slow downward glide. Inaya and her mother rose from the bench along with Latoya, like they were obeying a silent solar command. Together they strolled down Fairmont, the way Latoya had taken to get there. It was still too early in the season for swarms of bugs, so on this gorgeous afternoon, they floated more than walked. They made it all the way to Kofi's before Inaya's mother spoke up.

"My name's Maria," she said in halting English. The two mothers observed each other closely, sharing unspoken feelings only lonely women born in different parts of the world, but similarly marked by war, could fathom. Their silence lasted mere seconds, but to Latoya it seemed her life in summary. *Folks knows so much, but understands so little*, she thought. As they walked ahead, Latoya kept quiet, but Maria talked on, now in Arabic.

"We were Ma'dan in Iraq. The English called us marsh Arabs. They were the first that tried to rid themselves of us. We had rivers like the Mississippi and lakes like this one, and ducks and geese," she began. She pointed back at Nokomis while Inaya searched for words in English. Remembering how young the girl was, Latoya wondered what horrors she had experienced. "We fished and raised buffalo. That was before Saddam drained our wetlands between the rivers. He was our country's leader but tried to destroy us because we opposed him. He turned our freshwater to salt."

Latoya wanted to express sympathy but couldn't identify with the struggle Maria described, so they wandered slowly on until the rattle of traffic blended with the bustle of daily commerce. Kofi's reappeared at 50th and Fairmont and Latoya sat down on a concrete abutment to rest her stocky legs, which ached from all the walking. She peered back toward the lake and pulled her bag's drawstring again. Digging ever deeper inside it, she finally hauled out a handful of crinkled dollar bills. She put the bag aside and set off for Kofi's.

After a while, Latoya returned carrying three large drinks. "You folks thirsty?" she asked.

Inaya and Maria said thanks and accepted their drinks. The three women wiggled their straws and clinked their ice cubes before savoring the cooling concoction of coffee, whipped cream, chocolate syrup, and sugary sauces. They sipped and simultaneously let out a long, refreshed ahhhhh.

"Tastes like a malt," Inaya said, but Maria didn't understand what she meant and Latoya could only reply with a mellow *hmmmm* as she sucked her straw. Receiving so little response, Inaya looked at the storefront and commented, "Kofi loves Allah. His boy's in my school. We pray together."

Allah. Iraqis' name for God, Latoya guessed. They worship in Mosques. Otherwise she didn't know about any such stuff. Instead, she focused on the passing traffic, which led her thoughts back to Kamren. He was slow as a child and the docs found a hole in his heart. She and Walter had no money, but the medical folks were good to the boy at Shriners Hospital, so he grew up fit. He ran like a gazelle and Walter said he chased the wind and would one day outrun it. As a small boy, Kamren loved nothing so much as cars. He sat for hours with Latoya at bus stops proudly naming each model that whizzed by.

Why he later set his heart on the Armed Forces was a mystery. The only thing Latoya knew was that their lives gradually veered in different directions following his deployment. After he died, Gudiva cried for weeks, but eventually found a new life with another man. Walter faded ever farther from people's memory till finally they quit asking about him. Latoya found her new home in the basement room, where the sun streamed in and woke her harshly, like it had this very morning. The *koficcino* finished, she studied her reflection in the empty glass and continued thinking how Kamren loved watching *Animorphs* on TV as a child. He smiled and snuggled up next to her on their sofa.

After several minutes, the noisy traffic recaptured Latoya's attention. A #10 bus pulled up at the stop where she got off earlier, and she wondered if it would take her home, like the #22. Inaya saw the bus, too, and began to recite city routes from memory and each bus's final destination. Latoya looked at the girl and said, "I be goin' to Seven Corners."

"Ten isn't yours," Inaya said with a confident shake of her head.

When Maria nodded at their empty glasses, the girl protested but soon gave up and bused them back to the counter inside. Clearly ticked off by her daughter's reluctance to help with the glasses, Maria continued talking rapidly in Arabic. Puzzled, Latoya looked to Inaya for help when she returned, but mother and daughter became silent. Inaya was especially sullen until she finally turned to Latoya and spoke, paying only scant attention to Maria. "Mom talks a lot abut me. I know her words by heart. She told you, 'Inaya's aware what's up around her and she lets people know about it.'"

"Like at the sign? You strong?"

Inaya nodded yes. "And so are you," she said.

Having discovered a new neighborhood so different and welcoming, Latoya felt content for the rest of the fading afternoon. She and her new friends sat together. Their anger with each other having cooled, the Iraqis talked softly in Arabic, while Latoya thought about tomorrow's city market and the items she had to sell. Finally, the #22 bus ground to a halt opposite Kofi's. With little time to lose, Latoya gathered her belongings and boarded the bus. Once she found a seat, Inaya approached her open window. "Mom says the war sent me to Minnesota, and someday Minnesota'll send me to Washington."

Latoya didn't know how to respond, so Inaya added with a becoming wink, "Next time, our treat."

As the bus chugged away, Maria and Inaya waved 'so long.' Latoya waved back. To relax her aching legs, she stretched out across her seat and the vacant one next to it, but she couldn't slow her mind. Iraq and Minnesota. Kamren and Inaya. *Him there, an' her here*, Latoya thought, imagining the courage it took to live so far away from home.

She rode the rest of the way with her mind on remote. As the #22 crept through the hustle and bustle of downtown, Latoya felt a sudden intense longing for the safety of the street. At its last stop, the bus emptied, but she remained seated and remembered yet again: Kamren, gone forever. Walter, too. And Yani. When she finally got off, she hoisted her bag and marched across the market square. Her heart still hurt, but she was home among her people and smiling. *Maria and Inaya*, she reminded herself. *Their treat, next time.*

SPEED
CLEAN

JANUARY TORNADOES. A snowy Memorial Day. Stan Scribbling had seen it all. As dead leaves swirled in the September wind and rain, he and Kristine sipped their coffee in his mother Louisa's vacant Twin Cities apartment. She had died two weeks earlier and they were trying to sell the last of her possessions, which wasn't proving easy. Among the items were her ornate silver flatware and an outdated 40-inch Sony TV. A 1990s Speed Clean washing machine, with a mounted hand wringer, seemed more antiquarian than useful. They'd received a few calls, but no one cared to venture out in such dreadful weather.

"Darned washer," Kristine lamented. "Getting rid of it will be a tale to tell."

"So what else is new," Stan replied.

Ever since he moved up north, one strange occurrence involving his mother had followed another. Along with him marrying Kristine and helping her raise their two girls in Minneapolis came repeated visits to Louisa in Paducah. As newlyweds, they visited the Old Slave House in nearby Illinois, which Louisa insisted couldn't have existed in a Northern state, but Stan's photos of ghastly shackles and whipping posts proved her wrong. Then came the time he convinced Louisa to sell her home and try subsidized government housing, but she tripped over a fellow renter's tail-wagging dog and broke a leg. Other times he treated her to meals in fancy restaurants, only to watch her sob over the waitresses' friendly comments, which she took as jabs about her advancing years. Finally, Stan decided to move her to Minnesota, and so began the long and trying experience that taught him more about growing old than he ever knew existed.

Stan found Louisa a one-bedroom apartment in an over-55 building in St. Paul, but his drive down south to help her move was somber. The endless ribbon of highway through Iowa, the aloneness he felt on the Illinois prairie, and the return to his hometown unnerved him. Childhood acquaintances in Paducah stared at him like a space traveler lost in time. Young and old alike were talkative but entrenched in their opinions, while Stan had undergone a change up North. Like a good Minnesotan, he had heaps of new ideas but said only what was needed and kept his feelings to himself.

The drive back to the Upper Midwest took place in sunlight and silence. It was the loveliest of springs and Stan gloried in the lengthening days, while Louisa stared blankly ahead, enduring what she surely viewed as a voyage into nothingness, the end of life as she knew it. Her building, Bridal Veil Towers, was a modern but misnamed complex of one-story senior flats between St. Paul and Minneapolis. The building overlooked Bridal Veil Falls and the Mighty Mississippi, which Louisa declared no match for Paducah's Ohio River, on whose banks she had grown up and spent her life admiring. The Mississippi snaked confusingly between the Twin Cities, so she soon gave up trying to understand where one city ended and the other began, or what place this was that Stan had chosen as his home—and now rudely plopped her down in as well, without asking. Bridal Veil's brown-skinned East Asian staff met Louisa with broad smiles but had trouble understanding her Kentucky English.

Despite the difficulties, it was here near the 45th parallel north that Louisa toughed out the first few years of the 21st century. Minnesotans' reticent speech and lack of public eye contact were bothersome, so she retreated within herself and silently stared at strangers. Glaring wide-eyed became, in fact, the one thing she excelled at. Louisa had suffered through cataract surgery by a small-town Kentucky doc who knew nothing of inter-ocular lens implantation and gave her thick eye glasses instead. From her St. Paul apartment patio, she peered through Coke-bottle lenses at the carefree cyclists and skateboarders dashing along Mississippi River Boulevard on mild summer evenings, keenly aware she looked as alien to the passing youth as they to her.

Stan remembered Louisa's first taste of Minnesota snow during a three-day November blizzard. Swiftly she declared herself a staunch doubter of global warming and a stranger to city life, with all its snow and ice-induced fender benders. When the blizzard began, Stan called Kristine to ask if she'd join them for dinner out, but Louisa wept with indecision over how they'd manage the task of taking her to a restaurant. Plus, when and where? Once Kristine arrived and Stan guided his mother through her front door, a Canada wind blew fearsome flakes horizontal to the ground and knocked the goggles off her face. Confused and teary-eyed, she refused Stan's efforts to nudge her onward, so he helped her back inside.

"While Ma sat and sniffled, I used her wall phone to call Pasta Pit and hoped you'd stay on for pizza," Stan announced.

Kristine, who read Stan's mind as well as he read hers, sat down and studied her husband. Her own mother had suffered through the sudden family loss of Kristine's sister when she drowned as a youth, just as Louisa had never quit mourning the unexpected death of Stan's father, who was only 50. Through years of marriage, Stan and Kristine had internalized each other's family tragedies and learned to make associations from the slightest hints given by the other.

"Yes, I remember," Kristine explained. "You ordered pineapple pizza and I went to pick it up." After a pause, she continued with a sly smile, "and *I* paid for it."

"Thick crust. What we always order. We ate here, in Ma's kitchen," Stan recalled. "It was incongruous watching an aging woman, clearly out of step with the times, delicately hold up huge triangular slices and devour them. To her, the pineapples in Italian dishes seemed like products of a new time, a South Seas dispensation invading even the wildest of climes."

The wall phone rang and Kristine reached out to answer it, pressing the receiver to her ear like she'd forgotten how to use land lines. She exchanged a few words with the caller and shrugged when Stan asked who was on the line. Barely a month ago he'd found Louisa chatting on that exact phone, her grip slacker than Kristine's. She was discussing dinner with a friend from her senior center, first announcing she wasn't well enough to go out, not even on the neighborhood shuttle bus, but then changing her mind.

"I came here to take her for a flu shot," Stan remembered. "She seemed happy to see me, but kept touching the top of her head and saying it hurt. She told me, 'Doc Dancy said, why, Louisa, it's that arthritis, it affects every part of your body.' Later she claimed the flu shot laid her low. The next day she was in good spirits after I took her shopping, again talking to me about going to dinner with her friend, but when I drove her home, she complained how hard it was to see in the late afternoon darkness. At the back door, she turned to me and said in this plaintive voice, 'It's awful to want to die and not be able to.'"

In only a few weeks she *was* dead, Stan reflected. The death certificate Doc Dancy signed stated the cause of death was cancer. Kristine reasoned the doctor knew all along her true malady wasn't the flu or arthritis, and realizing her cancer was too advanced for surgery, he concealed the cause of the headaches from Louisa. Kristine questioned the doctor's ethics, but with no proof of wrongdoing, she and Stan had let the funeral proceed. Stan, Kristine, their daughters, and a handful of seniors from Bridal Veil Towers gathered and heard a perfunctory sermon from a Lutheran minister, "about this and that," as Kristine later summarized it. The pastor didn't know Louisa and assumed she was only one in a long list of aged and stoic Minnesota Swedes. A few souls in Paducah sent cards, all of whom attested to Louisa's kindness in helping the poor, the sick, and underprivileged.

"Yes, your ma," Kristine sighed. She rolled her eyes humorously to mimic Stan's word for 'mother.' She found his use of the term 'ma' reminiscent of his youth down South, a time she felt he'd long ago outgrown in every other way.

"True, she was a tangle of complexes, but as kind to folks as she wished them be with her. That is, those as disadvantaged as she became," Stan continued. "She wasn't prepared to have her body fall apart all at once, as she put it."

Kristine looked long and hard at Stan. She wondered if he blamed himself for tearing Louisa away from her hometown and leaving her to hunker down in this clean but featureless apartment during long stretches of wintry hibernation. Any Border State native would have deemed such treatment cruel and inhumane, as though harsh wind and snow understood human feelings. Stan decided he'd done his best.

Stan and Kristine were seated in Louisa's nearly denuded apartment, locked in an introspective staring duel, when the phone rang again. "Yes, your mother cared for everybody around her who needed it," Kristine said as she picked up the receiver.

Stan discovered he was watching Kristine talk on the phone more than listening to her. Her blonde hair hung down loosely without fully covering the birthmark on the left side of her face. In their younger days, after meeting at Lake Nokomis in Minneapolis, they quickly became good friends. Kristine regaled him with tales of Swedes settling in Minnesota and her own immigrant great-grandmother surviving a shipwreck by clinging to a rock off the coast of

Newfoundland. After their love blossomed, Stan grew acutely aware of her birthmark, proud of it, in fact. When they made love, he felt doubly endeared because she'd explained how bearing up under the social stigma of the birthmark strengthened her mentally. He studied it often, noting how it seemed to grow darker when she was under pressure or perplexed, and right now it was virtually black. Kristine grimaced in her frustrated efforts to hear or understand the current caller.

"You do what? You wash them how?" Kristine asked, incredulous at what she thought she'd heard on the other end. "Yes, that's our address, all right. We'll be here, for sure."

Kristine hung up and sighed. Stan could see she was weary, just like him. Not for us, he thought, this lonely vigil, auctioning off goods no one needs or bothers to come and look at. His wife nodded at Stan, who muttered, "I guess," which was his laconic way of agreeing to more coffee. The brew grew steaming hot and Kristine was busy filling Stan's cup when a timid knock at the back door caught their attention.

Stan got up and opened the door to a subdued and nervous-looking lady in faded jeans and denim jacket. *Goodwill Store purchase,* flashed through his mind as the visitor looked past him toward Kristine. "It's Ellie. I called earlier."

"Oh, yes, you're here for the sale?" Kristine asked.

Ellie nodded, then glanced around the apartment like a curious child. Kristine smiled at her in a kindly way and Stan backed off to let his wife show her the goods. She began with pots and pans, which Ellie bought for a few cents each but showed little interest in. When they emerged from the kitchen, Stan bagged the items and placed her payment money on the table. Showing no signs of leaving, Ellie hesitated and then glanced toward the doorway.

"Your daughter?" Kristine asked.

Stan saw a young woman standing outside with a baby. Without waiting for a welcome, she let herself in.

"Yes, this is Nellie," Ellie answered.

Stan found himself facing what looked like two young sisters, Ellie and Nellie, both a tad heavy and frazzled, but smiling in eager anticipation. The baby slept in a sling over Nellie's shoulder. They were roughly 5' 3" with short dark hair and blonde highlights. Both were dressed in matching jeans and jackets, even if Nellie's looked store-bought, likely from a discount super-mart, unlike the second-hand outfit worn by her mother. Neither was inclined to say much more until Kristine urged them on.

"I'm afraid I didn't catch what you were looking for, exactly," she said to Nellie, mistakenly thinking she was encouraging Ellie. "Over the phone, I mean. A stove? Our washing machine?"

"You mean Ellie, that's her over there, my mom. I'm only 18," Nellie responded and pointed to her mother.

"Why, Nellie here found herself in a family way and look what we've got, little Jacob," Ellie interrupted, pointing to the baby. "We're shopping for goods for her 'n our little one."

Despite the gold ring in her lip, Ellie was well-spoken, even if a habit of constantly shifting her feet while talking showed she was ill at ease. Grandmother or not, she was yet to pass her mid-thirties, Stan figured. He glanced through the window and spotted a rusty Ford pickup in the driveway. He guessed the women had borrowed it briefly or bought it for a song at Poke's Salvage Yard across town.

When Kristine tried speaking to Nellie, Ellie interrupted. "Her fellow's in the clinker. For meth."

"But not his fault, somebody framed him," Nellie was quick to add. She brushed some lingering raindrops from her hair and revealed a couple of tattoos on her arm. One showed a fiery dragon, its claws wrapped around a flailing girl. The second was a simple name, *Danny*.

Curious about the visitors, Kristine looked over her shoulder at Stan for encouragement, which he gave with a nod, so she led mother and daughter into the living room,

where she showed them Louisa's ancient Sony. Ellie flipped
the set on and acted surprised that it worked. Lacking chairs,
the four stood around the TV and stared at the screen.

"Louisa, Stan's mother, watched lots of reruns," Kristine
explained. "Stan insisted on replacing it with a newer model,
but she said no, it was like a friend to her."

Ellie fumbled with one of the knobs and watched a sales
commercial for new cars as Nellie pulled out her iPhone
and began to text. Ellie frowned, switched off the TV, and
gazed distractedly at the silver flatware. Finally, she set off for
the kitchen, clearly ticked off at her daughter for using her
phone instead of talking to Kristine or Stan. Nellie followed
her and both mother and daughter sat down quietly, at their
own invitation, without looking at each other. The silence
was broken when Nellie's baby began to cry. She bared a
breast to nurse the child and Ellie suddenly got impatient,
darting glances toward the utility room.

Seeing the women and baby settled in, Stan moved
to make fresh coffee for the four of them, suspecting the
visitors would say yes to refreshments. He gave them
cups and served them where they sat so they had no
need to get up.

"You mentioned something special?" Kristine asked.

"It's the baby," Nellie answered instantly.

"No, the lady means their washing machine," Ellie
corrected her daughter.

"Yes, for Jacob," Nellie agreed.

"Well, we certainly have one. It was Louisa's gem. We're
asking a hundred fifty for it, or best offer," Kristine replied.
Without spilling their coffee, Ellie and Nellie rushed to
see it, and Kristine explained the Speed Clean's wringers.
"The washer's electric. It washes the clothes, but you
wring them by hand."

Mother and daughter ignored the wringer, but examined
the power cord closely.

"It's magnificent!" Nellie screamed so loudly the baby

broke out crying in his mother's arms. The girl gave her coffee cup to Kristine to hold. Irritated by the commotion, Stan left for the kitchen.

After a few minutes, Ellie appeared by his side. She jiggled her coffee and sipped at it quickly, before discovering the cup was empty. "We don't have much, we've been washing diapers by hand," she said in a near whisper, nodding toward the other room. "Her man's a wreck. Gives us no support. In and outa county jail."

Ellie grew quiet and Stan refilled her cup just as Kristine and Nellie returned to the kitchen. By now, Nellie was wrapped up in a tale of her own about cleaning diapers. "This is how we do it," she said, asking Kristine to hold her coffee cup again. Her eyes darted back and forth between the kitchen and utility room. "The diaper's square, you know, they all are, so we hold it up and scrape the poop off with a knife or cutter, then we soak it in hot water." She produced a hankie and imitated the scraping with her free hand. Soon she remembered the coffee in Kristine's hand, accepted it from her, and luxuriated in a long drink, though it was surely was cold by now. She sighed in satisfaction before nodding yes to a coffee roll Stan offered up. After consuming it and giving her cup back to Kristine, Nellie revealed a breast to nurse Jacob and quiet his crying, while she jealously eyed the additional rolls Stan held on a platter in one hand. Holding the coffeepot in his other hand, he refilled her cup.

"The diapers, I mean. We soak the diapers, not the poop," Nellie added with a laugh. "They get pretty brown. Swishing around like that."

"You can imagine the water," Ellie hastened to explain. She had sat down but squirmed in her seat and fixed her eyes on the wall clock. Her determined concentration signaled she knew exactly what she wanted, and how soon she needed it, and who in the room she wanted it from.

Still, Stan thought he saw a flicker of worry in Ellie's expression as he himself eyed the clock. The day was slowly moving along with wilder winds but lighter rain. He wished to step outside for a breath of fresh air, but the visitors remained. He guessed he might need to make more coffee.

"Once the diapers've soaked, we heat more water and scrub 'em clean," Nellie explained. "A sink full of that nasty junk, you can't imagine. Load after load. But we get'em sparkling white."

Judging by the disgruntled look Ellie flashed at her daughter, Stan suspected Jacob mostly had his grandmother to thank for the sparkling diapers and clean butt. Nellie was likely too busy with her phone to help out.

For her part, Kristine shot another knowing glance towards Stan, then addressed the visitors. "Wouldn't a nice automatic washer help you ladies?" she asked bluntly.

"Yes, ma'am!" Ellie exclaimed, glancing at the idle Speed Clean and then staring straight at Kristine, while her daughter continued to eye the tasty treats Stan still held. "Yes, ma'am, for sure!"

And so they sat, as morning became afternoon, chatting over cups of steaming coffee. Once the rolls ran out and her hands were free, Nellie showed them how she folded diapers into squares or triangles and poured out the dirty water. Ellie described the trailer park they lived in, which Stan remembered local TV reporters calling "a home for the homeless." Greedy developers kept eyeing the property and now promised glitzy high-rise condos within a year. With razing of the present rental buildings already in the plans and renewed homelessness staring them in the face, residents feared for their future.

At last, Kristine rolled the Speed Clean out in full view. "All yours," she said in a cheerful, yet tired voice.

"Best offer? Fifty, maybe a hundred?" Ellie asked anxiously. "Will that do?" When Kristine nodded, Ellie dug in her pockets for the cash but came up empty.

"Sorry, we'll have to wait to pay you," she admitted with deep disappointment.

Not surprised by their hardship, Stan still found it difficult to envisage their living conditions or the nearly unimaginable miracle they must have prayed for, a primitive electric washer, which would seem a useless trifle to most. The few cents Ellie used for her earlier purchases from Kristine were surely the last coins she had to her name.

"Sorry," Ellie repeated imploringly.

"No, it's yours," Kristine insisted. She looked at Stan. When he smiled and nodded in agreement, she leaned forward and patted Ellie soothingly on the shoulder. "Free. For you, no charge. It was Louisa's. She would've wanted you to have it."

Ellie leaned back. "The answer to my prayers," she said with a sigh.

In awe Ellie and Nellie ran their hands along the gleaming washer top like it was a prize from Above. Ellie turned toward Kristine, tears welling in her eyes, her lips quivering. She was unable to speak.

Sensing what she wanted to say, Kristine rested a hand on her shoulder. "No thanks needed. You were meant for it."

"It had your name on it," Stan added.

Ellie wiped at her tears, but still no words came from her.

Stan loaded the Speed Clean onto the truck. Graciously Ellie shook hands with Stan and Kristine through her driver's window as Nellie piled in up front with Jacob. After their pickup disappeared down the street, the rain tailed off and a pale sun peeked out. Watching sunrays mix with the lingering clouds, Stan grew melancholy about his mother. The Speed Clean was the very first of many treasured possessions she brought with her from Paducah and among the last she would've parted with.

"They didn't even hear you when you spoke Ma's name," he said to Kristine. "She was here. Now she's gone."

River Boulevard was nearly empty of people after the rain.

Kristine looked distractedly at the few souls who ventured out, but she didn't speak until she and Stan started back inside. "They call it the cycle of life, or some mysterious-sounding thing," she said. "Best of all, the washer'll let Jacob grow up with a clean bottom, and eventually the washer will die, too. Speed Clean's only a name."

Stan turned to Kristine. "D'you ever wonder how things'd be if your great-grandma hadn't grasped hold of that rock off the coast of Newfoundland?"

Quietly Kristine cleaned the coffee maker, shooed Stan out the front door, and locked Louisa's apartment behind them. They were in the car heading home when she finally replied, "Or if you'd never moved here from Kentucky?"

Kristine was driving, so she could only glance quickly at Stan. They smiled broadly at each other in the fading September light. They hadn't experienced *everything* that day, but they outlasted the rain. While it came and went, they did their bit to keep Louisa's spirit alive. More colossal matters could wait for another day.

"Yeah, lotsa questions don't have answers, I figure, but we ask them anyway," Stan reasoned. "Like if Louisa never owned that washing machine, what then?"

Kristine pulled into their driveway, turned off the ignition, and spoke softly, "But, my love, she did."

ACKNOWLEDGEMENTS

In his *Fable of the Spider and the Bee*, Jonathan Swift wrote of the spider, who gathers past information in his gut and spins stories from second-hand details, while the bee, energized by curiosity, finds narratives springing from Nature and his own imagination. This literary construct partly describes my approach in *Hopeful Monsters*.

The spider in me has emerged in various stories. Minnesotan **Joann Walstedt** told me, for example, about a Swedish forebear, who made it from Sweden to America by surviving a ship wreck and clinging to a rock off the coast of eastern Canada. I used that episode as a motif in *Genuine Souls*. Likewise, my description of refugee life in *Sixteen* comes from tales told to me by Somalian immigrants, now residents of Minnesota. My fictional account of The Old Slave House, as related in *Down the River*, is based on information from my tour of the former Civil War era slave house in Gallatin County, Illinois, before it was closed to the public.

The bee in me is reflected by the fantasy *A Place in Space*. For that story I speculated about what might have caused a former neighbor in Minneapolis to obsess about ridding his neighborhood of squirrels, who were apparently harming no one. The title story *Hopeful Monsters* arose from my watching a forlorn mourning dove tough out three days of an April snowstorm on a bare tree limb in Minnesota - and then at last flutter blithely away. *The First, Best Bus* is my white man's attempt to imagine, even a wee bit of, what it's like to be an ethnic or racial minority in America.

Several colleagues have supported me in writing this collection. With careful discussions of narrative style, my writer friend **Gerri Buchanan** has helped me improve the various texts. **Helena Karlsson** has read my stories and given me insights from her Swedish perspective. While working in Hungary and writing her own stories about life in Budapest, she encouraged me to keep interpreting people and events my own way. I offer thanks to my Swedish friend **Annika Strandell**, who once told me that she felt perfectly at home traveling in Minnesota, because "like in Sweden, Minnesotans don't say hello to newcomers; they just stare at them." I used that motif in *Speed Clean*.

Others who've commented on my texts are **Barb, Kathryn Anderson,** and **Rosemary Zurawel. Donna Bieg, Savannah Bieg,** and **Rob Pearce** also deserve credit. Above all, I deeply appreciate the skill and encouragement of editor/publisher **Tomek Dzido**. Thanks for believing.

COMING SOON FROM
STORGY BOOKS

SONAYA NIGHTS
BOOK ONE

THIS RAGGED,
WASTREL THING

A NOVEL BY
TOMAS MARCANTONIO

AVAILABLE WINTER
2019

ALSO AVAILABLE FROM STORGY BOOKS

...EXIT EARTH...

EXIT EARTH delves into dystopian worlds and uncovers the most daring and original voices in print today. With twenty-four short stories, accompanying artwork, afterwords, and interviews, EXIT EARTH is a haunting exploration of the sanity of our species...past, present, and future.

Featuring the fourteen finalists from the STORGY EXIT EARTH Short Story Competition, and additional stories by award winning authors M.R. Carey (The Girl with all the Gifts), Toby Litt (Corpsing, DeadKidSongs), Courttia Newland (The Gospel According to Cane, A Book of Blues), James Miller (Sunshine State, Lost Boys), and David James Poissant (The Heaven of Animals). With accompanying artwork by Amie Dearlove, HarlotVonCharlotte, and CrapPanther.

To discover more about EXIT EARTH visit STORGY.COM

ALSO AVAILABLE FROM STORGY BOOKS

SHALLOW CREEK

This is the tale of a town on the fringes of fear, of ordinary people and everyday objects transformed by terror and madness, a microcosm of the world where nothing is ever quite what it seems. This is a world where the unreal is real, where the familiar and friendly lure and deceive. On the outskirts of civilisation sits this solitary town. Home to the unhinged. Oblivion to outsiders.

Shallow Creek contains twenty-one original horror stories by a chilling cast of contemporary writers, including stories by Sarah Lotz, Richard Thomas, Adrian J Walker, and Aliya Whitely. Told through a series of interconnected narratives, Shallow Creek is an epic anthology that exposes the raw human emotion and heart-pounding thrills at the the genre's core.

To discover more about SHALLOW CREEK visit
STORGY.COM

STORGY
MAGAZINE

ONLINE ARTS & ENTERTAINMENT MAGAZINE

BOOKS - FILMS - ART - MUSIC
INTERVIEWS - REVIEWS - SHORT STORIES

For more information about STORGY Magazine visit our
website.

STORGY

www.storgy.com

@fb.me/morest0rgy   @morestorgy   morestorgy